WHITE LIES
DEADLY LIES

WHITE LIES
DEADLY LIES

Peter Tickler

ROBERT HALE

First published in 2018 by
Robert Hale, an imprint of
The Crowood Press Ltd,
Ramsbury, Marlborough
Wiltshire SN8 2HR

www.crowood.com

British Library Cataloguing-in-Publication Data
A catalogue record for this book is available from the British
Library.

ISBN 978 0 7198 2803 4

Typeset by Chapter One Book Production, Knebworth

Printed and bound in India by Replika Press Pvt Ltd

AUTHOR'S NOTE

I TRY TO DESCRIBE Oxford as accurately as I can, although obviously I do make places up from time to time.

My Hull may well be less accurate and for that I apologize. The Bricklayers Arms does not exist as far as I know, though its name is inspired by a pub of the same name across the Humber in Grimsby. The Bricklayers Arms in Nelson Street seems to have been quite notorious in the nineteenth century. One publican was charged with refusing to let the police in and another was charged with allowing drunkenness in his house. I rather like the idea that my fictitious pub may have had a similar history!

Of course, all persons in this story are totally fictitious. The dog was inspired by one I encountered while walking by the river in Abingdon – hopefully he will not object to his depiction in the story.

PROLOGUE

The Crash

DOUG MULLEN SPOTTED THE girl approximately forty seconds before all hell was let loose. That he noticed her was nothing to do with her looks. Sulky Goth teenagers who have eyes only for the mobile phone in their hands were of no interest to him. It was the car which caught his attention – a bright pink Fiat Uno which was moving serenely past him. He had had a Fiat once. It was not pink, and he would never have described it as serene. But it had been his first car, and first cars – like first girlfriends – are not easily forgotten.

His Fiat had never let him down, unlike the battered metallic blue Ford Focus which was now his proud (ha!) possession. His right foot was hard down on the accelerator, but it was wasting its time. The black-eyed, black-haired, black-clothed girl glanced up from her electronic device, smiled smugly and gave an unregal one-fingered salute.

Fiat and Focus were both heading up the M40 towards Oxford and the weekend. Mullen had spent a fruitless day tracking the gay partner of his only current client around London and he had had enough. The rain had increased in intensity and was drumming angrily on the roof of the car. More seriously, the heater fan had given up the ghost and it was proving impossible to clear the windscreen of condensation. The

Fiat had pulled across into the inside lane in front of him, and now a stream of much larger SUVs was speeding past him, spraying torrents of water with abandon. Mullen could feel the resentment and anger rising in him, not least because he knew that the disgusting people churning past him in their oversized four-by-fours were – quite apart from being disgusting – at this precise moment a good deal safer than he was.

It was only much later, watching the news and reading the accounts on the internet, that Mullen realized quite how it had all started. A low flying pheasant – which for some bizarre reason had decided that this was the moment and these were the weather conditions in which to cross the motorway – had crashed into the windscreen of a lorry. The lorry driver – so the assumption went in the all-knowing media – had been checking a text message on his mobile. There always has to be someone to blame. The thump of the bird, the few moments of inattention, maybe also the tiredness of the driver (again an assumption, but one which the driver, dead before the firemen got to him, was never able to deny or confirm) combined to deadly effect. The lorry twitched dramatically to one side and then the other, dancing in the rain. Then the dancer became a drunken reveller, staggering wildly from side to side before sprawling full length in the gutter.

The first Mullen knew of the incipient disaster was that the tail lights of another lorry, the one just in front of the pink Fiat, were flashing bright red as its driver went into emergency mode. He saw its frame shudder and twist, realized it was looming larger and larger in his vision and rammed his foot hard on the brake pedal. And that was it. The next thing – or so it seemed when he later tried to describe what had happened – was that he was standing in the rain next to his Ford Focus staring at the confusion and carnage all around him. Physically, he and his car were untouched. Immediately behind him, however, a white van and a saloon were locked in a crumpled embrace; a squat bald-headed figure emerged from the van and then stood clinging onto the open door, overwhelmed but alive. Beyond them, there were more vehicles and shouts and a blaring horn. He turned 180 degrees. The lorry which had been in front of him was upright, but slewed across the carriageway. The driver was still in his cab, upright and immobile, shaken but not stirring.

There was a car stuck under the body of the lorry just behind the cab. It was a small car, a Fiat – Mullen could identify a Fiat Uno's rear end from a hundred metres. Only it wasn't just any old Fiat, it was that gloriously pink one. Mullen began to run towards it. In the air he could smell the acrid fumes of things burning and then, from beyond the lorry, he saw a ball of flame hurtle up into the swirling sky, like Greek fire launched from some ancient war machine. He ducked his head and ran faster. The Fiat was jammed underneath at an angle. It was a three-door job, as his own had been. That much had already registered with him. Mullen headed for the passenger door, conscious that there was smoke coming from somewhere close by. He could smell petrol too. He grabbed the handle and wrenched it open. Goth girl was sitting upright but apparently unharmed. She stared at him uncomprehending.

'Out!' he said, taking her by the arm. She nodded and fiddled at her seat-belt, then got out. He could feel the trembling in her body.

'Wait!' he said, as if she was a dog.

The driver of the car, her mother presumably, had blood on her forehead and the nearside of her face. She showed no sign of moving.

'You've got to get out!' Mullen said loudly, leaning in and snapping open her seat-belt. Nothing. Not a moan or a nod or a word of acknowledgement. Mullen felt the stirrings of panic in his gut. The smoke was stinging his eyes and the intense smell of petrol was alarming.

He took the woman's hand in his and gently tugged.

'Come on, now!' he said, changing tack, coaxing her. This seemed to work. She turned and stared at him. 'Come on,' he repeated. 'You need to get out.'

She nodded. He let go of her hand, and backed out of the car as she started to clamber across the passenger seat.

'Good girl!' Mullen said, reverting to dog-training mode.

Soon the three of them were standing up outside the Fiat. Mullen surveyed the chaos around it. There were one or two other people now visible, walking as if in a dream through the wrecked vehicles and drifting smoke. A man in a grey and red anorak was standing some fifteen metres away, observing and – or so Mullen reckoned – filming it all for his Twitter feed. Mullen would have liked to ram the guy's mobile up where the sun couldn't shine, but he had more important things to do. He linked arms with his two charges and together they stumbled away from the carnage. Only when they were halfway up the embankment did Mullen allow them all to collapse on the sodden grass. It was still raining cats and dogs, but that seemed irrelevant.

He rubbed at his forehead with the back of his hand. His head, he now realized, was hurting like hell, a cacophony of bass drums hammering away inside it without any sense of rhythm. He looked at his hand. It was covered with sticky red liquid. He tried to stand up, but both mother and daughter were still firmly attached to him. He slumped back down. He could hear sirens. He looked to his right and saw flashing blue lights emerging from the murk along the hard shoulder.

'Thank God!' he said loudly, though he wasn't a religious man. But he had learned from experience that sometimes God seems to be the only answer.

CHAPTER 1

Fallout

THERE ARE CONSEQUENCES TO appearing memorably in a car crash which has been plastered (thanks to a guy in a grey and red anorak) across the media outlets of the world. Lots of people see you and quite a few of them recognize you.

One such person was Jade Sawyer. Mostly she ignored the TV. Mostly she slept or stared at the ceiling, waiting for death. For death would come soon. That much she knew. It couldn't come soon enough for her. There was no-one to stay alive for. There hadn't been since Lucy. Certainly not the feckless Alex who had turned up out of the blue shedding false tears and fake regrets. Now after years of absence, he sat in the hospital room for hours on end, pretending to the nurses how much he had loved Jade and how sorry he was.

Jade didn't have the energy to argue with him or to tell the nurses that in reality Alex Pike was a pile of treacherous shit who had walked out on her and Lucy as soon as things had got difficult. It had been her, not Alex, who had carried and given birth to Lucy and who had loved and cared for the child despite everything. Whereas Alex had got more and more distant until one day he had just disappeared, leaving behind a one-word note: *Sorry!* Jade wondered why he had come back here now. Of course, he had a glib story to tell. He had always been a teller of touching tales. He had bumped into an English girl in an Auckland bar, he said. She turned out to have come from that very same Cornish village that Jade had lived in all her life. Jade could believe the bit about meeting in a bar.

'It was like a message,' Alex had said very seriously. 'As you know, sweetie, I would never claim to be a religious man, but it seemed like it was a message from God.' He had taken hold of Jade's hand at that point. 'It felt like I had been given a chance for redemption. It really did. So I came back here to care for you.'

If Dr Holt ('do call me Rebecca') hadn't come in at that moment, Jade might have said something. Instead she waited patiently while Rebecca studied her notes and fended off a few flirtatious comments from Alex. Alex hadn't changed in that respect. Always did have an eye for a good pair of female legs. And the chat-up lines to go with it.

After Rebecca withdrew, Jade resumed her thoughts. The cynic inside her insisted that Alex was only after her money and that he had come back from New Zealand in the hope that after a deathbed reconciliation she would leave all her worldly goods to him. She wouldn't. She had already made her will and she had no intention of changing a single word of it.

Her thoughts meandered. How on earth had she been so stupid as to fall for Alex? Actually, she knew the answer to that. She had been overwhelmed by the fact that someone as good looking as Alex should want her in preference to anyone else. Looking back on it, she realized that it was she who had wanted a child, not Alex. He had agreed reluctantly, but once she had got pregnant, the cracks in their relationship had started to become apparent. Eight and half months after conception, Lucy had been born and within a few more, the cracks had become chasms.

She knew now that the underlying problem was that they were so different. They were alike in one way only: she, like Alex, wasn't religious. But that didn't stop her hoping with every feeble fibre of her being that, despite her disbelief, heaven existed and that her Lucy would be there, waiting for her. And that Alex would end up in hell.

'I just want to make it up to you.' It was Alex, butting in again. He had taken hold of her hand. Jade wanted to drag it out of his grasp, but she had neither the strength nor the will.

'Shall I turn the news on?'

Jade thought it was a stupid question. Why would she want to watch the news when it was so irrelevant to her? She shook her head.

But Alex was already picking up the TV remote control. He wanted to watch the news. No change there: asking a question and not listening to the answer. Doing what he wanted. Probably what he wanted was to have an excuse not to look at her. Maybe he was regretting coming back. Maybe he was wondering how long it would take for her to die. Not yet, Jade hissed silently. She would hang on for as long as she could just to spite him.

The main news story was all about a monster car smash. The BBC had got hold of some pretty spectacular footage from someone who preferred standing in the middle of the disaster to actually helping anyone. Temporarily her anger transferred from Alex to that unseen photographer. Fire, smoke, wrecked vehicles, people stumbling around in confused panic, the flashing blue lights of police cars, ambulances and fire-engines, but the arsehole was only interested in filming it. Unlike the man in picture now who had just rescued two females from a tiny car and was stumbling with them through the chaos to safety. The report ended with a shot of the three of them collapsed on the grass embankment. Something about the woman was familiar, but she couldn't think what. The cameraman zoomed into a close-up of the group. She gasped. She stared hard at the screen, unable to believe what she was seeing. She knew the woman!

'Natalie and Eleanor Swan,' the newsman was saying, 'will be forever in debt to …'. But Jade wasn't listening anymore. It was as if a nail bomb had gone off in her brain, sparking a thousand splinters of pain. She let out a moan of agony and dug her nails hard into the back of Alex's hand. It must have been hard because Alex swore loudly and dragged himself free of her grip.

'Jesus, Jade.' He studied his hand. 'What the hell did you do that for?'

Less than twenty-four hours after Jade Sawyer almost suffered a cardiac arrest in Cornwall, somewhere in South Yorkshire Paul Reeve saw the self-same news clip on the BBC website. He didn't often get access to the internet and when he did the first thing he did was to do search for Gemma Reeve. For the umpteenth time, he had failed to come up with anything interesting. He had on previous occasions come across various people called Gemma Reeve. There was a sculptor in the Lake District whose photograph revealed her to be both very arty (long grey hair piled haphazardly on top of her head, dangling silver earrings and tie-dyed scarves and floaty dresses) and old (at least seventy-five, Reeve reckoned). A second Gemma Reeve turned out to be a very attractive young woman looking for 'an open but committed relationship' – whatever that meant. But she wasn't the woman he was looking for either. As he had many times before, Reeve searched Facebook too, both for Gemma Reeve and Gemma Partridge (her maiden name), but again without success.

Of course, there were some references to *his* Gemma Reeve, but these were all from ten years ago, when she and he were briefly a news story, but it was as if she had, a few months later, just disappeared without trace.

'Changed her name, ain't she?' said Phil, who slept in the bunk above him and was pretty full of himself because he was only a couple of weeks away from his release. 'Easy enough to do.'

Paul knew he was very probably right. But that didn't stop him searching. You never know, he told himself as he lay on his back listening to the unedifying sound of Phil's snoring. One day she might do something which gets her in the news.

She already had, of course. That very afternoon, Paul Reeve had seen the video in which his ex-wife and her (and his) daughter had featured. But he had completely failed to recognize them. People change a lot in ten years – especially if they want to. Hair colour, length and style, body size and shape (his ex-wife had lost five stone since he had last seen her and had taken up a gym membership which she made use of at least twice a week). As for his daughter, she had grown and changed out of all recognition. The irony was that even though Paul Reeve still hadn't given up on finding her, when God or the Devil or Lady Luck did offer him the opportunity one uneventful April afternoon, he literally didn't notice.

CHAPTER 2

Later

IT IS A LONG time since I have been to London and I am determined
to enjoy it. Of course, I have no idea where I will go, but that doesn't
matter. The four of them go upstairs on the coach from Oxford, so I sit
downstairs. I pull my cap down over my head and pretend to sleep. In
the end I do sleep and I wake later with a start and have to ask my neighbour where we are. Shepherd's Bush.

Thank God! My guess is that they will get off at the Marble Arch stop
rather than go on to Victoria where the coach terminates. I am right.
They stumble off the bus chattering and giggling, and I wait until the last
moment before getting off myself, behind my balding neighbour. Already
they are plunging into the heaving mass of tourists and shoppers and I
plunge after them, anxious not to lose sight. The tall girl is overdressed in
red. She will be the beacon I will follow.

By the time we reach Bond Street, they are each carrying a bag which
declares their fashion allegiances. What next? More shopping? Madame
Tussauds? The Tower of London? None of them as it turns out. They disappear into the Underground station. This is harder for me. If I get too
close, they may notice me, and if I am too far behind I may miss whatever train they catch and lose them altogether. I feel my anxiety build.

Losing them is not the end of the world, but I want this to carry on for as long as possible. I want to see how they operate together. I want to observe their behaviour. Already I know which of them is the dominant female and which is the one who is always out to please. Who is strong and who is weak. I also know that all three girls like the boy.

We end up at the Tate Modern. That is a surprise to me. It was not on my list of things that teenagers do in London. Is this something connected with school work? They begin by going to the toilets and then to a café. Only when they are queueing for their food do I finally take the opportunity to go to the toilet myself. As well as peeing (phew!), I also change my appearance. It is easy enough to do if you come prepared.

Tate Modern is a huge space, but they seem to know where they are going. I follow at a distance, but once they are in the exhibition rooms it is harder to do so. But the truth is that I want to get as close to them as I dare.

The girls behave much as young teenage girls do, the boy joins in with gusto. I try not to disapprove, but this is after all a museum – albeit a museum of modern art, a place where the normal rules of art and behaviour don't apply. I am compelled to follow them. I am fascinated and appalled by the four of them. I cannot stop myself. I find myself admiring the things they ignore and vice versa until they come to the mirror installation. It is a large cube constructed of mirrors and in each side are small holes which invite the visitor to look inside, into a world of multiple reflection, where you see miniature images of yourself and of others looking in. Two of the girls have already moved on, but when I peer in, I see the girl in the red dress (she has very red lips too) and the boy and in that moment I make my decision. I linger at the installation, watching them as they pursue their friends. The girl briefly takes the arm of the boy. He turns and leans down and whispers in her ear. Then, as they enter the next room, she releases him. I know that the longer I follow them, the greater the danger of me being noticed. I ought to leave them and go back to Oxford, but I am not ready yet. They have entered a room of cages. I have no idea what the point of them is, but the Chinese girl is already sliding into one of them alongside her girlfriends while the boy takes a photograph of them. I am a long way from them, but I do the same. A photograph of them in a cage. The idea appeals to me a lot.

They are restless as a wild sea and soon they are off again. The black-haired girl seems to have taken charge now and they enter a lift. At the last moment, behind a large American couple, I slip in as well. It is a risk, but a low one I reckon. They exit at the fourth floor and head for the Louise Bourgeois rooms. Like so many people, they head straight for the large spider while I keep my distance, studying the walls near the entrance. I have, I decide, taken sufficient risks. I have seen what I need to see. I slip away, the outline of a plan now firmly in my head, and I bump into the boy.

I duck my head and apologize and make my way to the escalator, cursing myself for my stupidity. The girls had been thronging round the spider, but he had not. That should have put me on my guard. As I step onto the escalator, I glance across to where I had come from. The boy is still there, and he is talking to another teenager, a little taller than himself. They are engrossed with each other, and I realize that I have got away with my stupidity.

Getting your heroic actions splashed across the media has its advantages when you're a private investigator with a shortage of work. Not that 'heroic' was a word that Mullen would ever have used to describe what he did that day on the M40. 'Instinctive' maybe, 'human'. Or 'what any normal person would have done'. Those were the words which he uttered when badgered by members of the press corps. But such modesty only encouraged their hyperbole as they gushed effusively about the 'simple heroism' of what Mullen did.

Mullen was only human. Initially he was sucked in by all the adulation, by the journalists wanting to speak to him, by the people of Oxford who stopped him on the street or talked at him on the bus.

'Hey, aren't you the guy who...?'

By day three he – like the press pack – had had enough. He felt a fraud. Nine people had died that day on the M40, with many more injured. He, like Natalie and Ellie, had been lucky. And he felt as if he was trading on all that misery. He felt dirty to his core. Especially when it became apparent that Natalie had not been so lucky after all. She had suffered a stroke within hours of being rescued.

But whatever Mullen's misgivings, the fact was he was now in demand: first a man who wanted his male partner tracking; then a woman who thought her male colleague was conniving with a business rival; and soon after that a London-based couple 'in property' who wanted Mullen to conduct a week-long surveillance of their daughter who was studying PPE at Oxford University and supposedly skipping lectures and even tutorials. All of this was easy money, and Mullen was glad of it, but it was like gorging on ice-cream and soon enough he was feeling extremely queasy. What good would come of any of this snooping? The bottom line was that Mullen was at heart a sentimental do-gooder, and he found it hard to believe that any of these jobs he was being paid to do would bring any good to anyone.

He explained this to Rex one morning as they took an early morning stroll across the fields above Oxford. It wasn't quite 7.30, but there was plenty of traffic ploughing along the A34 and so plenty of noise to spoil the silence. Not that Rex cared. Being a dog, he didn't care about Mullen's introspective monologue either. He stopped dead, sniffing at the trail of a rabbit. Mullen stopped too. He had kept Rex on his lead so far. He had been tempted to let him run free that morning. But two nights previously he had dreamt that Rex had been savaged by a huge husky, so he continued to play safe. Just in case. Mullen waited patiently for the dog to finish sniffing and only then resumed his slow walk.

A few metres further on Rex stopped again. He cocked his leg and at that same moment Mullen's phone rang. He fumbled in his pocket.

Who on earth would be ringing him at this hour? Another person wanting to hire him to follow their not-so-beloved?

Unknown flashed up on screen. For a moment or two Mullen hesitated to answer it. If it was the woman who had stood him up the previous day, who had summoned him to a meeting across the other side of the county and then not turned up, he wasn't sure he would be able to be polite to her.

Mullen breathed in, then out, and then he answered.

'Doug Mullen Detective Agency,' he said.

'It's Ellie.'

'Oh.' Mullen's brain froze momentarily. As did his tongue.

'I thought you'd like to know that Mum is coming home today. At last.'

'Oh. Yes. That's … great.'

'I'm sure she'd like to see you. If you aren't too busy?'

'Of course,' Mullen burbled. 'Yes indeed. When would be…?'

But Mullen was talking to a digital void. Ellie had hung up.

It was the fourth time since the crash that Doug Mullen had been to visit Natalie Swan. On the three previous occasions she had been in a hospital, where flowers were discouraged, and he had taken grapes because he couldn't think of anything more original. After all, he didn't really know the woman at all. But this time he was going to her house and it felt different. So he set off with a large bunch of flowers in his arms because surely in her own house she would be delighted to receive them. Actually, Mullen was more of a vegetable man than a flower man. Give him a kitchen garden any day. Growing things that you could eat – or you could give to others to eat – seemed infinitely more valuable and beneficial than growing flowers. But you don't pay a visit to a sick woman brandishing a bunch of carrots. Mullen knew that, even though he had some fine young carrots and broad beans which he could have brought from his garden.

Not that it was his garden in the legal sense. It actually belonged to a Professor Moody, as did the large modern house which Mullen was going to be occupying for the foreseeable future until she returned from her year at Yale. Mullen was house-sitting. He couldn't initially understand why Professor Moody had opted for a sitter when the house could have been rented out very profitably in her absence. Very profitably indeed given the going rate for rented property in Oxford. But when the professor had listed the conditions, things had become clearer.

'Take your shoes off at the front door.'

'Do not enter my bedroom or en-suite bathroom under any circumstance unless there is reason to believe that there is a leak.'

'Do not use my study. Only enter it to reset the wifi.'

'You must maintain the garden properly.' She had handed him nine pages of printed instructions which defined in detail what she meant by 'properly'.

'Do not have sex on the Afghan rug.' Mullen wasn't sure which of the several rugs around the house the Afghan was, but he wasn't planning sex on any of them.

'And you must, above all, look after Rex.'

Mullen had been briefly confused by this too, but at that point, as if he had been waiting offstage for his cue, Rex shambled in – short legged, rough black hair, upright ears which suggested an intense curiosity in the world.

'He's a Westie Poodle,' the professor announced proudly. 'Usually they are white. But Rex is rather special.' Special? Did that mean she spoilt him rotten? 'He's lazy,' she continued, 'so needs taking out for his exercise and he's a little fussy with his food.'

Mullen's enthusiasm for the house-sitting role was plummeting fast. He hoped 'a little fussy' didn't mean he'd have to cook 'special' food for the little blighter.

If Mullen had had any other options open to him, he might well have made his excuses and scarpered. But beggars can't be choosers and in any case, Mullen quite liked living in an environment where there were very clear rules of behaviour. It felt a bit like the army, but without the bad food. The only bit he was uneasy about was the dog. He didn't dislike dogs. But looking after one seemed a considerable responsibility.

The flowers which he was taking to Natalie Swan were hand-picked from the professor's garden that morning. They were a mixture of wild flowers – he knew that because they were all from the 'wild flower area' (as designated on page eight of the professor's instruction booklet). He thought they looked pretty, but he hoped he wouldn't be quizzed on what each of them was.

Mullen paused on Natalie's doorstep and rang the bell. It was late July and although it was only mid-morning, it was already threatening to be a stinking hot day. He wiped his forehead with the back of his hand. It was damp with sweat. He rubbed his chin and realised with dismay that he hadn't shaved that morning. Or brushed his hair. He ran a hand over it. It needed a cut. It was slightly over his ears, something he would never have allowed in the past. He knew too that there were plenty of grey hairs, but he wasn't going to resort to dying them. Even so, he made a mental note to get a haircut.

There was a tug on the lead. He turned to look behind him. Rex, who had already crapped halfway along Arnold's Way, was completing the job on Natalie Swan's path.

'Shit!' he said, as the door opened. He didn't have a second plastic bag on him.

'Oh!' The apparition which opened the door was Ellie Swan. Her black hair had now sprouted purple tufts. Despite him having rescued her as well as her mother on the M40 some months previously, she greeted him with the level of hostility which most people reserve for Jehovah's Witnesses on their doorsteps. 'It's *you*.' She pushed past Mullen. 'Oh my God!' she exclaimed. 'What is *that*?' She was gesticulating at Rex rather than the poo. Then, 'I'm going to be late.' She spoke as if her being late was all Mullen's fault. Then she was gone, stomping aggressively along the pavement in her purple Doc Marten boots.

Mullen peered inside the house, wondering if Natalie or someone else might come and invite him in. Nobody did. Rex pulled on the leash, keen to explore, and so Mullen allowed himself to walk cautiously forwards until he found himself in an empty kitchen. The patio door was open and he advanced towards it. The thin garden stretched away down a slight slope, surprisingly long. He pushed his head out. To his left, on the patio, sat a motionless figure.

'Hi!' he said.

Natalie Swan was sitting in a patch of sunlight softened by the shade cast by a false acacia tree. She was seated on a large green chair stuffed with cushions. She was studying the palms of her hands as if they held the secrets of the universe.

'Hi!' Mullen said again, more loudly.

This time she turned her head and looked up at him. Her expression was blank.

'I've brought you some flowers.' Mullen held them up, more in self-defence than triumph.

There was a long pause.

'Oh! How nice!' she said finally. She smiled. It was the sort of smile that might have launched a ship or two if only Mullen had had some at his command.

He advanced onto the patio and handed the flowers over to her. She took them, smelt them and then lay them on the table.

'We need a ...' The smile melted into nothingness. Mullen waited awkwardly, uncertain whether to say something. Natalie squeezed her eyes tight and several seconds passed before she opened them.

'A vase,' said a much deeper voice, close by Mullen's right ear. A woman, small and square, in a crisp light-blue uniform, had materialized. 'My name's Mercy,' she said. 'Mercy McAlister.'

'Doug Mullen.'

'Ah! You Mr Mullen? Natalie's knight in shining armour.' Mercy was on the verge of exploding with delight. 'Sit down, Mr Mullen. I'll deal with these beautiful flowers and make us all a nice cup of tea.'

Natalie seemed happy to sit in silence. Mullen tried not to feel uncomfortable. He still hadn't got used to Natalie's condition and he still hadn't accepted the brutal unfairness of what had happened. He had rescued her – no big deal, he kept telling himself – and by the time she had been transported to the hospital for a check-up, she had had a stroke. It could have been worse but it could have been better too. The stroke had brought on aphasia. Mullen had looked it up on the internet. Essentially it affected communication; in Natalie's case this was most apparent in her inability to locate simple words in her brain. There wasn't, as far as Mullen could see, any rhyme or reason. She could produce words like 'circumlocution' and 'aardvark' (and apparently know what they meant), but words like 'vase' and 'table' refused to surface until someone else prompted her.

'You've got a nice sun-trap here,' he said eventually, trying to start a conversation.

Natalie had been looking up at the leaves of the false acacia, the ship-launching smile restored to its full glory. But it faded as she focused back on him.

'Spade,' she said.

It was Mullen's turn to frown, but Mercy appeared just in time, bearing a tray with mugs of tea and three pieces of sponge cake.

'She struggles with your name,' she said as she dispensed her goodies and pulled up another faded plastic chair. 'Doug doesn't register for her. But you're a private eye, aren't you? And I understand you like gardening. So we've decided to call you Spade, as in Sam Spade.'

'Doug Spade,' Natalie said brightly.

Doug or dug? Mullen was getting confused himself.

'Spade is good,' he said and bit into the cake. Coffee and walnut, one of his favourites.

He was about to ask Mercy about her own name when the doorbell rang. She got up and went to answer it, stuffing a piece of cake in as she did.

She was soon back. 'Look, a parcel for you, sweetie.'

She placed a brown jiffy bag on the table, plus a pair of scissors and demolished the last piece of her cake.

'You going to open it, sweetie?' she said as she stood up. 'Just got to pop upstairs for a private moment.' She winked at Mullen. 'Mr Spade will keep you company.'

Natalie eyed the package as if she hadn't a clue what to do with it. Eventually, she pushed it across the table towards Mullen.

'I'll open it,' he said, and picked up the scissors.

Thirty seconds later he had sliced his way through all the brown tape and eased open the flap. Then he passed the jiffy bag back to her.

Natalie slipped her hand inside and pulled out something wrapped in white tissue paper. She placed it on the table in front of her and carefully unwrapped it with intense concentration, one fold at a time. Mullen couldn't help but think of how childlike she looked. When she pulled back the final fold to uncover the contents, she gave a gasp.

At first Mullen couldn't make out what the objects were. But it was clear that Natalie didn't like them. Another sound, a low groan, emitted from Natalie's throat, and then with a violent sweep of her arm, she sent the package and its contents flying across the patio. Then she lay her head down on the table and began to whimper very softly.

Mullen paused, thrown off balance by the sudden development. But the army had taught him a few things, and one of them involved making a decision and then acting on it. He got up, moved a couple of steps and knelt down to see what had caused Natalie's wild reaction. White stuffed toys, he thought, and then realized it was more than that. Two swans, one larger than the other. But not very swanlike now, because in each case the head of the swan had been cut clean off the neck. Mullen picked up the two heads. Each was white, as you might

25

expect, but the stump of each neck had been daubed with some sort of red paint or dye.

Mullen slipped all four pieces and the paper packaging back into the jiffy bag and then stood up, holding it behind his back. Natalie raised her head and stared him. She opened her mouth, but nothing came out. Mullen felt at a loss. Was this her aphasia kicking in, her wanting to tell him something, but unable to find the words? Should he wait for her to say something or should he be talking? He wished Mercy would return from the loo.

At last Mullen decided he had to say something, but Natalie beat him to it. She opened her mouth and emitted a scream which started high and loud and got higher and louder until the heavy feet of Mercy came pounding down the stairs, through the kitchen and into the garden.

'Mary, mother of Jesus,' she said, flinging an accusatory glare at Mullen. He stepped backwards, suddenly panicking that Mercy might think he had done something to Natalie.

'It was the package,' he said, holding it up before him. If looks could kill, Mullen would have been vaporized by Mercy's glare. She enfolded Natalie in her dark brown arms, and Mullen took the opportunity to flee to sanctuary inside the house, the jiffy bag still gripped tight in his right hand.

'I'll be wanting a word with you, Spade,' Mercy bellowed after him. 'Don't you go running away.'

Rex was silent all the way home, as if conscious that he had pushed his luck with his new master. He no longer had an urge to void his bowels or bladder, but as soon as he reached the familiar front gate with his own territorial smells he uttered a fearsome growl. Intruder! There was someone on his patch. He pulled against the restraining lead and sniffed hard at a foreign scent on the gravel path. He stood as tall as his short legs would permit and stared ahead. There was a stranger sitting on one of the two stone benches which stood in front of the house on either side of the porch.

The stranger was on his mistress's bench, the one she often sat on and the one he always lay under, basking in her protection. But the person on the bench was most definitely not his mistress.

'Rex!' That was his master's voice, but Rex didn't much care. He knew better than his stupid master. So he barked again. He knew trouble when he smelt it, and this intruder was trouble.

'Can I help you?' Mullen said. Not that he much felt like helping the woman who was sitting on the bench as if she owned it. She had brown hair, cut into a bob. A neat fringe which hid much of her forehead. Thin eyebrows, a mole on her chin and blue eyes which surveyed him as if he was a previously undiscovered species of creature. Mid-forties, he guessed. Or maybe older than that, but trying to look younger. She had a piece of material in her lap – a scarf Mullen reckoned – and her hands were twisting and wringing it as if it had just been extricated from a bowl of hand-washing.

She stood up as he drew near. She detached the earphones which had been plugged into her ears and stood up. 'Sorry, I was miles away. What did you say?'

'This is private property,' Mullen said and immediately regretted it. How pathetic his words sounded as they came out of his mouth. Mullen had never owned his own property, but being Professor Moody's house-sitter had imparted in him a particular sense of responsibility. It was his job to look after the house. And if there was one thing that Rex's aggression told him, it was that the woman was not a friend of the professor. And therefore that she shouldn't be sitting in the front garden as if it was a bench in a public park.

The woman straightened herself and looked at him calmly. Mullen had the impression that she was finding him a disappointment. When she spoke, she did so calmly. 'I understand you are a private investigator.'

Mullen was taken by surprise. He didn't advertise where he lived on his single-page website or his business cards. Only a mobile phone number and an email address.

'How on earth…?' he began, but she had anticipated him, and was already pulling a piece of newspaper out of her pocket. She unfolded it and held it up in front of him. He recognized it. It was the *Oxford Mail* double-page report on the accident, which featured a photo of himself with Natalie and Ellie.

'You're quite a celebrity round here. I only had to show it to the guy in the newsagent down the hill and he immediately told me what a wonderful chap you were and where you lived.'

Mullen nodded.

'Is that Professor Moody's dog?'

Mullen said nothing, but the dog, right on cue, emitted a low growl. Perhaps Rex, like Mullen, was rather unnerved by the amount that the woman seemed to know about them.

'Do you know Professor Moody?' he said.

'It doesn't matter whether I do or don't.' Her face was dead serious now. Her skin was stretched tight across her cheeks and jaw. Eyes narrowed. 'What matters is this: are you any good at finding people?'

The woman's name was Elizabeth Durant. Once she had given up that amount of information, Mullen decided it was OK to let her into the house. He guided her through into the kitchen.

'Tea or coffee?'

'Just hot water, please. Can I use the loo?'

Mullen could hardly say no. But he felt uneasy nevertheless. After switching on the kettle, he positioned himself in the corner of the room by the gas hob. From there he could see right through to the door of the downstairs toilet as well as the bottom of the stairs. The last thing the professor would have wanted – or so he told himself – was for a complete stranger to go snooping around the house.

Elizabeth Durant reappeared from the toilet after five minutes and sat meekly down at the table where Mullen had placed her mug of freshly boiled water.

Mullen sat down opposite her with his mug of builder's tea.

'So who is this person you want to find?'

For a second time, she produced a piece of newspaper, a much smaller cutting. There was a photo of a youth, his mouth slightly open, eyes looking away to his left. *Saad Ismat* the caption said. Syrian refugee. Mullen read the short article carefully. He remembered hearing about it on BBC Radio Oxford a week or two previously, but the information had not lodged in his brain any more than the many other sad stories which make the news for a day or two and then disappear down a black hole of public indifference.

Saad had disappeared too. He had gone to school as normal and left at the end of lessons, but had never arrived home. Home, as far as the *Oxford Mail* was concerned, was a house in the village of Kennington, just to the south of Oxford. Though as a refugee from Syria, he may still have considered the Arabic for the word 'home' to be a bombed out flat in Aleppo.

'There was no reason why he should have run away,' Elizabeth Durant had told the journalist. 'He had some friends at school and he felt really happy. I would have known if he hadn't been. Something terrible must have happened to him.'

'I'm sorry,' Mullen began. 'It must be very difficult for you.'

Durant said nothing. She had cupped her mug in both hands and was staring into the water.

Mullen tried a question. 'What have the police done about finding him?'

She gave out a single hoarse laugh. 'Added him to a list of missing persons. Asked me a lot of intrusive questions. Put out a press statement. And told me that if he doesn't want to be found, it will be very difficult to find him.'

'Have you any ideas? About where he might have gone or why?'

'He wouldn't have just run away.'

'I did once,' Mullen said.

She looked up sharply, her eyes boring in on his. She wanted to know more. Mullen knew that. But he could see that she didn't know whether to believe him.

'When I was fifteen,' he explained, 'I spent about a month on the streets in London. Then I went back home.'

'Why did you run away?'

Mullen wished he hadn't opened this particular can of worms. It was something he preferred to keep the lid on, very tight. If he did so, his thinking went, he might eventually forget it altogether. But he hadn't.

'Family problems,' he said finally. 'My dad mostly.'

Durant nodded and finally took a sip of her water. Then she looked up, peering through the disobedient strands of her hair. 'And what made you return home?'

'I met someone. He had been living rough for ages. He looked after me and he persuaded me to go home to my mum.'

Durant fell silent. She pulled some tissue out of her sleeve and dabbed at her eyes. Mullen waited. He was in no rush. He had the rest of the day. Even Rex had settled down in his basket, as if accepting that this was no time to be demanding attention, that there was another being in the room who had greater needs than his. Mullen sipped at his tea. He knew he would have to help Elizabeth Durant. How could he not?

'People do return,' he said, trying to open up a channel of communication. He was living proof, after all.

Durant howled. Like a wolf. Mullen jumped. He had been cradling his mug in his hands and the tea flooded across the table. He swore and got up, grabbing kitchen towel off its roller. He began to wipe the table, anxious to stop the tea dripping onto the floor. But Durant seemed oblivious. She had relapsed into deep sobs which were causing her body to twitch violently. Mullen scrabbled in his back pocket for a handkerchief. He always kept one there. White with his name tape sown in. He still had several of them left, a memorial of his mother's love for him. He handed it over to her reluctantly before resuming the clear-up operation.

Eventually he sat down. 'It's important to hang onto hope,' he said, surprising himself. He wasn't sure where that piece of pop psychology wisdom had come from. He waited for her to react.

She looked up and peered at him through tortured eyes.

'There's no hope for Saad,' she said, defying his optimism. 'Saad is dead.'

Both of them fell silent again. Mullen drained what was left of his tea before venturing another question. This was unknown and dangerous territory – like walking through hostile territory, conscious there are unexploded landmines all around.

'What makes you think he is dead?'

Durant didn't say anything. She opened up the bag on her knees and pulled out the scarf which she had been twisting like a piece of damp washing when he had first seen her. She tried to straighten and smooth it out on the table, then folded it into a neatish pile. It was blue and yellow – standard Oxford United issue. She bent down and buried her face in it. Then she sat up and gently placed her two hands on it. Out in the hallway, the professor's grandmother clock chimed sonorously. Rex growled softly in his dream-filled sleep. Mullen tried not to make any sound at all. Finally, Elizabeth Durant looked up at him, her face a crumpled mess. But when she spoke, she did so with absolute seriousness.

'This is Saad's scarf. He loved it. We went to watch the football together. He was so happy. But now as I feel it, I know that he is dead and gone forever.'

Mullen was bemused. This was beyond his experience. 'What do you mean?'

'There is no life in the scarf. None. Saad is not in London, sleeping on the streets, getting into bad habits. He is dead.'

Mullen's mouth was half-open. He felt he had to say something. God only knew what. But then the phone rang.

For the second time that day, Mullen found himself on Natalie Swan's doorstep. Elizabeth Durant had reacted to Mullen's phone ringing as if it was a starter gun. She had been up on her feet and out of his front door before he could hope to stop her. It had been Mercy's distinctive voice on the end of the phone and she asked him very politely and firmly to come round again, at six o'clock.

'Mrs Swan is in a terrible state,' she said. He could have replied that Elizabeth Durant was too, but it wouldn't have helped.

For the second time, it was a sour-faced Ellie who opened the door.

'Have you brought that dog?'

'Left him at home. He's not that keen on exercise.'

She gave a grunt. Not exactly gracious, but a slight improvement on their previous encounter. 'You'd better come in.'

Natalie looked up as he entered the kitchen. She was sitting at the kitchen table, cradling a mug in her hands. She frowned.

'Would you like a...?' Her mouth froze. She was looking over Mullen's shoulder now, searching for that elusive word.

'Beer, tea or coffee?' Ellie was emitting waves of impatience.

'Beer would be nice.'

Mullen took off his jacket and sat down opposite Natalie. She was hugging her mug again, as if desperate for the heat that it gave off. He waited until she looked up at him.

'Mercy said you wanted to see me.'

Ellie banged the bottle down in front of him and herself sat down. 'Mum's scared.'

'The two swans, you mean.'

'The two headless bloody swans. How would you feel if you had

32

received them through the post? Wouldn't you be scared shitless if you had received them and your name was Swan?' Not so much angry or impatient as terrified. The girl's hands were twisting and pulling at her hair. 'And in case you haven't noticed, there are two of us named Swan and two headless swans.'

'Have you reported this to the police?'

Ellie didn't answer. Mullen turned back to her mother. Natalie was looking at him now.

'I thought maybe you—' She spoke slowly, one lumbering word after another.

Ellie butted in. 'You're a private investigator, Mullen. And you're an all right sort of bloke. We thought maybe you could help us.'

Mullen took a sip of beer from his bottle. An all right sort of bloke? That seemed like high praise from Ellie's mouth.

'I know people in the police. I—'

Natalie slapped a hand hard down on the table. 'No police.' No hesitation either. No searching for the word. 'Definitely no police!'

Mullen took another sip from his bottle. Unless he was in an unfamiliar pub, he preferred drinking from a glass. 'Do you mind telling me why?'

'They aren't going to take it seriously.' Ellie had taken over again.

Mullen sighed. 'Why do you say that?'

'It's hardly going to be a priority, investigating two swans.'

Mullen was inclined to agree. He tried a different tack. 'If you give me the jiffy bag and the swans, then maybe I can use my contacts to get it checked for DNA.'

Silence. An embarrassed sort of silence. Then Natalie spoke. 'Not … not possible.'

Mullen waited. Was an explanation going to come?

Ellie took over again. 'Mum was so distressed that Mercy took them into the garden and put them in the brazier which the gardener uses to burn stuff.'

'You mean Mercy burnt them?'

Ellie nodded.

Mullen nodded back, largely because he couldn't think of anything to say. He changed the subject. 'Could I possibly have a glass for the beer?'

Actually he was beginning to think he should have opted for a cup of strong tea. He needed a clear head. Mother and daughter were both frightened. Why? There had to be a reason.

He poured the beer carefully down the side of the glass, trying to work out how best to approach questioning Natalie.

'I'll try to help,' he said finally. How could he turn them down? He should have stated his terms and conditions then, or at least how much he charged per day, but he didn't want to sound like he only helped if the money was right. The bottom line was that Mullen was a soft touch. And at this moment his focus was on finding out why on earth Natalie was so afraid. 'Natalie,' he said, speaking slowly and softly. 'Do you have any idea who might have sent you the swans?'

Natalie glanced across at her daughter and then back at Mullen. 'The only person I can think of is my ex-husband.'

It took Mullen four and a half hours to get from Oxford to Hull, even though he set out long before any sensible person would want to be out of bed. But that didn't guarantee a good journey. There are a surprising number of lorries on the road at 5.30 in the morning, but being on the road that early doesn't mean the drivers of these vehicles are fully awake and alert. A smash somewhere north of Leicester left him and his car motionless on the A46 for almost an hour.

One silver lining to the cloud was that it gave Rex an opportunity to do his business on the verge. Another was that it gave Mullen an opportunity to think about what he had learnt and what he was trying to achieve. Natalie (with less and less help from Ellie) had eventually told him about her ex-husband Paul Reeve, who had been jailed for fifteen years for physically abusing her and three-year-old Ellie. That had been over ten years previously. Was he out of prison? That was the first question. If he had behaved himself inside, the chances were he would have been released on licence by now. Besides, as Mullen knew from the news, prisons were getting ridiculously overcrowded. The pressure to release inmates early must be enormous.

Revelation number two was that Natalie and Ellie Swan had once been Gemma and Sally Reeve. They had changed their names soon after Paul Reeve had been sentenced and had moved a long way from Hull to start a new life. That was the starting point that Mullen had needed. If the toy swans had been sent by Paul Reeve, then he must have discovered their change of name. Had he recognized them from the TV and press reports of that M40 accident? That seemed unlikely. Quite apart from their change of names, mother and daughter had changed a lot in those intervening years. So how might Reeve have discovered their new identity? Natalie had apparently had no family members who needed to be party to their secret. She had ruthlessly cut herself adrift from all of her friends to ensure their safety from her ex-husband. No-one knew who or where she and her daughter were – except for Mr Ray Costa, the man who had helped them achieve their disappearing act.

Ray Costa LLP had an impressive address, but the reality was less so. It was one of a number of businesses based in an unexciting modern block opposite a bed shop and DIY store. Mullen made his way up to the fourth floor by the stairs, keen to galvanize his legs into life after their extended immobility in his car. He found the relevant door, knocked and entered. A woman looked up at him from behind an immaculately tidy desk. Grey blouse, grey rimmed glasses, silver earrings, platinum grey hair cut into a bob. Her nails were grey too. If Mullen had been a psychologist, perhaps he would have known what all that meant. The woman's name, according to a small plaque on the desk, was Linda Wiseman.

'Can I help you?' She spoke brusquely, as if casual visitors were an intolerable intrusion on the order and calm of her working life.

'I was hoping to have a quick word with Mr Costa.'

'Appointments only.' She stared unblinkingly into Mullen's eyes.

Mullen launched what he hoped was a winning smile. 'I've come a long way. It really would take only a few minutes.'

'He's not in today. But if you would like to make an appointment, I've got one or two gaps next week.'

Mullen unzipped his leather jacket and pulled a piece of paper from the inside pocket. 'Maybe *you* can help me. Save me bothering Mr Costa.' He attempted another winning smile. 'Do you recognize this man?'

It was a photograph of Paul Reeve, but Paul Reeve as he had appeared in the press ten years previously. An unflattering mugshot. Mullen had found and printed it off the internet the previous evening, because Natalie (understandably) had removed every trace of her ex-husband from her life, and that included every single photograph in which he had appeared.

'Look, who are you exactly?' If Linda Wiseman had been a dog, she would have been emitting a low warning growl.

'Doug Mullen.' He plunged in. 'I'm a friend of the woman who was once married to this man. That was until ten years ago, when he was imprisoned for beating her black and blue. And stubbing his cigarette out on his own child.' Mullen had picked up that detail from the press reports. He hoped it was the sort of horror that would persuade Linda Wiseman to co-operate.

'I can't say I recognize him.'

'His name is Paul Reeve. I have reason to believe he may have visited Mr Costa in the last few weeks.'

'I don't recall the name. And I do know most of our clients.'

'He might easily have used a false name. Come in and had a single meeting with Mr Costa. No follow up. No legal documents that you had to process. No letters to type. Cash payment maybe, if he paid at all. Any or all of that.'

Linda Wiseman looked at Mullen again, but differently. This time the hard edge had gone from her manner, as if what Mullen had said was ringing a few bells. He did hope so.

'Would you mind getting me a coffee from the machine in the corridor?' she said. Buying some time to think – or possibly to summon security. 'White, no sugar.'

Mullen nodded. 'Of course.'

When Mullen returned, bearing two coffees, Linda Wiseman was leaning back in her chair, staring at the ceiling. She was looking rather pleased with herself.

'You're smarter than you look, Mr Mullen.'

Mullen tried not to take offence.

'I mean, you come here in that rather tired leather jacket and a creased shirt and a little boy lost face, but behind that facade there's a very sharp little brain whirring away.'

'So you've found something?'

'A Mr John Smith. Original, don't you think? Made an appointment over the phone. Stayed only eleven minutes. Last Friday.'

'Mr Costa didn't say what the meeting had been about?'

'No, nothing.'

'And do you think Mr Smith is the same as the man in the photo?'

She looked at the newspaper clipping again and nodded. 'Very possibly.'

'Look, I really need to speak to Mr Costa. I know this is out of order, but perhaps you could just dial him up for me now. I don't need to know the number. But for the safety of my client, I need to know what Paul Reeve wanted.'

Linda Wiseman looked at Mullen as if he had asked her to strip naked and dance on her desk. She sank her face into her hands and began to wail. Mullen sat motionless. When the sobs had subsided, she began to talk. She told Mullen how Ray wasn't answering either his landline or his mobile. How she had been trying to get hold of him ever since Monday morning. How she was really worried that something might have happened to him.

'He was in a real state after Mr Smith came to see him. I could see that. And he went home early. That was completely out of character.'

Mullen listened until eventually the storm inside Wiseman subsided. He drained his half-cold coffee, not sure when he might get anything else to eat or drink.

'I wonder, Linda,' he said, turning on his little-boy-lost charm, 'if you happen to have a spare key for Ray's house?'

Linda Wiseman didn't have a spare key, but she had Ray Costa's address firmly lodged in her brain, and to judge from the ease with which she directed him to it, she had visited him there. She seemed to know plenty about his personal life too. Costa, she told Mullen, was separated from his wife. It had been an acrimonious parting of the marital ways. He had managed to keep in touch with his two teenage kids, but only just – alternate weekends if he was lucky. He lived in an unexciting semi-detached house in a cul-de-sac in the north-western extremities of Hull. Wiseman was out of the car as soon as she had switched off the engine. She marched briskly along the side of the house. Just beyond the back door there was a terracotta pot containing long neglected Chrysanthemums, and it was here that she bent down, lifting the pot and recovering a key.

'I sometimes feed the cat for him if he's away,' she explained, opening the door.

'Shall I go first?' Mullen had unpleasant images of what they might find inside, but Wiseman unlocked the door and pushed her way in without hesitation.

Flies! That was Mullen's first anxiety, but there was no host of bluebottles buzzing around the kitchen. Nor was there the stench of decaying flesh. The only smells were a general mustiness and the odour of fetid food waste.

Wiseman paused in the kitchen, as if the adrenalin in her system had suddenly run dry and had been replaced by the bleak realization of what they might find.

'It doesn't look like he's here,' Mullen said, trying to project an optimism he didn't feel. 'Maybe he's gone bird-watching.' For that, as Linda had mentioned in the car, was his one true passion.

Mullen moved past her through to the living room. All neat and tidy. There was a paper on the coffee table, apparently unread. He checked the date. Three days ago. Evidence of sorts. He turned to say something trite and comforting to Linda, but she wasn't there.

He moved back into the kitchen, but she wasn't there either.

'Linda?' he called, and began to move back through the living room.

Linda didn't reply – or at least not in any normal sense. Instead Mullen heard her wail – a soft distressed moan which grew in intensity and volume until, by the time Mullen had reached the bottom of the stairs, it had reached a crescendo of distress.

Wiseman was staring up the stairs. Mullen saw immediately – swaying ever so slightly – the highly polished black leather shoes, blue socks with pink spots, and the pin-striped trousers of a very dead man. He advanced a step, so he could check fully that there was nothing to be done. He caught a strong whiff of urine, but saw no sign of dampness. Ray Costa, he was pretty sure, had been dead for a couple of days at least.

Have you made a decision?

The text arrived almost as soon as Mullen and Rex got in the front door. By the time Rex had been ushered out the back door, another had arrived. *Do you think I am mad?*

Mullen presumed these were from Elizabeth Durant, though she hadn't put her name at the end and she had left his house the previous morning without giving him any personal details. He could truthfully have texted *Yes* to both questions, but he knew better than to do that. Instead, although it was just gone 10.30 p.m., he rang her. Better and safer to talk about it than fire texts back and forth.

'Is that Mr Mullen?'

'Sorry to ring so late,' he began.

'You probably think I'm crazy.'

'Not at all.'

'You're not in your pyjamas yet?'

'No.'

'Got company?'

'Only the dog.'

'Can I pop round now?'

'Erm ...'

'Actually I'm parked very close by.'

'Oh!'

'Just for a few minutes. I promise.'

Mullen hung up and went to the front door. By the time he had unchained and unlocked it, the external light had switched on automatically. When he opened the door, she was there, her hand poised to ring the bell.

She declined the offer of a drink and sat down at the kitchen table. Mullen let Rex in and he shambled towards her. She had ignored him last time, but now she helped him onto her lap and began to stroke and fuss him, as if they were long lost buddies.

Mullen sat down. 'You left Saad's scarf here.' He gestured towards it, lying on the work surface. He had put it in a see-through plastic bag. 'Actually, I'm afraid the dog got hold of it. He took it to bed with him. I was going to wash it, and then ...' He lifted his hands apologetically. 'Sorry!'

'Not your fault. It was mine, and maybe Rex's too. But you can't blame a dog for behaving like a dog.' She bent down, burying her face in Rex's coat and uttering soft mewing noises. Mullen waited, wondering what on earth he was letting himself in for. Eventually, she straightened up and looked at him. 'Anyway, to get down to business, how much will you charge to find Saad?'

'I can't promise to find him. As for how long it will take to explore every avenue ...' He shrugged. 'I mean, how long is a piece of string?'

She gave a harsh laugh. 'So how much string will £500 buy me?'

Mullen got up and went to the sink. He poured himself a glass of water and drank half of it. 'Quite a long piece. I'll tell you when it runs out.'

'I expect you prefer cash?'

'Not necessarily. I can give you my bank details if you prefer.'

'OK, I'll make a transfer when I get home.'

He nodded. She was very trusting. Or maybe just desperate.

But Elizabeth Durant was, despite her somewhat shambolic air, also very focused. 'Have you had a chance to research the case yet?'

Mullen took another sip of water. 'I had to go to Hull today. On another job.' He felt bad admitting this. As if he had better things to do than start looking for her missing boy. 'I left very early and only got back a short while ago. It's a long way. The traffic was bad.' He dribbled to a stop. He had run out of excuses.

'I understand,' she said. 'You're helping Natalie Swan, aren't you?'

Mullen felt thrown off balance again. 'You know her?'

She leaned forward, fixing him with her blue eyes. 'Ellie and Saad were friends. Nothing inappropriate. There was an age gap, of course, but teenage girls tend to prefer older boys, and Saad was a bit different from most of the other lads. As well as being very good looking.'

It was Mercy who opened the door. She beamed. 'Mr Spade!' She ushered him in.

'Natalie is rather late getting up this morning, but why don't you go and sit in the garden and she'll be down shortly.'

It was 9.45, but already there was the promise of an overheated day in prospect. Mullen made his way through the kitchen and out through the patio doors.

'Hi!'

There was a figure kneeling down on the edge of the lawn.

The man turned his head, revealing a tightly clipped beard, a slightly asymmetrical face and weathered skin.

'I'm Doug. Doug Mullen.'

The man nodded, but didn't move from his spot.

'Rick North. Gardener and odd-job man. I'm making a start on the weeding. It's a surprisingly long garden, so there's plenty to be done. '

'Don't mind me. I'm just waiting for Natalie.'

'You a friend, are you?'

Mullen considered this. He didn't really think of himself as a friend, but maybe that was what he was becoming.

'Sort of,' he said, hedging his bets.

'Sorry, none of my business. I always have been someone who asks too many questions. Learned it off my mother, I guess.'

'I'll leave you to it,' Mullen said. He turned and headed back into the kitchen, leaving North to get on with his work. He didn't want to be responsible for distracting him and he didn't want to be asked too many questions either.

There was an unopened copy of the *Oxford Times* on the table. He picked it up and started to leaf through it carefully, just in case there was anything about Saad in it. He rather doubted it, but you never knew.

Two sets of footsteps on the stairs – one pair light and one heavy – heralded the arrival of Natalie and Mercy.

'Hello, Mr Spade.' Natalie seemed bright and more on the ball than Mullen was expecting.

'We've been a bit naughty this morning,' Mercy said. 'Had breakfast in bed. Now for a cup of tea.'

While Mercy busied herself, Natalie sat down. She looked at Mullen expectantly, but didn't say anything. Mullen waited for the tea to arrive. Ellie was apparently out – or in bed – and for a moment he thought Mercy was now going to take over the role of prompter. But instead she went outside with two mugs of tea in her hands and shut the door. Mullen saw her give a mug to Rick and realized that this was his opportunity to talk. He wondered how much Mercy knew.

'I have been making some inquiries about your ex-husband,' he said.

Mullen had already decided to keep things simple, and certainly not to go into any detail about his trip to Hull. 'Making inquiries' seemed like a good way of avoiding awkward questions. He didn't want to lie unless he had to and he certainly didn't want to cause Natalie to get alarmed.

'Is he ... is he still in...?' Her eyebrows were arched in concentration, but the word wouldn't come, obvious though it was to Mullen.

'Paul Reeve is out of prison. I'm not sure when he was released. It might have been weeks or months or even longer ago.'

'Do you think he...?' Again there was a long pause.

Knew of her name change? Knew she was living in Oxford? Had sent the decapitated swans and was now biding his time? She could have asked any of those things, but she didn't. In the end she gave up trying to finish the sentence and held her head in her hands. She began to sob softly. Mullen turned. Mercy was outside, watching them through the glass. He gestured for her to come in.

Mercy gave Natalie some tissues and then took her out in the garden, where she seated her in the green chair.

Mullen was tempted to leave immediately, but he had things he needed to say to Mercy. So he waited, bracing himself for Mercy's telling off.

'What is it with you and Natalie? It always seems to end in tears.'

'Yeah,' he said.

'Actually, she is often in tears.' Mercy sat down abruptly on the chair opposite Mullen. She leaned forward, lowering her voice. 'Especially when Ellie's around. She's a right little madam, that girl. Honestly, if she was mine I'd have boxed her ears years ago.'

'I guess everyone's under stress,' Mullen said, even though he pretty much agreed with Mercy's sentiment.

'So what were you up to yesterday?'

It was a straight from the hip question, but Mullen ignored it.

'I need you to keep a look out for any strangers, for anyone hanging around in the road. Especially when you go out for a walk with Natalie. If you do see anyone that makes you suspicious, try to memorize what he looks like and then let me know. You can ring me any time of the day or night.'

'And who is this I am looking out for?'

Mullen had been wondering whether or not to say, but in the circumstances and for everyone's safety, he felt she needed to know.

'Her ex-husband,' he said. 'He has a history of violence against her, so don't take any chances. And if anyone calls at the house, be very careful. Keep the security chain on at all times. Make a note of time, place, clothes and so on. All right?'

Mercy nodded. 'Don't you worry, Spade. No-one's gonna hurt Mrs Swan. Not on my watch.'

Mullen nodded back. Mercy was a good ally, but when dealing with violent men, he wondered if she wasn't just a tiny bit naïve.

Ellie was fifty metres from McDonald's when she stopped suddenly and knelt down on the pavement. She undid her right-hand lace and then pulled it tight. It hadn't been loose, but she did it up even tighter this time, finishing with a double bow. She stood up, and as she adjusted the rucksack on her back, she glanced back towards the bridge. It was Mullen. Complete with stupid little black dog. She had been going to continue on to McDonald's and pretend she hadn't seen him, but she changed her mind. She slipped the rucksack off and dug around in the side pockets until she found the one with the cigarettes. She removed one, stuck it between her lips and slipped the rucksack back on.

She wondered if he would suddenly cross the road, pretending that he hadn't been following her after all. Or maybe he would feign amazement that he should just happen to be taking exactly the same route as her.

Mullen kept walking. His head was down. He seemed to be talking to the dog. Only when he was a couple of metres away did he look up at her. He stopped still and pulled Rex tighter to him.

'Hello,' he said.

'Got a light, Spade?'

'No.'

'You couldn't check the pockets of my rucksack?' she said. 'See if you can find mine.'

She turned around and waited. Would he or wouldn't he?

She felt a slight tug which indicated that he would.

'Here.' He held the box of matches out.

'You light it.' She thrust her face forwards. She puckered her lips so the cigarette jumped around.

'Not my job.'

She felt anger flare in her. The boys who tagged around her and Trish and Alice at school would have been fighting to be the one with the matches.

She snatched the box from his hand and lit up. She tossed the match away and blew a cloud of smoke into his face. He didn't react.

'Is my mother paying you to follow me, Spade?'

'What are you up to, Ellie?'

'Just on the way to McDonald's. You fancy joining me?' She blew another smoke cloud in his direction. 'You could buy me a burger if you like. I'm a bit short of cash.'

'I think you're taking advantage of your mother's condition.' He was continuing to look at her full on, eyes unblinking.

She took another drag, sucking the smoke deep into her lungs. She coughed. For a moment or two, she felt sick, as if she might cough up bile or food.

'Are you going to tell on me, Spade?' she snapped. 'Tell Mummy that you caught me smoking? Cause if you do, that would be the most pathetic thing ever.'

She tossed the cigarette on the pavement and stamped on it, taking out on it all her anger, frustration and fear.

Mullen said nothing.

'Well, are you buying or not?'

'I'll buy you a burger if you tell me about Saad.'

'Saad?' She felt her stomach lurch. It was the last thing she had expected to hear him say. The last thing, and yet the best thing. 'Actually I'd prefer a milkshake,' she said.

Mullen placed the milkshake in front of Ellie and sat down with his coffee. The aggressive teenage bravado had disappeared. As he studied the pale face under the black and purple hair, he half expected her to burst into tears – like everyone else in his life.

'Elizabeth Durant has asked me to try and find Saad.' He spoke slowly, one word carefully placed after another. 'I am hoping you can help me.'

She nodded.

'Perhaps I should say at the outset that this is strictly confidential. I don't tell your mother and I don't tell Elizabeth anything unless you agree to it.'

'Why should I believe you?'

'No reason. Except that I promise it. You'll have to trust me.'

She didn't respond, so Mullen tried an easy opening question.

'You were good friends, I understand.'

'Yes.'

'Best friends, maybe?'

'One of them.'

'And who were his other best friends?'

'Alice Dong. And Trisha Robinson.'

'And how did that work?'

She frowned. 'We girls were best friends.'

'But he was older than you.'

'So?'

Mullen let it hang. He was in danger of getting into areas of pure speculation when what he needed were facts.

'Do you have any idea where he might have gone?'

'Not really.'

'Did he ever talk about running away?'

'No.'

'Was he happy living with Elizabeth?'

'I expect so. She had given him a home.' Ellie sucked hard on her straw. Her face hardened. 'He damned well should have been.'

Mullen had another question on the end of his tongue, but he reeled it in. The girl was on edge, no longer the teenager who blows smoke in your face just to prove how tough she is. More a girl who didn't know what the hell was going on in her life. She seemed scared too. He knew what fear looked like. So what, he wondered, was she afraid of? He sipped his coffee and tried a different approach.

'I'm a bit stuck,' he said. 'I'm not a magician. I don't have access to CCTV systems or police records. I'm not even a whizz on computers.'

He paused and sipped again.

'The fact is that I don't really know where to start.'

He looked at her with what he hoped was a look of helplessness, but she wasn't impressed. There was a toughness about her that he rather admired. Fatherless and a single child, she had learnt about life the hard way. Eventually she replied with a shrug.

'You should ask Trisha. He really liked Trisha.'

'Where does she live?'

'I'll tell you when you've bought me a burger.'

CHAPTER 3

Previously

WHEN ALEX PIKE ARRIVED at 4 p.m. that Tuesday, he was confronted by a *Do not enter* sign on Jade's door. His first thought was that perhaps she had finally died. But he could hear sounds from within the room. One of the nurses he guessed. He shrugged. He was in no rush to go in. He continued along the corner and round the corner until he arrived at the visitor's day-room.

He made himself a coffee. There was an honesty box, but he didn't put anything in. He picked up a copy of the *Daily Mail* which someone had abandoned and began to read it. He had pretty much brought himself up to date – on the iniquities of the EEC and the risks posed to the UK by the swarms of migrants and refugees who were reported to be flooding into the UK and taking all the jobs – when someone walked into the room.

He looked up and saw a tall lean man studying him.

'Are you Alex Pike?'

He nodded.

'I am John Tolman. I am Jade Sawyer's solicitor.'

Alex eased himself up out of the armchair he had sunk into. Solicitors were serious stuff.

'Pleased to meet you.' He held out his hand, but the solicitor showed no sign of shaking it. He looked around, checking to see if they were alone.

'If anyone comes in, we'll have to stop, but until then this will do.' He moved to the other side of the low table and sat down.

Alex sat down too, but this time he didn't slump.

'Jade has made a change to her will.'

'Has she?'

'She has every right to do so. Despite the pain she is in, she is still fully *compos mentis*. To put it briefly, you are now a beneficiary.' It was clear from the tone of his voice that he disapproved of his client's decision. Indeed it was clear from the tight set of his mouth and the way that he refused to look Alex in the face that Tolman the solicitor disapproved of Alex the prodigal – full stop.

'You mean she's giving me some money?' Alex was struggling to keep the surprise and delight out of his voice.

Tolman didn't answer immediately. Instead he stood up and went and got himself some water from the dispenser. He drank it hurriedly, dropped the plastic cup in the bin, and finally looked at Alex.

'Not *some* money.' His face had turned a glaring red. It was as if he was in the process of choking on a large lump of gristle. 'Half. You and her sister will be equal beneficiaries.'

Alex swallowed. He had to be hearing things. Jade hated him. He knew that. Jade owned her own house on the north coast. Not overlooking a beach or anything like that, but close enough to the coastal path to be very desirable. He guessed Tolman was talking about an extremely substantial six figure sum of money even when it was split two ways.

'She is making this bequest in the hope that you will do one thing for her,' Tolman said.

'Of course,' Alex said, his head nodding as if he was one of those toy dogs that people used to proudly place on the back windows of their

Ford Cortinas. 'I would do anything for Jade,' he said. Which wasn't entirely true, but it wasn't entirely untrue either. Even he wasn't such a bastard that he didn't realize that he owed Jade.

'She wants you to find out what happened to her daughter, Lucy.' Tolman paused and skewered him with his eyes. 'Your daughter too, as I understand it.'

'My daughter too.' Alex gave the slightest of nods, but beyond that he refused to yield to Tolman's overt hostility. Who was Tolman to pass judgement on him? What did the man know? Only what Jade had told him. Which was, of course, not the whole story.

Tolman continued to stare back. They were like two schoolboys vying for supremacy, seeing who would blink first.

It was Alex who gave way, but that was primarily because he suddenly realized that he didn't understand what he was being asked to do.

'Anyway, what do you mean Jade wants me to find out what happened to Lucy? My daughter fell off a cliff, didn't she? That's what Jade told me.'

'I understand that it may not have been as simple as that.'

The train eased to a stop at the Hull Paragon Interchange and Paul Reeve got out. He felt a sense of purpose. It was the first stop on his journey, though whether reconciliation or revenge lay at the end of it, he wasn't sure.

He knew exactly what he was going to do. He had been planning and thinking about it for ages, so the detail was pretty much hardwired into his brain. Visit the bank first. That took longer than he had expected, but it worked out eventually. The divorce had stripped him of a lot of his assets, but he still had some money awaiting him. But he needed cash and he needed a debit and credit card. Then it was a case of finding somewhere cheap and inconspicuous to stay. Not that he expected to be staying there long. It was a long time since he had lived in Hull, so he spent his evenings walking, reacquainting himself with the place. On his second evening he saw Phil roll out of the Bricklayers Arms, a pub which he had talked about in prison endlessly. Phil had a surprisingly young blonde on his arm. For a while Reeve followed, until they got onto a bus. He didn't try and follow. He was in no great rush.

It was three days after that that he finally caught up with Phil properly – minus the blonde.

'So have you got the business done?'

Phil's lips curled up. 'Course I have. You got the money?'

'Sure. But I've got a little job to do this evening,' he lied, 'so I can't meet you until later on.'

'I'll be at the Bricklayers. Come and find me.'

Reeve got there at 9.45 to find Phil already well settled at a small round table in the corner of the pub. He had a curry and a pint in front of him.

'Sit down, Paul, my old mate. Do you want the same?'

'Dodgy stomach,' he lied.

'Don't be a lightweight.'

They didn't leave until closing time.

'Let's do the business, now,' Reeve said, 'but not here.'

He headed off into the night while Phil followed, wheezing noisily and staggering erratically. Reeve didn't stop until they reached the Humber. It was a bleak night, with rain in the air and a cool wind blowing in off the North Sea. A young man, all skin and bone and old before his time, came whirling past them, high on crack, but after that they were free to make their exchange.

'So what have you got for me?' Reeve said.

Phil belched and laughed. 'Some nice photos. Like you said. But what have you got for me?'

'What we agreed, Phil. I'm a man of my word.' There were two or three seconds when nothing happened, as greed and distrust began to bite. Then, 'Here.' Reeve handed over a brown envelope. 'Count it while

I take a look at the photos.'

Reeve took the white envelope which Phil pulled out of his coat pocket. He peeled open the flap and removed the contents. He began to leaf through the photographs using the torch application on his mobile phone. They weren't the most skilfully taken pictures, but... He stopped suddenly on the fourth photo. He froze, suddenly realizing what he was looking at. He leafed through some more, studying them intently, before pushing them back into the envelope and then into his own pocket.

'Who's the woman?' he said.

'Woman might be stretching it.' Phil laughed. 'She's only thirteen. Caught her bunking off school. Easily persuaded. Offered her a bit of alcohol and some cash. Thought it'd give you a bit more leverage. And Costa was very pleased with her.'

'Right.' Reeve clapped his arm around the man's shoulders. 'You've been a real star, Phil. I owe you.'

'No problem, mate. Any time.'

Reeve sighed. 'It's hard to believe, isn't it, us two here. You know, sometimes I thought I would never get out.'

'I know what you mean.' Phil belched again and laughed. 'Sorry.'

Reeve laughed too. Then the two men were hugging and giggling like two drunk old men and Reeve's left hand was slipping inside Phil's coat pocket and grabbing hold of the end of the brown envelope. Meanwhile his right hand (now clenched inside a knuckle duster) had detached itself from Phil's coat and was looping round in a wide arc into the side of his friend's head. Phil juddered and staggered, but he remained on his feet. He swore and swung his own right fist in the direction of Reeve. But he was groggy with shock and drink and Reeve ducked underneath. Then he stepped forward and gave Phil a single sharp push with both hands. Phil sprawled backwards, arms akimbo, through the air and into the blackness below. There was a splash. Reeve didn't look down. Instead he lit a cigarette and stood there smoking for a minute or so, ears alert for any sign that Phil might have survived. But not only was Phil half drunk, he had also (you learn a lot about a man when you share a prison cell with him for nearly a year) never learnt to swim. There were, of course, other sounds: distant traffic, some men singing tunelessly and, closer by, a pair of cats yowling. But there was nothing to cause Reeve any alarm. Satisfied, he tossed his half-smoked cigarette out over the river Humber and started walking.

He kicked viciously at a beer can lying on the path. He was thinking about his daughter. She, like the girl in the photos, would now be thirteen. Suppose it had been her.

'You shouldn't have used a kid, Phil,' he said very quietly. 'You really shouldn't.'

CHAPTER 4

Monday

WHEN TRISHA ROBINSON OPENED the door, Mullen found himself taken by surprise. Perhaps he was secretly expecting to encounter a clone of Ellie, all black spiky hair and attitude, but instead he found himself facing a model in the making, long fair hair, high cheek bones, welcoming smile and, in her heels, at least four inches taller than her friend.

'Can I help you?' Posh voice. Ridiculously polite too for a hormonal teenager.

'I do hope so,' Mullen said, catching the mood. 'My name is Doug Mullen, and I assume you are Trisha. Your friend Ellie suggested I get in touch.'

Her eyes flickered up and down, in a rapid assessment. Mullen was half expecting her to slam the door, but she didn't. But she didn't invite him in either. She moved closer to him and lowered her voice. 'So this is about Saad?'

'Yes.'

'You've been hired to find him? By Mrs Durant.' She was whispering now.

'I can see you've been well briefed by Ellie.'

'So what do you want to know?'

'If you have any idea where he might be.'

She didn't answer immediately, but her immaculately made-up face went into a slow-motion crumple. Her eyes moistened with tears. 'I don't know. London maybe. But he's not answering his phone. He didn't tell me anything or warn me. He just...'

'Who are you?' A tall, broad-shouldered man with slicked-back dark hair and emanating aggression had appeared from inside the house.

Mullen stood his ground. 'Are you Mr Robinson?'

'You haven't answered my question.'

'Doug Mullen. I'm a private investigator and I'm looking into the disappearance of Saad Ismat.'

'Him!' He gave a harsh laugh. 'Done a runner, hasn't he. You'd have thought, after the kindness people have shown, he'd have given some back. But not the likes of him. He's no idea how to behave.'

'Dad! He behaves perfectly well. He—'

Robinson held up his hand, closing his daughter down, but his eyes remained fixed on Mullen.

'Look, I don't care where the guy is. As far as I'm concerned, it's good riddance. He was always sniffing round my daughter and her friends as if they were bitches on heat. Trish is only just fourteen, for crying out loud. Maybe he's gone to London to try his luck there. With a bit of luck, someone there will teach him a lesson. Anyway, I want you to leave my property right now and not come back. Or I'll be reporting you to the police.'

Rex was flagging. If he was a resentful dog, he would have been hating his new master by now, what with all the long walks he forced him to go on. Rex liked getting out, of course, all the interesting smells and places to explore, except that no sooner had he found a place he wanted to scrabble around in than there would be a sharp tug on his lead and he'd be forced to move on before he had had a chance to investigate further. His master liked to walk fast too. Not like his mistress, who was always stopping to chat to someone or admire a front garden or sniff at a flower. At least they were nearly home. He was tired, but even so he managed to speed up a little. Home was good. Home was a place to lie down and sleep.

He sensed the woman even sooner this time. That perked him up even more. He hadn't liked her at first. But she had lifted him onto her knees and stroked him and talked to him properly. She had even left her scarf in his basket, which was nice of her. Lots of interesting smells on it. So he had slept on it until his master had discovered it and taken it. As before, she was sitting on the bench outside the house. Rex pulled on the lead and gave a welcoming yap.

Elizabeth Durant was agitated. She had a book in her hand and was holding it up as if it was a trophy.

'I think I've found something,' she squealed. 'I really do.'

Mullen had poured himself a glass of water and was drinking it as she said this. Rex too was lapping up water from his bowl in the rather pernickety way that he did. Durant was looking more scatty than the previous day. Batty even. Mullen put his glass down and turned to face her.

What on earth was he doing with this woman who divined that someone was dead on the basis of feeling a scarf? When the likelihood was he had done a runner, maybe gone to London or Birmingham to try and hook up with other Syrians. Mullen pressed these thoughts back down.

'What have you found?' he said in his calmest, I'm-going-to-humour-you-if-it-kills-me manner.

'His Koran.'

'Right.' Mullen fought against his feelings of scepticism and tried to assess this information. If Saad was doing a runner and was a devout Muslim, he wouldn't have left his Koran behind. Was Saad a devout Muslim? Maybe Durant was onto something. Maybe.

'I gave it to him. I'm a Christian, but I knew he should have a copy of the Koran. It's not my job to convert him, just to look after him and give him some sort of security. But what's important is what I found inside.'

She thrust the book towards him. Mullen opened it and looked at the piece of card inside it. But it wasn't a bookmark. At least it wasn't only a bookmark. He read the words on it: *16.00 Bagley Wood*. A rendezvous presumably. No sign of with whom, or even on which day. Had it been given to him in the morning by someone? At school? A pupil? A teacher? A parent?

Mullen frowned. It was written in English, not Arabic.

'It's not Saad's writing,' Durant said, answering a question that Mullen might eventually have got round to asking. He was feeling light-headed and hungry.

'Are you sure?'

'Of course I'm sure. I wouldn't say it if I wasn't sure.' It was the first time she had spoken sharply to Mullen, perhaps a sign of the stress she was under.

'So what's Saad's English like?'

'Very good. He came from a middle-class family. So he learnt English and also some French. A clever lad.'

'But the handwriting is someone else's and you've no idea whose?'

'It tells us that he was due to meet someone in Bagley Wood. A meeting which he never mentioned to me.'

'A girl perhaps? Perhaps he's run off with a girl. It would explain a lot, why he's not contacted you, why ...'

Durant screeched and grabbed her head as if she was in the process of having a seizure or wanted to pull it off with a single yank.

'He's dead. I've told you he's dead. Don't you believe me? You're like all the others. You think I'm mad, don't you?'

'Of course not,' Mullen replied hastily, anxious to avert whatever emotional explosion was about to go off.

'In that case, why don't we go and look for him there?'

'OK.' Mullen raised his hands in front of him. He had walked right into her trap. However batty she was or wasn't, Durant clearly had animal cunning. 'I really need to make a quick sandwich,' he continued. 'I never got round to breakfast. Then we'll go and look.'

'Sorry!' It was as if a current had suddenly been switched off at the main supply box. Durant melted into tears. 'I'm so sorry.'

They drove to Bagley Wood in Mullen's car.

'Mine's playing me up,' Durant had said at least three times in different ways over their brief sandwich lunch. Given the intensity with which she talked, Mullen wondered if she wasn't rather lonely. Or was she one of those people who is always able to talk the hind legs off a donkey?

Rex didn't care about her chatter. He sat contentedly on her lap. They might have been friends for life. Rex clearly shifted his loyalties quicker than the most venal mercenary soldier. Durant held Saad's scarf close to her bosom, but still in its see-through bag.

They parked and got out, Mullen firmly re-attaching the lead to Rex's collar. He had a dread of the dog escaping and getting lost or else falling down a hole like Alice's white rabbit and never reappearing. Though actually he knew the most likely horror would be for Rex to run slap bang into a Rottweiler which believed all short-legged canines were an affront to his authority.

They started walking along a rutted track roughly parallel to the A34.

'You see deer here occasionally,' Durant said. 'Roe and muntjac. Less than you used to. They cull them to protect the young trees.'

She strode on in front of Mullen and Rex, who had apparently decided that a second walk so soon after the first (and on such a hot day) required some sort of go-slow to demonstrate his dissatisfaction. Mullen happily dawdled with him. He sided with the dog.

Durant was oblivious to the incipient industrial action behind her, stretching her legs with a will. As they moved further away from the noise of the traffic, car noise was replaced by the song of various birds and the raucous alarm calls of, Mullen reckoned, squirrels. He looked around hopefully. If there were any deer, he'd hate to walk past without noticing them. The undergrowth was thick. Ferns and low bushes provided plenty of cover. Could Saad be camping somewhere out here? If so, there was a lot of ground for them to cover.

Up front, Durant had stopped and was looking back at them. She was standing near a pile of logs, the second such pile along this stretch, laid out in a triangular stack over a drainage ditch which ran parallel to the track. Signs warned people against clambering on them. Duly warned, Mullen shortened the lead and switched to the right-hand side of the track.

When he reached Durant, she was standing very still, apparently wrapped up in her own thoughts. Then very gradually, she turned through 360 degrees, as if she expected Saad to come walking out of the greenery. He didn't. She sighed and knelt down on the ground and began fussing over Rex. Saad's scarf was no longer in Mullen's plastic bag. She had it wrapped around her hand, as if she was an Oxford United fan and wanted to make sure she could wave it around and yet ensure that no-one could grab it from her. Rex sniffed at it. He could probably smell himself on it, Mullen reckoned. Rex would have liked that, he thought. Rex, he had decided some weeks ago, was rather fond of himself. Mullen was so taken up with his own thoughts that at first he didn't realize what Durant, in all her battiness, was doing: a quick flick of finger and thumb and Rex was free, charging away from them with an alacrity which he never even hinted at when attached to his lead.

'What the hell are you playing at?'

But Durant wasn't playing at anything. She locked her fingers round Mullen's wrist.

'Wait!' she ordered. She might have been a sergeant-major on the parade ground. Mullen pulled against her grip, but she hung on.

'Let me go!' he demanded.

'Let him go,' she said quietly. 'I'll let you go, but give him a chance.'

Her fingers went slack. Mullen gave his wrist a surreptitious rub. 'If he gets lost, I'll never hear the end of it. If...'

'He won't. As soon as he's tired, he'll come home to Daddy. Dogs always do.'

Rex had disappeared into the bushes and out of view. Mullen fought the urge to run after him.

'It's quite obvious that you'll never find Saad in this vast wood,' Durant said. 'But Rex is a dog. Why do you think I put my scarf in his basket the other night? Why was I letting him have a sniff now before I released him? Because if Saad is in the vicinity, especially if he is dead, then Rex is much more likely to find him than you are.'

Mullen was about to say something in reply, but right on queue Rex reappeared out of the undergrowth about thirty metres away next to a third pile of logs. Durant took Mullen by the arm, but this time much more lightly and only for a second or two.

'Let's walk very slowly and give him a chance. For the sake of Saad.'

They walked slowly. In front of them, Rex had stopped moving. His head was down, as he sniffed at a particularly intriguing smell. Occasionally his tail wagged vigorously for a couple of seconds.

Yet again Durant's hand alighted on Mullen's arm and then moved away, like a robin disturbed by a sudden movement.

'Mullen.' Her voice was breathless. 'Do you think?'

Rex had begun to move forward again, with purpose, head down and straight towards the log pile. Mullen was stirred into life and started forward, but Rex hopped down into the drainage ditch and ran along it. Within moments he had disappeared under the logs. The last thing Mullen saw was his waving tail.

'Holy shit!' Mullen broke into a run. When he reached the logs, he bent down on his knees, peering along the ditch into the darkness. He couldn't see a thing.

'Suppose he gets stuck in there?'

'He won't.' Elizabeth Durant seemed very sure of it. 'He got in there, so he'll be able to get out. Just give him time. Trust me.'

Mullen looked up at her, into her wild eyes and decided that if she wasn't mad, then it was he who was crazy for allowing himself to get involved in such a foolhardy escapade. Not only crazy, but stupid too. He wondered if she had yet paid him any of the promised money. He should have checked his account.

'Rex!' Mullen whistled. He had had enough. He had to get the dog back out and on his lead. But he had no confidence that, when there was a competition between himself and a rabbit, Rex would opt to obey him.

He whistled and called again. And then, quite suddenly, there was whining and growling from somewhere under the pile. Mullen wondered briefly if the dog had encountered a badger, because if he had Mullen wouldn't rate his chances very high. There was a bark, then silence and then Rex came rushing out, tail wagging and head up. For a moment, he stood stock still, looking at first Mullen and then Durant, as if uncertain which of them was currently his boss.

'Good boy, Rex,' Mullen called, as insincere as a conman. He held the lead behind his back. 'Here, boy!'

Rex gave a muffled grunt and ran straight up to Elizabeth Durant. And there at her feet he laid down his piece of treasure.

She bent down and shrieked. 'Oh my God!'

Mullen moved closer to her, knelt down and grabbed Rex, deftly reattaching the lead to him. First things first. Then, 'What have you got there, boy?' He spoke as if Rex was a curious two-year-old, into anything and everything.

'Oh shit!' he said, as his eyes focused on the stubby little object which Rex had recovered from under the logs. It was messy and covered in slobber and dust, but there was no doubt what it was. A human finger.

'Oh my God! Oh my God!' Elizabeth Durant was disintegrating into shock.

'I'll ring the police and stay here,' Mullen said firmly. Old army habits were kicking in. Don't panic. Make a plan. Carry it out.

But Durant hadn't had military discipline knocked into her. She started to run back along the track towards the road, her arms flailing either side of her.

'You wait by the car,' Mullen called. 'Direct the police down here.'

She raised one arm in acknowledgement. She shouted something too, but Mullen wasn't sure what. She was freaked out. That was clear from her helter skelter progress as she weaved from side to side like someone pursued by demons from hell.

Mullen dialled 999. The police arrived within fifteen minutes, which seemed pretty good to Mullen. First some uniformed plods and then two detectives, one female and one male.

'Detective Inspector Holden,' the woman said, brandishing her ID. She peered at the finger, still lying on the ground and then confronted Mullen. 'Your dog found this?'

'Under that pile of logs.' He had already decided that it was easier at this stage to describe Rex as his dog. For the next month or two, at least, that was the reality.

'You often walk here?'

'No.'

'Why today then?'

'Elizabeth Durant suggested it. She's the woman waiting on the roadside. I'm a private investigator and I'm looking for a missing refugee. Saad Ismat.'

DI Holden looked at him for three or four seconds without responding. He guessed the words 'private investigator' were the dirtiest words in the book as far as a Detective Inspector of the Thames Valley Police was concerned. Then, 'You live locally?'

'Off Cumnor Hill.'

WHITE LIES, DEADLY LIES

'Right.' She gestured towards her colleague. 'Well, you give a few details to Detective Constable Trent and then toddle off home. We'll be in touch.'

Mullen nodded.

'One more thing, Mullen. Try not to go talking to the press. I know it's very tempting for anyone hoping for a little cash bonus, but it really doesn't help us.'

Anger flashed through Mullen. Who was she to assume that he was that sort of person when she didn't know him from Adam?

'Come on, sir.' It was Trent. Posh voice, but calm and ever so slightly condescending. 'Let's just move away from the crime scene, shall we, while I take down a few details.'

When Mullen got home that evening, he was feeling confused and frazzled. He was pretty sure he was dehydrated, so he drank a pint of water and took two paracetamols before giving the exhausted Rex a larger meal than usual.

'Don't tell the professor,' he said to the dog as he put the bowl in front of him. 'And if you decide to be sick, do avoid all the carpets, especially the Afghan one.' Whichever the Afghan one was.

Mullen sat in a chair for twenty minutes before realizing that he too was hungry. He made a sandwich, ate it greedily and then went into the garden. He had been neglecting it and in the heat, it desperately needed water too. The tomato plants in particular needed some attention before they keeled over. He had allowed them to grow too many trusses for their own good.

Gardening was therapy as far as Mullen was concerned, and watering and pinching out tomatoes was pretty easy therapy at that. Ideally he wanted to talk to Elizabeth Durant, but when he rang her mobile there was no ringing and no message-answering service.

When the well-spoken DC Trent had let him return to his car, he had been surprised that Durant hadn't been there waiting for him. A

PETER TICKLER

uniformed constable was standing in the gateway, on guard and very officious, keeping all other humans and dogs away, but when Mullen asked him about Durant, he had told him that he had only taken up this post ten minutes previously, and if sir wouldn't mind, would he please get in his car and go home because the whole area was now being treated as a crime scene. At that point, his radio had crackled into life and he had waved Mullen away.

The result of all this was that Mullen was stuck at home, his mind in turmoil, and unable to talk it all over with the one person who would have understood and who might well herself be wanting to talk it all over. They could have had a bit of mutual talking therapy.

By the time Mullen was finished in the garden, the light was beginning to fade. He was tired, but his brain was spinning like a top. He slumped in front of the TV and found, to his delight, that *The Bourne Supremacy* had just started on Film4. It was perfect viewing for his mood. He knew that because he had seen it before: fast paced, well acted, a strong lead with a woman to protect; in short, an easy watch with a happy ending. Actually, he wasn't sure he could remember the precise ending. Maybe the girl ended up dead, but he was damned sure that Bourne didn't. He allowed himself to sink into the sofa and into a fantasy celluloid world. Rex, perhaps sensing his indulgent mood, hopped up beside him and, when Mullen made no attempt to dislodge him, lay triumphantly there, his nose pushed companionably against Mullen's knee. Soon enough Rex was asleep, whimpering occasionally as he dreamt of chasing rabbits – or maybe human fingers. And soon enough Mullen followed him into the land of Nod.

The doorbell rang at 9.30 a.m. precisely. Mullen had only just finished his breakfast and was busy wiping the surfaces ready for the day. Keeping things clean and tidy was part of his DNA, or maybe it was the army which had drilled it into him. He wondered who it could be. People rarely came to call on Mullen. It was too early for the postie and he had no outstanding online purchases. Perhaps it was Elizabeth Durant. He sure as heck had some questions for her.

But it wasn't Durant. It was the detective and her sidekick. Holden and Trent. He had the previous day made a point of logging away their names for future reference. You never knew when it might come in useful, to have someone in the Thames Valley Police you could contact directly.

'Mind if we come in?' Holden gave a tight smile. She almost made it seem like they were paying a social visit.

Mullen responded in the same vein. 'Fancy a tea or coffee?'

'No, thanks.'

But Mullen was going to have a coffee anyway. He stuck a pod in the professor's fancy machine and waited. Meanwhile the two detectives had sat down at the table in the kitchen and were making small talk that wasn't small talk at all.

'Nice house you've got here,' Trent said. Which, translated, meant: how the hell can you afford this? Mullen ignored the opportunity to explain.

'Cute dog, isn't he?' Which meant: he's a woman's dog. So what sort of man are you?

'You have a bit of a history of finding dead bodies.' That was Holden, making it clear that she had researched his background. Mullen wondered if she had spoken to Detective Inspector Dorkin about him. Dorkin would surely speak up for him.

Mullen placed a jug of water and two glasses on the table, but didn't pour any out. If they were thirsty, they could pour it themselves.

Holden straightened herself up and started the questions. 'Tell me about Elizabeth Durant.'

'I told your constable last night.' He nodded towards Trent.

'Humour me. And let's keep it simple. I ask the questions and you answer them. When did you first meet her?'

'A few days ago.'

Holden poured herself a glass of water and took a sip. 'A bit more detail would be good.'

Mullen scratched at his chin. 'Three nights ago, I think. I came home from walking the dog and she was sitting on the bench outside the front door.'

'And she asked you to find Saad Ismat.'

'Yes.'

'And you agreed.'

'Not immediately. She came back the following night. That was when I agreed.'

'Has she paid you?'

'We agreed a fee, but I don't know if she's paid me.'

'You don't know?'

'I gave her my bank details. She said she'd pay yesterday, but I just haven't got round to checking it out.'

'So where does she live?' Holden was relentless. Mullen couldn't help wondering how many questions she had up her jacket sleeves. Zillions?

'I don't have her address,' he replied.

'Phone number?'

'Yes, a mobile. I've tried ringing it, but there's no answer.' Mullen felt like he was taking an exam and scoring very badly.

Holden glanced across at Trent, and in that instant Mullen knew that something was wrong.

'Didn't one of your officers get these details off her yesterday?' he said.

Holden pursed her lips. 'Actually, Mr Mullen, none of my officers saw Elizabeth Durant yesterday.'

Mullen tried to take this in. 'But she went up to the road to make sure you found us easily. I made the phone call and stayed by the wood pile while she ran off along the track towards the road. She was a bit freaked out. I shouted after her and told her to wait at the gateway to guide you in.'

Holden took another sip of water.

'I believe you served in the army.'

'What on earth has that got to do with anything?'

'Afghanistan? Iraq?'

'Afghanistan.' Mullen's brain was in free fall. What was this all about? He'd found the body of a missing youth and the police were quizzing him about his military background.

'What was it like?' Trent had joined in now. Was this pre-planned or had he merely got bored with being the poor sap who sits quietly in the corner playing second fiddle for a living?

'Not much fun.' He wasn't inclined to expand on that.

'I don't suppose it was.' Trent leaned forward. Smooth, expensively dressed, well spoken, a graduate from a posh university who had been put on the fast track. Mullen could feel resentment balling in his stomach. 'I guess that in a place like Afghanistan you see things which stay with you for years?' It was a leading question and Mullen wasn't going to be led. He sipped at his coffee and said nothing.

Holden cleared her voice and as soon as Mullen turned towards her, she launched the question which they had clearly been working towards. 'Ever suffered from PTSD, Doug?'

Post-traumatic stress disorder. Mullen didn't need to ask what the initials stood for. He'd seen people who had copped it badly and never recovered.

'You had a friend who killed himself, didn't you? You found him after he had blown his brains out. That must have been tough.'

Mullen stood up abruptly. The last thing he wanted to do was remember that. That was before Afghanistan. What the hell right had they to be bringing all that up? It was getting hot in the kitchen. He moved to the patio door and pulled it wide open.

He turned round, but he remained standing, at a distance from the table. 'What exactly is this all about? I found the body of Saad Ismat. You should be thanking me, not giving me the third degree.'

'Do you know how old Saad is?' Holden said. She was sitting unmoved at the table, though Trent had got up from his chair as if ready for any possible trouble.

'Sixteen, I think. He's just taken his GCSEs.'

'Well, whoever the person is whom your dog found under those logs, it's not Saad Ismat. The wrong age and the wrong sex.'

Ellie looked up from her Mandarin book and for the third or fourth time, her glance took in the man sitting by the window. For some reason, she had a distinct sense that he was watching her, and yet every time she checked him out, he was head down over his newspaper. This time, he had a biro in his right hand. He was doing – or pretending to do – a crossword or maybe sudoku. In his forties, she thought, close-cut hair, broad shoulders, and looking like he worked out.

She had been practising Mandarin with Trisha and drinking a milkshake. The holidays stretched in front of her and she knew if she didn't keep up the Mandarin, she would have forgotten half she had learnt by the next term. Trisha had gone to the toilet. Ellie allowed her eyes to dwell on the man for two or three seconds and that was when he glanced up and across the room. Ever so briefly, their eyes met. An infinitesimal nod, then he looked down again at his newspaper. What was that about?

Trisha returned. 'Got to go. Or I'll be getting the third degree. You coming?'

'Mercy's at home. I'll hang about a bit longer. Maybe have a burger.'

'OK.' Trisha swung her fancy rucksack over her shoulder. Everything which Trisha wore, carried or applied to her body was fancy. 'Zai jian,' she said. 'See you later.'

A minute or so later, a shadow fell across the table. Ellie looked up, wondering what Trisha had forgotten, but it wasn't her. It was the man. He *had* been watching her.

'Mind if I join you?'

'Of course I mind.'

She looked down, waiting for him to clear off, but instead he scraped the chair back and sat down.

'If you don't get up, I'm going to start screaming. They know me in here. I'm a regular. And I'm only thirteen.'

She half opened her mouth, but the scream didn't materialize because he was already getting to his feet.

He pulled on his thin windcheater and zipped it up, but he didn't leave. He looked at her. 'Actually, to be precise, you'll be fourteen in six days' time.'

It was as if something, an alien hand, was in her gut, twisting it tight. Ellie gasped for breath as panic and fear swept over her.

'Don't you know who I am?' He spoke softly now, surprisingly so.

But Ellie was in freefall, and no words would come.

'Of course I know how old you are,' he continued. 'I'm your father.' And with that he turned and went out.

For twenty minutes Ellie barely moved. Stunned. Disbelieving. Then partially believing. She had been only three when she last saw her father, and she had absolutely no memory of what he had looked like then. Her only memory was of him carrying her on his shoulders in the sea. She could remember the salt and the wind and the smell of his hair and the fact that she was being carried high above the waves like a princess. But she had no memory of his face. There wasn't a single photo of him in the house. In fact there was only one of herself as a little child, aged about one, sitting on her mother's lap on some grassy knoll. Was it him who had taken the photo? She imagined it must have been. But the fact was that her mother never talked about him. She had excised every trace and memory of him from their lives. Ellie didn't even know what her father's name was. Just as she had no idea what she had been named when she was born. Because her mother had got rid of their names too and started them off with new ones.

'I don't want him to find us,' Natalie had said. 'Never, ever, ever.'
But now, it seemed, he had.

It took Mullen less than half an hour to track down where Elizabeth Durant lived. Or where he reckoned she must live. After Holden's visit, he was convinced that he urgently needed to speak to her. He needed to ask her why on earth she had run off the day before. Why did she not wait to speak to the police? Why would she not want to make sure that the police came down the right track into Bagley Wood when Rex had just found the body? It made no sense.

But above all he needed to speak to her and tell her that the body wasn't Saad's and that he could very well still be out there somewhere. Alive! Mullen had this terrible feeling in his gut that after the shock of yesterday, she might go and do a Ray Costa – hang herself or else throw herself off one of the many bridges over the A34. Or there was the mainline railway track running through Kennington too. Messy but instant. That was why he had frantically checked the *Oxford Mail* website and the local news on the BBC website in case there were any reports of suicides in the last twenty-four hours. He had been enormously relieved not to find any.

There was an E. Durant in Kennington according to the online BT phonebook. It might not be her, but it was a fair bet, given that the address was Bagley Wood Road in Kennington. More than a fair bet, he reckoned.

Fifteen minutes later, he was parked opposite outside a bland semi-detached house. Brick built, bowed front-windows, blue front door, an immaculately clean paved area in front of the house on which was parked a small, smart, red Vauxhall Corsa. He surveyed the scene. Not what he had expected. Not that he knew what he was expecting.

Mullen eased himself out of his own car and made his way to the front door. He paused. He took a deep slow breath in and then out, preparing himself for whatever came next. He had to remind himself that he wasn't in Hull and that there wouldn't be another dead body hanging in the stairwell. He took a second deep breath and pressed on the buzzer. Almost immediately the door opened.

Mullen's first thought was that he must have got the wrong house. He prided himself on his ability to remember names, addresses and even telephone numbers, so to have come to the wrong house threw him off balance.

'Sorry,' he said. 'I was hoping this was the house of Elizabeth Durant.'

'It is.' The woman in front of him was slim and little more than five feet tall. She had dark brown hair pulled up onto the top of her head and sunglasses perched above the neat fringe. Mid-forties Mullen reckoned, trying to take in as much detail as he could. She lowered the sunglasses against the light of the morning sun. Whoever this was, she wasn't Elizabeth Durant. A friend? Lover? Even her sister, because as Mullen looked at her, he thought that maybe he could see a family resemblance.

'Is Elizabeth in?' Mullen said.

The corners of the woman's mouth curled slightly. 'As far as I know, I am in!' Then she laughed.

Mullen gave his impersonation of a fish newly landed on a fishing boat, opening and then closing his mouth. How on earth could this be Elizabeth Durant? Could there really be two of them? After all, he had found no other Durants in the Oxford area in the phone book.

'I'm sorry. There must be a mistake,' Mullen said finally.

'A mistake? You mean I've made a mistake, that I don't know my own name?' The smile flickered for a few moments longer, then disappeared. 'Look, without wishing to be rude, can I ask who *you* are? And why exactly are you standing on my doorstep?'

'My name is Doug Mullen and I'm a private investigator.'

'And?'

'And someone called Elizabeth Durant came to my house and asked me to find someone for her.'

Despite the protective layer of make-up on her face, the woman paled visibly, and Mullen saw a spark of something close to alarm in her eyes.

'Who?' She spoke breathlessly. 'Who did she want you to find?'

'A sixteen-year-old refugee called Saad Ismat.'

'Oh my God!' Elizabeth Durant didn't move. Her body seemed to stiffen, and she stared into Mullen's face as if he was an apparition. Then, in slow motion, her face contorted and her eyes rolled upwards in their sockets. Mullen thrust himself forward and caught her before she could crash to the ground.

Mullen knew his first aid, so an epileptic fit didn't alarm him. He cushioned Durant's head with his arms to prevent her hurting herself and put her in the recovery position. When a passer-by rushed over to offer help, he stuffed the man's rolled-up coat under her head. The seizure passed within a few minutes, and for ten minutes Mullen remained on his knees, waiting for Durant to wake up from her heavy sleep. Eventually she opened her eyes.

'Look, the police have arrived,' the passer-by said. (Mullen never learnt the man's name.) His first thought was that the guy had over-reacted by calling the police. It was a purely medical situation and Mullen was pretty pleased with the way he had handled it. But when he looked up and saw the tall figure of DC Trent and a uniformed officer, he realized he had got it wrong.

'Mr Mullen, is everything alright?'

'Yes, she had a seizure. She's just tired now, I think.'

'And, is this,' his public school voice continued, 'by any chance your Elizabeth Durant?'

'No and yes,' he replied, because that seemed the easiest way of explaining.

'I see,' Trent said, although he clearly didn't. 'Well, anyway, let's get the poor lady inside and give her a nice cup of sugared tea, and then you can bring me up to date with things.'

*

When Mullen got home, it was to find Rex had pooped on the rug in the living room. It was, he decided, going to be one of those days and he pulled open the patio door to let the dog out. It was his own fault. He had rushed off to Kennington without thinking of the poor chap's needs. Mullen reckoned that it served him right.

He had barely cleaned the rug before the bell rang. He wondered what other misery was about to be visited on him. It surely couldn't be the police again. Who else? Mullen had a negative fantasy. He'd done a surveillance job at the beginning of the month on a man – a very big man, as it happened – who had turned out to have two mistresses. Maybe the guy had tracked him down and come to teach him a lesson.

He opened the door. He didn't immediately register who it was standing in front of him, but at least it wasn't the big guy.

'I'm Rick. Do you remember?' the man said, spotting his confusion. 'The gardener.'

'Of course, sorry. It's been a bit of a day.'

'Well, I've just finished at Natalie's for the day.' The sentence hung uncertainly in the air, much like Mullen's willingness to engage with any other human being. Was Rick hoping to be invited in, offered a drink? Tea? A beer? A three-course meal?

'Actually,' Rick said, 'I'm worried about Natalie.'

'Yes.' Mullen's small talk had gone AWOL.

'Maybe you'd like to call round. She likes you.'

'OK.'

'If you need an incentive, Mercy has made a very tasty carrot cake.'

'Why are you worried about Natalie?'

Rick shrugged. 'Quiet. In her own world a lot of the time. But she seems very anxious too. Gets up suddenly and paces about. Comes and stands over me when I'm weeding, but doesn't say a thing. Wrings her hands. Talks to herself too. It's like there's something really eating away

73

at her, but …' He didn't finish the sentence. Instead he left it hanging there, demanding a response from Mullen.

But Mullen didn't want to discuss the swans with anyone except Natalie or Ellie. Not even with Mercy who had found them so alarming, and certainly not with Rick. It was private and sensitive. Presumably Rick didn't know about them or he would have said so.

'She has a medical condition. Aphasia. The result of a mini-stroke following the car accident. I guess she's still rather confused.'

'Mercy has told me a bit about that. But even so.' He shrugged. Mullen couldn't help thinking he was digging for information, but he didn't want to give him any more.

'Do you have many gardening clients?' Mullen was changing the subject.

'A few. Natalie's my best one at the moment. The garden has been allowed to get in a bit of a mess. But there are plenty of gardens round here owned by people who would rather someone else did all the work. The only problem is that they have a tendency to quibble about my rates.'

If that was a cue for Mullen to ask him what his rates were, he wasn't going to pick up on it. Instead he said, 'I love gardening. I find it very therapeutic.'

'A bit different from being a private eye, I guess.'

Mullen didn't answer. The two of them stood in silence for several seconds. Sticky and uncomfortable as the weather.

Rick clearly wanted to talk. Maybe he wanted to snoop around Mullen's garden and then offer him helpful hints on how he would do it better. Mullen was feeling guilty. He knew he was being pretty bloody unfriendly. Even so.

'Maybe I'd better head over now and see how Natalie is,' he said, drawing a line under their meeting. 'The dog could do with a walk too.'

CHAPTER 5

Previously

RAY COSTA TOOK HIS jacket off the back of the door and eased it over his bulky torso. He preferred to work in his short sleeves, mainly because his office manager Linda felt the cold and therefore always kept the heating higher than he would have chosen. But, cold or hot, he had the rule to always wear a jacket while dealing directly with clients. He sat back down at his desk and rang through to Linda. Seconds later she was showing his new client in.

'Mr John Smith,' she announced and then she was gone, shutting the door behind her.

'Unusual name you've got there.' Costa liked to think he was funny.

Smith didn't laugh. He didn't even ask him if he was related to the coffee people. Plenty of other people did and Ray Costa was always ready for it. 'Wish I was!' he'd say. But Mr Smith didn't seem like he was a man who did jokes. His face was emotionless, with grey eyes that stared out at Costa from under dark eyebrows, a sharply rectangular face, number one haircut, and just the hint of a snarl around the thick lips.

'Please,' Costa said, waving him into the chair. 'What can I do for you?'

Smith settled himself in his chair, as if testing it out for comfort and value. But his eyes never left Costa. 'I'm looking for someone.'

Costa resisted the urge to make another funny comment. Instead he said, 'I'm a lawyer, Mr Smith. It sounds like you need a private investigator. I could put you in touch with one.'

Smith slid an envelope across the smooth surface of the reproduction desk. 'Open it.'

Costa frowned and picked it up. He opened the envelope and pulled out the contents: half a dozen photos. Despite the heat and his jacket, Costa shivered. For a few moments he thought he might vomit, but he fought back the urge.

'I expect you recognize yourself.'

Costa nodded.

'You know how old the girl is? Or rather how young she is?'

Costa licked his lips. Terror gripped him.

'Not good for you if these fall into the wrong hands.'

'She said she was seventeen.'

'Yeah, right. Do you think a court will believe you?'

'She was all made up. She didn't object. I paid her what she asked for. But if I had known—'

'Cut the crap, Costa. As far as I am concerned, I have come here today to transact some business with you. This is the deal on offer. I will let you keep all these photos of you and the girl if you will write down a name for me.' He paused, enjoyed the moment. 'The name I want is the name by which Mrs Gemma Reeve is now known.'

Costa's head jerked up, and jumped back ten years to the man who had beaten his wife senseless and stubbed out a cigarette on his little daughter's thigh.

'I've no idea what it is,' he whispered.

'In that case, I'll just have to make sure these photographs get delivered into the hands of the police.'

'No!' Costa felt his chest tightening. He began to panic. Was he having a heart attack? He could hardly breathe. He pulled open a drawer, scrabbled around for his asthma inhaler and sucked hard on it.

'Let's not get in a state, Mr Costa.' Smith remained motionless in his chair. He spoke with exaggerated calm. 'We don't want Linda rushing in here all aflutter and seeing all these nasty photos, do we? So this is what we'll do. You will write down Gemma's new names – all of them – and then I'll disappear out of your life for ever.'

'I bet you've got copies of the photos,' Costa gasped, trying to buy a few seconds of time to think.

'I'm a businessman, Mr Costa.' He continued to speak in the controlled manner of a therapist dealing with an agitated patient. 'I'm not interested in ruining you and I would hate to upset Mrs Costa unnecessarily. All I want is Gemma Reeve's new identity.'

Costa nodded furiously, as if he was considering every aspect of a complicated legal agreement. Then he tore a piece of paper off his pad and wrote the name *Natalie Swan* on it.

'Middle name?'

'She hasn't got one.'

'Where does she live?'

'I don't know.'

'Don't piss with me, Ray. Where does she live?'

'Oxford. I think. That's where she went anyway. She didn't give me her address.'

'You're sure about that, because if I discover that you do know her address, then it'll be a case of all bets off.'

Costa shook his head vehemently. 'She wouldn't tell me. A few months after she left, she came back to Hull and made me give her all the documents relating to her. "It's safer that way," she told me. I've not seen or heard from her since. You've got to believe me.'

Costa fought to control his breathing again. He didn't dare look up. He couldn't bear to look again into the eyes of the man who claimed to be John Smith. Paul Reeve. He remembered the name and the face hadn't changed that much over the years. How could he have forgotten?

'OK.' Smith took the piece of paper and tucked it into his inside pocket. 'As I said, you keep the photos.'

Costa nodded inanely.

'One more thing,' Smith said, 'what is my daughter called now?'

'Eleanor, I think.'

Smith stood up. He took a tissue from the box on Costa's desk and blew his nose loudly, before dropping the tissue on the floor.

'Well, nice doing business with you, Ray,' he said.

Dr Rebecca Holt was called to Jade Sawyer's bedside at 10.53 p.m. It was obvious that her patient was dead, but she checked the pulse anyway. Alex Pike was curled up asleep in the armchair which he had been inhabiting intermittently for the last four weeks.

'I didn't want to wake him,' Nurse Jamila Karim said when she saw Dr Holt's gaze fall unhappily on Pike. 'I thought it was best that you came and …'

'Thank you, Nurse.' Dr Holt gestured for her to leave. 'I'll break it to him.'

Nurse Karim left. Dr Holt shut the door softly behind her and moved back over to the bed.

This time she made a more thorough physical examination of the dead woman, checking eyes, mouth, hands, arms, neck, everything. Eventually she straightened herself up. Her back was aching, but that wasn't what was causing her cold sweat. She found a tissue and dabbed at her forehead. She drew a sheet up over Jade Sawyer's face. She didn't want to look at her any more.

'You can wake up now, Alex.'

Nothing.

She moved over and leaned down low over him, so that her mouth was only inches from his left ear. 'She's dead, Alex.'

Pike shifted and raised himself up, as if from the deepest of sleeps.

He blinked. He looked at Dr Holt. He looked at his ex-wife, or rather the white sheet covering his ex-wife.

'She'll be at peace then,' he said. 'Out of her misery.' But there wasn't even a hint of emotion in his voice.

'I can see where you injected her,' Dr Holt hissed.

'I don't know what you're talking about.'

'Morphine, was it?'

'And where would I have got morphine from?'

'You bloody well used me.'

'I didn't recall you objecting at the time.'

She turned away. She felt sick. She had always thought of herself as being clever, but he had played her for a fool and she had fallen for it.

'Let's hope nobody is as sharp-eyed as you,' he continued. 'Because if they did spot it, then I guess they might think the injection had been given by a psychopathic nurse. Or even a doctor like yourself.' He picked up the denim jacket off the back of his chair and folded it over his left arm. He smiled at her. 'You know where to find me if you want a bit of R and R after your shift is over.'

He pushed the door open and went out, closing it carefully behind him, as if any sort of loud noise might wake Jade Sawyer.

CHAPTER 6

Tuesday

DI ALAN BRYCE HAD never got used to viewing bodies. Every visit to the pathologist brought back memories of finding his mother dead in bed. She had been so still. She hadn't answered when he had told her that he was going to be late for school if she didn't get up. He had assumed that she was asleep. But when he had put his hand on her shoulder to wake her up, she hadn't even flinched. He had touched her again, on the bare flesh of her arm, and that had been when he had realized that something was very, very wrong. She was stone cold.

'I wouldn't have bothered to call you,' the pathologist was saying. 'But I thought you might like to take a closer look at this one.'

Bryce nodded, as if he was agreement. As if he was delighted to have been summoned to 'take a closer look'. The body in front of him looked nothing like his mother's had. It barely looked like a body at all. A monstrosity was more like it. But Bryce looked at it, if only to show the pathologist – and himself – that he could.

'Name of Philip Stubbs. He still had his wallet on him. Not much cash on him, mind you. Just a fiver. He was fished out of the Humber, as you know. By my reckoning, he'd only been in there for three or four days. As you can see, not a pretty sight, but cold salt water slows the decomposition process down. My assessment is that he had been drinking alcohol.'

He paused, rather melodramatically in Bryce's opinion.

'Are you saying he fell in while drunk?'

'I believe he took one hell of a punch to the right side of the face.' He pointed at the cheek.

Bryce wasn't sure he wanted to take a close look himself. He'd take it on trust. 'You're sure it's a punch? Couldn't he have hit something as he fell?'

'Not questioning my interpretation, Alan?'

'Course not, Bill.'

'Take it from me: it's a punch. Assisted by a knuckle-duster, I suspect.'

Bryce nodded. 'Send me all the details.' Then he walked out, desperate for the fresh air. It sounded like a drunken brawl that had gone wrong, but it still needed to be investigated. A perfect case to give to DC Knight. He could cut his teeth on it.

Trisha Robinson wished she had brought her headphones. There was a guy sitting at the back of the bus who was talking very loudly on his mobile. He was the sort of guy you can't miss – a large round bloke, unshaven, in a black shapeless tracksuit and he had started his conversation almost the instant she sat down. She had noticed him as she made her way to her seat. She was sitting two rows in front of him because the bus was almost full and that was the furthest away she could sit. But that didn't protect her from his smell. She wondered when he or his clothes had last been washed.

Eventually he finished his phone call, but that didn't mean he was now going to be quiet. The bus pulled up at its next stop and a woman in a head cover got on. She seemed agitated and confused, thrusting some piece of paper at the driver, and then arguing when he refused to accept it.

'Less talking, or you'll be walking,' the big guy said loudly. 'We've got places to go and people to meet.' The woman glared along the bus and Trisha wondered for a second if she was going to shout back, but all she did was wave her hand and get off the bus.

Trisha shrugged inside her head. The fat guy had a point, disgusting though he was. The trip along the Botley Road was a slow one at the best of times and this was definitely not the best of times. Stop, start, crawl. Stop, start, stop. People ought to be ready with their money or ticket or at least know where they were going.

'Too many foreigners, if you ask me.' The guy hadn't finished. 'The sooner we're out of the bloody EU, the better. Taking all our jobs.'

'Nobody was asking you,' someone right behind her said.

Trisha was only fourteen, with little experience of the world, but she had a sharp brain and she knew instinctively that this was a stupid thing to say, especially to someone exhibiting a mixture of mental health problems and overt racism. A red rag to a bull.

'Butt out, you four-eyed git.' The bull was clearly up for a fight.

'You're upsetting people,' the man continued, trying to reason.

'I'll say what I like. It's a free country. I was born here. I've as much right as the likes of you to say what I think.'

'No-one wants to hear it.'

'Says who? Shall we ask them all? Call a referendum on it? Let's start with the girl in front of you. Pretty, ain't she? I wouldn't mind...'

At that point Trisha turned round and glared at him. To her surprise he shut up. But that wasn't because he was ashamed. It was because he was devouring her with his eyes. She knew immediately that she, like the guy with glasses right behind her, had made a mistake, allowing herself to get drawn into a situation she couldn't control and certainly couldn't win. Trisha was starting to get used to men looking at her, especially now her breasts were very obvious. She didn't mind the looking. After all, she had a good body, so why not? But this guy wasn't just looking. It felt like he was undressing her and slobbering over her as he did it. She felt violated. And yet not a single person on the bus seemed to give a damn.

'If you can't be civil maybe you should get off the bus,' the guy immediately behind her said. Maybe he was the one person who did care and had the balls to try and do something about it.

'Well, Blondie, what do you think? Should I shut up or can I say what's on my mind?'

Trisha stood up, jabbed at the bell and made her way to the front of the bus. She wasn't even half-way down the Botley Road, at least a mile from home, but she had had enough.

'Are you all right, dear?' an old woman said as she passed.

Of course she wasn't, but Trisha didn't even look at her, let alone reply. She pressed on forward, and as soon as the bus lurched to a stop and the driver released the doors, she was out onto the pavement. She felt like she was about to burst into tears. The bastard man. The silly old lady. Damn them all.

'Hey, are you all right?'

It was a woman, platinum hair pulled up onto her head, heavily made up, trying hard to look younger than she was. She had been at the front of the bus when Trisha got on. A rather sad looking figure then, but now full of fury.

'What a horrid man. It makes me ashamed to be human and ashamed to be British. People like that. Insulting foreigners, insulting women.'

That was all it took – a few kind words. Trisha began to cry. 'Not your fault,' she mumbled.

'Here.' The woman produced a packet of paper tissues from her bag. 'That was a beastly thing to happen to you. In the old days, he'd have been thrown off the bus, but nowadays we have to be endlessly tolerant.'

Trisha finished wiping her nose and passed the unused tissues back to her. 'Thanks.'

'Have you got a long way to walk?'

'Up Cumnor Hill.'

'My car is in the park and ride. If you like, we can walk some of the way together.'

They walked in silence, heading west along the Botley Road. Trisha was glad of the companionship and glad too that the woman had now stopped talking. She knew that if she asked any more questions along the lines of 'are you all right?', the dam would very likely burst again.

They came to a brief halt at a side road. The west-bound traffic had stopped, allowing a stream of east-bound cars to turn across in front of them into the retail park. That was when the woman broke her silence. She touched Trisha gently on the elbow.

'Look,' she said, 'if you like, I could give you a lift to your house.'

Ellie picked a chip off her plate and ate it, before returning her gaze to the page of Chinese characters. She couldn't concentrate at all. She needed Trisha's help, but she hadn't turned up and Alice, of course, had gone swanning off to Shanghai for a month.

She picked up her mobile and sent a plaintive text. *Ni qu nar?* Where the heck had Trisha got to? She might be ridiculously beautiful and clever, but she was not always reliable. Damn her!

She looked up and her stomach did a somersault. It was her father. Again. He was at the counter, ordering himself some food. She looked down again, hoping he hadn't noticed her staring. She didn't want to encourage him. She didn't want him to stalk her all round Oxford either.

She tried to focus on her Mandarin textbook, but failed to take a single word in. She was safe here. If her father wanted to talk to her, then this was the best place to do it. It was very public and very safe. But he wouldn't, would he? She certainly didn't want him to. Or did she? Oh God, she didn't know.

She looked up. He was standing there, one metre away, a tray in his hands, silent and unmoving, as if he too was wracked with uncertainty. He had two drinks and two food items. She suddenly realized that he was waiting for her. She nodded. He sat down. 'Cheeseburger or normal? Diet cola or milkshake?'

She took the cheeseburger and the cola. They ate in silence. She found that odd. She thought he'd be asking her a load of questions about her life and making lots of apologies about what a crap father and bastard husband he had been, but he didn't. She ate the burger gladly – the chips she had eaten while waiting for Trisha had stimulated rather than quelled her appetite. But she felt her irritation rise. Who did he think he was, creeping back into her life after what he had done? Why the hell had he come to Oxford anyway? If he thought he could wheedle his way back into their lives, he must be crazy.

When she had finished the burger and half-finished the cola, she straightened herself in her chair. This silence was ridiculous.

'Why exactly are you here?'

He didn't answer immediately. Even though he must have been expecting the question, he seemed unprepared for it. He wiped his mouth with his paper napkin and shrugged.

'I wanted to see how my little girl had grown up.'

'So now you've seen, you can clear off out of our lives and never come back.'

'I'm your dad.' He was pleading. Pathetic!

'I don't need a dad like you.'

'Everyone deserves a second chance.'

Fury rose within her, a deep tide which swept away all compassion and left behind only bitterness.

'You beat the shit out of my mother. You stubbed your cigarette out on me. Have you forgotten? Because we sure as hell haven't.'

His red face deepened in colour. He looked down at the table, unable to look her in the eyes. When he spoke, it was as if he was addressing her hands, which were fastened tight round her cardboard cup.

'I was in a bad place then. I was drinking. A lot. Much more than I should have been. And me and your mother, things were really bad between us. I was smoking forty or fifty a day. She hated that. I hoped the fags would calm me down. It was stupid, I know that now. Especially when we were so short of money. It was like I was caught up in a crazy spiral and I had no way of stopping it.'

He looked up and gazed at her with sad eyes. But she wasn't going to be taken in. Anyone can put on an act.

'Is that it? 'Cause I've got to go home and look after my mum.'

'You're angry,' he said quietly. 'I can understand that.'

'Can you? Did you do a course on pop psychology when you were inside? So you could come home and play happy families after all you did?' She was lashing out now.

'That night when I came home and hurt you, both of you, that wasn't the real me. It was another person. I can't even remember it. Christ, I was so drunk. I can't remember hitting her or doing what I did to you.' He held his head in his hands, full of contrition or more likely bullshit. 'I'm not saying I didn't hit her. I did. I admit that. But I swear to you, on my life, that I've given up the booze for good. That it'll be different this time.'

Ellie wasn't to be taken in. She pushed her cup away with a single push of her hand. It toppled over. Brown liquid fizzed across the table.

She got to her feet and began to pack her things away. She zipped her rucksack shut and then bent down close to him.

'They let you out of prison early, did they? For good behaviour?'

He nodded.

'So,' she hissed, 'if I were to tell the police you had been hassling me and making threats about Mum, you'd go back inside?'

'Making threats?'

'That's right. You threatening us.'

Reeve was motionless on his chair.

'It would be my word against yours,' she continued. She swung the rucksack onto her back.' Who do you think they would believe? You or me?' A pause. Then a twist of the knife. 'Dad!'

*

'Going somewhere, Mr Mullen?'

Mullen was just locking the front door when from behind him the schoolmarmish tones of DI Holden cut into his thoughts. There had been plenty of them ping-ponging around the inside of his head that morning, but they had all terminated at the deadest of dead ends.

Rex uttered a proprietary growl, which apparently meant something along the lines of, 'Watch it, lady, Mullen and me are a team and this here is our territory.'

The Detective Inspector looked down at the dog. Her lips quivered with distaste.

But Mullen felt a surge of pleasure, not just at her obvious dislike of dogs, but at the loyalty of Rex. He looked her full in the face, a disarming smile plastered across his own.

'Actually,' he said, 'Rex needs a walk and I need some groceries.'

Holden was not a woman easily disarmed. 'I'm afraid you'll both have to wait.'

'Can't we talk as we walk?'

'No!'

Mullen paused for a few moments, as if weighing up his options. But there were, in reality, none. He shrugged, unlocked the door and moved back inside the house. She and her inevitable sidekick DC Trent followed him in. Mullen remained on his feet and kept Rex on his lead. Whatever this was all about, he wanted to keep it short.

'How can I help you, Inspector?'

Holden sat down on a chair at the kitchen table and waited. She gestured towards the one opposite her. Meanwhile Trent took up position by the doorway leading to the front hall, as if he expected Mullen to do a runner. No-one spoke. A battle of wills. Mullen sensed that this was going to get a bit silly if he didn't cooperate. And waste a lot of time. So he sat down.

'We've got an ID on the body which you and your dog found.'

'Oh?' Mullen couldn't hide his interest. If it wasn't Saad Ismat, then who on earth was it?

'Her name is Ruth Lonsdale.'

Mullen nodded, but said nothing.

'Ring any bells?'

'No. I don't think so.'

'Late fifties. With lots of her life in front of her. Only problem was someone fired a bullet through her skull.'

More silence. Mullen tried to get his head round this information. Who was Ruth Lonsdale? Was the name meant to mean something to him? Presumably it was. Because why else would Holden be telling him this? In his experience (admittedly limited), the police wouldn't normally share a mini sausage roll with the likes of him.

'I'm sorry about that. But I'm not sure why—'

It was Trent who responded, putting in his penny worth. 'She must have put her hands over her face, scared as hell, just before the killer pulled the trigger.' He paused, letting his words sink in. 'Poor woman.' Another pause, then a vicious change of gear: 'I guess you must have fired a gun or two during your time in the army, Mullen.'

Fury mixed with anxiety ripped through Mullen. 'What the hell are you implying?'

'What do you think I'm implying, Mullen?' There was a smirk on Trent's face.

'Enough,' Holden snapped. She held up her hand. She might have been a primary teacher separating two squabbling schoolboys and trying to get the class back on track. 'We are here to establish some facts. One fact is that Ruth Lonsdale lives – or rather lived – near Henley. In the village of Nettlebed to be precise.'

Another pause. A meaningful pause. Mullen felt a flash of understanding. Nettlebed. He'd been there very recently.

'We understand you visited the Kettle and Cake café in Nettlebed eight days ago. In fact, thanks to automatic number plate recognition, we have a photograph of your car heading towards Nettlebed that very day.'

Mullen nodded. He could hardly deny it.

'You had a coffee there on your own and before you left, you asked the waitress if there was anyone she knew in the village whose name was Ruth. The waitress got the distinct impression that you'd been stood up by this Ruth, but she wasn't so daft as to tell a complete stranger like you where Ruth lived. So she kept quiet, even though she knew only the one Ruth in the village.'

The nausea rose in Mullen like a tidal wave. There was no warning, just a violent surge. He stood up and headed for the toilet. But DC Trent was standing in the way and as Mullen quickly discovered, DC Trent had no intention of letting his prime suspect escape. So Mullen stopped and vomited all over the floor, spraying the detective constable's trousers for good measure too.

Fifteen minutes later Holden and Mullen were out in the garden, sitting opposite each other on two wooden chairs. Trent had been deputed to clean up the mess, and was now busy sponging down his trousers in the kitchen. He had taken them off and was standing by the sink in blue boxers and grey socks. In any other circumstances, Mullen would have found it funny.

Holden had shut the patio door behind her, as if to insulate herself from the smell of vomit. Or was it her way of pretending this was a private chat and Mullen could say anything he wanted?

'Tell me,' she said, her voice suddenly soft and caressing, 'how exactly was it that you ended up in Nettlebed trying to meet Ruth Lonsdale?'

Mullen shrugged, conscious that his account wasn't going to sound too convincing. But he was determined to give it his best shot.

'Look, after I rescued Natalie and Ellie in that crash on the M40 and got all that publicity, it was like a free advert. Suddenly loads of people were contacting me, wanting to hire me. Some of this was the usual stuff – following partners and spouses and recalcitrant student offspring. Not exactly elevating work. But they were people who were willing to pay to get results. Of course there were the others too: one woman wanted me to find out what had happened to her long lost cat and a man begged me to track down the person who was sending messages to him via his television every night during the ten o'clock news.'

'What about Ruth?' Holden wasn't to be diverted.

'She rang me.'

'Do you have her number?'

'She said she was in a phone box.'

'Is that normal for your clients?'

'I guess if you don't want a spouse or anyone else to know, it's a good way.'

Holden nodded, but said nothing.

'Anyway, she said she was Ruth and would like to meet me in this coffee shop in Nettlebed.'

'Did she say what it was about?'

'She said she was very worried about her daughter Emma. She said Emma had gone travelling around Germany, but she had recently stopped replying to her emails and wasn't answering her mobile.'

'So you decided she wasn't an oddball?'

'There was no reason to suppose she was. She sounded distressed, so I agreed to meet her—'

'A damsel in distress?' The interruption came from behind Mullen. He turned around. It was Trent. He had his trousers back on, with several wet patches down both legs, but he hadn't managed to completely expunge the reek of Mullen's vomit. 'And you were the knight riding to the rescue?'

Mullen opened his mouth to say something in his defence, but

Holden beat him to it. 'Make us a cup of tea, Sergeant, before you sit down.'

There was a moment when no-one moved or spoke, a moment when DC Trent possibly considered arguing the toss with his superior. But then his common sense and breeding kicked in and he asked Mullen with exaggerated politeness how he liked his tea before retreating from whence he came.

'He can be a bit of a pain,' Holden said evenly. 'A well-connected pain, actually, as his uncle is a long way up the police hierarchy. But what I like about him is he's very acute. In fact, I think he's probably summed you up rather well.'

She paused, letting her words sink in before she continued.

'Did the woman who called herself Ruth not tell you her surname?'

Mullen shook his head.

'Just as she didn't give you any contact details. Yet you agreed to meet her in a café essentially because she told you a nice persuasive sob story?'

Mullen nodded. Holden leaned back in her chair, sipping at her tea. She seemed rather pleased with herself.

'I was speaking to DI Dorkin last night.'

'Dorkin?' Mullen was caught unawares by the sudden change of track. But he welcomed it. Dorkin and he had history and pretty good history at that. A nice guy, a bit old-fashioned perhaps, but a good bloke.

'He said lots of nice things about you. '

'That was kind of him.'

'He said to go easy on you until we were certain.'

'Certain of what?'

'Certain of the fact that you've been telling us a pack of lies.'

Mullen wished it was Dorkin sitting in front of him now. Holden was clever, devious even. He bet she was capable of playing the good cop bad cop all by herself if she needed to.

'I don't tell lies,' he lied. Everyone lied occasionally. White lies. Grey lies. To avoid a bollocking. To save someone's feelings. Out of embarrassment or shame. But Mullen felt confident that he didn't do big, black lies.

'Why don't you just start at the beginning again? With the first Elizabeth Durant.' She waited. A robin perching on a nearby shrub uttered a warning call. Rex, now released from his lead, lay silent at Mullen's feet. A red kite whistled from on high. 'If you don't mind.' DI Holden continued to wait.

So Mullen retold the whole story. And as he told it, he began to realize the glaring weaknesses and inconsistencies in it. By the time he got to the end, he was hoping without much hope that Dorkin's advice was still prominent in Holden's head.

Holden sat in silence after he had finished. She was cradling a mug of tea by this time, and Trent had sat himself down on a garden chair slightly removed from the two of them, a chastened observer rather than a participant.

Holden leaned forward. 'Tell me, Mr Mullen. What did Elizabeth Durant the First look like?'

Mullen knew exactly what Holden was thinking. It was so obvious. If he had done his research and looked at press reports and photos, he would have seen pictures of the real Elizabeth Durant alongside Saad and he would have twigged that Elizabeth the First was a fake.

'She was maybe four or five inches taller than the real Elizabeth Durant, but in some ways she was quite similar. Thin face. Dark round the eyes. Brown hair. A neat fringe. The big difference apart from the height however was the way she behaved. She waved her arms about and was very agitated.'

'Have you been in touch with her since yesterday?'

'No.'

'Why not?'

'She's not answering her mobile number. I told you that yesterday.'

'Did she pay you any money?'

'No.' Mullen had finally checked his bank account.

Trent chuckled. Mullen felt a sudden urge to grab him by his jacket lapels and give him a good shake, but of course he didn't.

Holden, to give her credit, merely flicked a dismissive look at her colleague before she continued.

'What sort of car was she driving?'

'I never saw it. She said she had parked round the corner the second time she came to see me, but...' Mullen dribbled into silence.

'So,' Holden said relentlessly, 'you're expecting me to believe that you took on this assignment to find Saad Ismat without any upfront payment, without knowing anything at all about this woman or being able to contact her by mobile phone, email or even carrier pigeon?'

'That's right.' Mullen tugged at the bridge of his nose with the thumb and forefinger of his right hand. He knew he needed to say something in his own defence. 'I felt sorry for her and for the boy. Refugee Syrian schoolboys who go missing don't get the Maddie McCann treatment, do they? After a few days, they are forgotten. So how could I possibly refuse to help Elizabeth Durant when she turned up on my doorstep?'

Holden looked back at him, though quite what she was thinking Mullen couldn't tell. She would have made a good poker player.

'Well,' he continued. He reckoned he needed to argue his case a bit more strongly. 'What sort of man would I have been if I had said no to her? You tell me that, Inspector.'

Holden pursed her lips. Several seconds passed and then, the interview apparently over, she got to her feet.

'Is that it?' Mullen said, standing up too and feeling rather relieved.

'Not quite, Mr Mullen,' she said. 'I'm afraid we need you to come down to the station and make a formal statement.'

Holden and Trent had retreated to the café in the central open space of the Templars Square Shopping Centre. It was almost two o'clock and only half a dozen of the tables were occupied. They ate their baguettes in silence. Lunch had been delayed by Doug Mullen, but now he had been despatched home. Time to recuperate and reflect.

Holden ate slowly whereas Trent devoured his at an alarming speed. She watched him with fascination. Was this a habit learned at boarding school? Scoff the grub before someone else nicks it off you? He finished long before her. He took other sip of his Americano, then picked up a paper napkin and wiped his mouth with surprising delicacy. Breeding will out. Then he looked across at her, suddenly boyish again.

'So what do you think, Guv?'

Holden's mouth was full.

But Trent wasn't really interested in Holden's thoughts, it was his own that he wanted to air. 'His story is a load of cock and bull. Two mysterious women allegedly wanting to hire him. No contact details, no car numbers, no witnesses to either of them. He must think we're idiots. Let's look at the facts. He went to Nettlebed to meet Ruth Lonsdale. She doesn't turn up for their meeting. Maybe she is scared. Maybe she's got wind of what he might do. Fact number two. Ruth Lonsdale turns up dead in Bagley Wood. Mullen claims he found her while walking his dog—'

Holden interrupted, 'Actually he said that his dog found her.'

Trent wasn't fazed by the correction. He grinned. 'Yes, nice touch that. Designed to distract us. But put the two facts together and what have we got? Mullen as our prime suspect.'

'He had the opportunity, I agree. But you're jumping the gun. What was his motive?'

'We'll find that out in due course.'

'Dorkin knows Mullen. He doesn't think Mullen has got it in him to kill.'

'Come off it, Guv. In the right circumstances, anyone can kill. You know that. Look at Mullen. He's a private detective. He knows the tricks of the trade. Easy enough for him to track her down in

Nettlebed, abduct her, bring her to Bagley Wood, then shoot her. It's a clever location to choose. Did you know that they cull the deer there at night? They shoot the squirrels too. Mullen would have known that. So another gunshot isn't going to be noticed. As for how he found the body – the mysterious woman with psychic powers, the missing refugee, the dog – well, it's all part of the charade, isn't it? Sooner or later someone else's dog would have found her, or the foresters would when they moved the logs, but if he finds her first with the help of a psychic and a dog, well, no-one could possibly believe that he had done it. Bloody clever if you ask me.'

'I wasn't aware I had asked you.' She pushed her plate away from her, abandoning what was left of her meal. She had had enough, and not just of her food. She wished she had come and had lunch on her own. Or at least that Trent had let her eat in peace.

He looked down at the table, overtly contrite. 'Sorry, Guv, I was just thinking out loud.'

'You were laying out a theory. Despite the fact that we currently have insufficient evidence.'

'We have to use what evidence we've got.' Trent wasn't going to lie down and be trampled. Besides, he was good at holding his own in an argument. He had been a member of the school debating team. 'How do you explain the fact that Mullen went looking for Ruth Lonsdale in Nettlebed?'

'One explanation is that Mullen is telling the truth. In that scenario, either Ruth Lonsdale contacted him because she had seen him on the news media or someone pretending to be Ruth Lonsdale rang him up.'

'One of two mystery women, neither of whom anyone else has seen.' There was derision in his voice.

'Actually, not necessarily two.' Holden spoke with exaggerated precision. 'Maybe only one. One woman pretending to be two different people. Which is why in the case of Ruth Lonsdale, she only contacted him by phone. So that he wouldn't realize.'

Holden stood up. She didn't want to discuss this any further. She knew that Trent wasn't convinced. But what the hell! As long as he didn't go muttering about her to his uncle, she didn't give a damn.

The pub was little more than a place to drink. Shabby, tired decor, cheaper alcohol than most of the competition in the area and busy. It was the seventh pub that Detective Constable Colin Knight had visited that afternoon in Hull, and despite the fact that he had drawn a complete blank, he hadn't given up. Far from it. The very dinginess of the Bricklayers Arms encouraged him. If Phil Stubbs, ex-con, drank anywhere – and he obviously did drink – it would be in a place like this. He walked up to the bar where a man with thinning grey hair was bent over a newspaper. The man looked up, as if surprised that anyone should be wanting a drink at this time of day.

Knight didn't say anything. He merely displayed his ID. He liked doing that. It still gave him a little thrill to see how people reacted – the initial flash of fear or distaste or worse before the shutters came down. This publican was definitely uneasy and very likely lived with his shutters half down.

'Yeah?'

'What's your name?'

'Harry.'

'So Harry, have you seen this guy recently?' Knight was now holding up a photograph, A5 in size, of Philip Stubbs.

'Yeah.'

'How recently?'

Harry sighed as if trying to remember – or maybe he was wondering how co-operative to be.

'He was a regular for a week or two. Called himself Phil. Not from round here. Manchester way, I'd say. But he hasn't been in for a few days.'

'Can you be more precise?'

The man scratched his scalp as if that might improve his recall. 'He was definitely here last Tuesday. He liked the curry. Tuesday is our curry night. Poppadoms, mango chutney, the works. Very popular. Not sure that I've seen him since then.'

'I see you've got CCTV. Does it work?'

Harry nodded.

'In that case, I'd like all your footage for the last week.'

Harry's faced dropped. 'Why?'

'Because I say so.'

Harry swore. Knight said nothing. He wasn't bothered. In fact, he almost smiled. He was starting to enjoy himself.

Mullen was beginning to feel the strain. It already felt like a very long day. Being interviewed in his own (as it were) garden by DI Holden had been bad enough. But the formal statement down at Cowley Station had taken a ridiculously long time and after that he'd had to make his own way home.

At least Rex had been pleased to see him, but after a very late lunch – during which he broke all the rules and deliberately dropped several small pieces of Danish salami onto the patio floor – Mullen had no option but to review the mess he had gotten into. And as he did so, he found himself driven to one conclusion. He had been played for a fool. Or to put it another way, Trent was right. He had been too eager to please the women who threw themselves at his feet. Too eager to be a knight in shining armour who rescued damsels, when in reality he was more like the guy who tilted hopelessly at windmills.

He stood up and wandered back inside the house, plate and glass in hand and as he placed them in the sink, the doorbell rang.

Not the police again! He was tempted to pretend he hadn't heard it. He stood in the kitchen motionless. If it was urgent, his visitor would press it again. Rex, unaware of the dilemma in Mullen's head, had heard the bell from the garden and was now at Mullen's feet. He gave his trademark little yap, and then padded along the hall corridor to the front door. The bell rang for a second time, and Mullen conceded defeat.

It was Elizabeth Durant. The real one whose house he had been to, the one who had collapsed into his arms, not the fake version who had led him by the nose into a right royal mess. If the real Durant was a damsel in distress, it wasn't outwardly apparent. She looked as though she was en route to an extremely smart party, where Pimms and canapés and a very high-class barbecue was on offer. In short, she was immaculately turned out: mid-calf summer dress (white flowers on green background), a plain green jacket, sandals with a multiplicity of thin straps, matching necklace and earrings, a serious covering of make-up and newly coiffured hair. Mullen felt a complete scruff. The only slightly off-key note in her attire was a capacious brown bag slung over her shoulder. Her face was impervious.

She launched straight in. 'Mr Mullen, I feel I owe you an apology.'

'Please …' he said.

'I behaved appallingly,' she insisted. 'Even though I was taken completely by surprise, there was absolutely no excuse for the way I behaved.'

Mullen wasn't quite sure in what way having an epileptic fit on her doorstep was appalling behaviour, but he wasn't going to argue the point.

'Why don't you come in? I was just about to have a cup of tea,' he lied. (But only a little white one.)

By the time Mullen had produced two mugs of tea, Durant had made herself at home at the garden table, on which she had laid out a sheaf of papers extracted from her bag.

She pushed them over to Mullen. 'I want to hire you to find Saad. Dead or alive, I need to know what happened to him.'

Mullen leafed through the first few bits of paper. Newspaper cuttings, print-outs from websites, a hand-written list of names headed

People Saad knew, and a print-out from a website headed *Missing Persons.* There was an image of Saad on the right-hand side, large startled eyes peering out of a soft brown face.

'I'm sure as a professional you have ways of finding out much more. But I hope this will help.'

'I can't offer any guarantees,' Mullen said, trying to get his excuses in first.

'Of course not. I fully understand. I am not an idiot.'

'No, of course not,' he replied quickly. He wasn't handling the situation well.

'If you give me your bank details, I'll make a payment now. Then you can make a start straight away.'

Mullen could barely believe his luck. While the real Durant completed the bank transfer using her mobile (unlike the fake one who had only promised to), Mullen started to read the documents in front of him. The first one was familiar – an article from the *Oxford Mail* which he had read online after the fake Durant had turned up at his door. He read it to the end, and then looked up, conscious that Durant's eyes were fixed on him.

'All done. Check your account in a couple of hours and the money should be there.'

Mullen sat back in his chair. 'I can read all this later, but I'd like you to tell me about the last time you saw Saad.'

'He went to school as normal. Last week of term. Left at 7.45, so he could catch the bus. He gave me a little hug as he always did, and then he walked out the front door and...' The words choked in her throat.

Mullen sat statue still, barely daring to breathe in case he should break into her grief and release a torrent.

'... and he disappeared,' she said finally. 'He hugged me and he disappeared.' Durant began to cry, deep silent sobs which wracked her body and caused tears to run untidily over her make-up. She removed a handkerchief from her bag and dabbed at her eyes. Mullen waited.

'Did he have some sort of school bag?'

'I gave him a rucksack. He always took that.'

'Have you been through his possessions since he left?'

She frowned as if uncertain where this line of questioning was going.

Mullen explained. 'What I would like to establish is whether he was planning to leave home that morning or whether it was something that just happened. So what were his lessons that day? Did he take all the books and equipment for a day at school or maybe did he put various spare clothes in his rucksack because he had other plans?'

'He never got on the school bus,' she said. Her fingers, complete with pale green nails, were interlocked tightly, the veins on the back of the hands raised. 'That is one of the things which the police did check out.'

'I read that. But it's Saad's intentions that I'm interested in. Was he planning on going to school that day or was he planning on running away?'

Mullen spoke more forcibly than he had intended, and for some time Durant didn't answer. Rex had previously jumped up onto the bench and was now sitting up close to Durant. He gave a little whine. She looked down at him and unclasped her hands. She stroked the dog. She spoke without looking up.

'I think he took a couple of pairs of pants, and his anorak,' she whispered, as if admitting this reality was just too painful. 'And his Oxford United shirt.'

'What about his school things?'

She shook her head. 'They are all in his bedroom.' Tears were trickling down her face again, but she made no attempt to mop them up. 'He loved his football shirt. We used to go to the games together sometimes. Not that I like football, but just to see the pleasure he got from it. It was worth it just for that.'

'Did you tell the police this?'

'No.'

'Why not?' Mullen said, and immediately regretted the stupidity of his question. The answer was obvious. If the police had known that he had planned to leave home that morning, then they would have been even less interested in his disappearance than they had been.

'I will do my level best to find him,' Mullen said, trying to smooth things over. 'I promise you.'

She stood up. 'Do you mind if I use your facilities?' She waved her hand to indicate her face. 'I need to repair some of the damage.'

'I want to report a missing person.'

Stella Robinson had put off ringing the police until 8.00 p.m., but when the clock in the front hall struck the hour, she caved in. She had already rung round everyone she could think of. All Trisha's friends. All her own friends in the area. She had sent five texts to Trisha's mobile and got not a single reply. She had left three voice messages too, the third of which she said she would ring the police if Trisha didn't respond within the hour. But no-one could help, no-one had seen her. Or at least none of Trisha's friends had admitted to seeing her. Even with her stress levels pumped up to maximum, Stella wasn't so gullible as to ignore the possibility that they might be covering for her. Maybe there was another boy on the scene. Maybe she had started having sex with him. Maybe she had run away with him? Or had Saad been in touch with her? Had he convinced her to run away with him to join Isis? Like those girls from that school in London. The fact that Trisha had shown not the slightest interest in Islam didn't feature in Stella's thinking. Her imagination, fuelled by fear, was going into orbit.

She had tried ringing her husband, Greg, too, but he had cleared off on a business trip to Liverpool and he wasn't answering his phone either. Stella was under no illusions that striking business deals wasn't the only thing he got up to while he was away from home. But the reality was that she didn't much care any more. She would rather he was away than he was hanging about the house, laying down the law and bullying his daughter. She wished she had had the guts to leave him years ago.

At the end of the phone line, a woman began to take some details. She was irritatingly calm, asking her questions and clarifying Stella's answers with such patience and precision that Stella felt like screaming down the phone in the hope of sparking some sense of urgency into the woman's demeanour.

'Do you think it is possible your daughter might have a boyfriend you don't know about?'

'Do you have a good relationship with your daughter?'

'What about your husband?'

'So your husband is away on business, but he's not answering his phone. Is that normal?'

'I know you are feeling stressed, but shouting really isn't helpful.'

'Of course we take missing persons reports seriously, but the fact is that lots of people are reported missing, and in the vast majority of cases there turns out to be a simple explanation.'

'No, not dead, Mrs Robinson. Statistically that is the least likely outcome. They come home after a few hours or a few days, saying how sorry they are for all the trouble they have caused.'

By the end of the phone call, Stella was in an even greater state of distress than she had been at the beginning.

She poured herself a whisky and downed it in one. She wasn't much of a drinker, but a slug of her husband's favourite and very expensive single malt seemed a much better bet than a calming cup of tea. Tea wasn't going to bring her daughter home. Nor was whisky, but she poured herself a second slug anyway and gulped half of it down. Then she tipped the bottle upside down over the sink and watched the amber liquid disappear down the plug hole. For a few seconds, she felt better, before fear and anxiety reasserted themselves.

She rang Natalie again. She knew Natalie had her own problems, but it was Natalie she needed. Ellie answered.

'Hi, Ellie. Is your mother there?'

'She's gone to bed.'

'Look, love, this is really important. Just take the phone upstairs. Wake her up if you have to. I must speak to her.'

Several seconds later she heard Natalie's voice, quiet and plodding. 'Can I help you, Stella?'

'I need to speak to your private detective.'

'Oh.' There was a long delay. Stella took another sip from her tumbler and this time savoured the taste. She could get used to whisky, she decided. She shouldn't have poured that bottle away. She would have to check the garage later and see where her bastard husband kept his supplies squirrelled away.

'Mr Spade, you mean.' It was Natalie again.

'Whatever his name is, I need his phone number, sweetie.'

After Elizabeth Durant had left, Mullen sat down and read carefully through every piece of paper which she had left with him. By the end he was certainly better informed about what the press and others were saying, but little the wiser when it came to the question of where had Saad gone – and why.

Then he belatedly gave Rex his supper, bunged a frozen pizza in the oven (what a stereotype you are today, Mullen!) and got out the hose. The heat had been close to insufferable and even now as the light was fading, it was sticky and uncomfortable. Mullen began to water all the plants he could reach. He imagined he could see the plants perking up as the moisture soaked down to their roots. He even turned the hose on his own face and hair, not caring that it also soaked half his T-shirt. The water cooled his body, easing the pent-up tension which had been building all day. Just in time he rescued the pizza, and then sat outside, eating it under the shade of the parasol, a pint glass of water and an expectant dog his only company.

After that, he visited the greenhouse, soaking the tomato plants, the chillies and the cucumbers, before retreating back to the house. He switched on the TV and found himself watching some trash that wasn't of the slightest interest to him. He sighed and closed his eyes and would have fallen asleep if his mobile hadn't rung.

It was Stella and she was close to hysterical, so fifteen minutes later he found himself outside her house, having towed an unenthusiastic Rex in his wake. Rex, it was clear, reckoned it was long past his bedtime.

Stella greeted him with a flurry of anxiety. 'Thank God you're here. I don't know what I'd do without you. The police just aren't interested. She could be dead in a ditch or have been abducted by a serial killer. They obviously think she's just gone off with a bloke and will return when she has had enough. But she wouldn't just go off and not tell me. I kept telling them that, but they weren't listening.'

Mullen tried to calm her down, not just for her own well-being, but so that he could get some clear information out of her. That proved to be easier said than done. Half the time, she didn't seem to be listening to his questions at all.

'Where's your husband?' he said, suddenly conscious that the man who had threatened him when he tried to talk to Trisha was nowhere to be seen. The question turned off the hysteria, but it was replaced with a gale of fury.

'Greg? That bastard. Shagging some woman, I dare say. His mobile's turned off. He's supposedly away on business. But why would he turn off his phone when he's on a business trip? Quite apart from his wife maybe wanting to talk to him, doesn't he need to be contactable by his clients and his colleagues? What do you think?'

Mullen wasn't going to share with her his own experience of what a turned-off mobile might mean. He didn't think it would help.

'Let me make us a cup of tea,' he said, trying to take charge. Anything to calm her down. He moved towards the kettle. 'After that, I'll need you to fill me in on some of the details.'

'Oh, God bless you,' she said, before bursting into tears. Mullen handed her a tissue and wondered if she was expecting him to be her knight in shining armour for free. He rather suspected she was.

CHAPTER 7

Wednesday

DC KNIGHT WAS AS high as a kite, though not on drugs or alcohol or caffeine. In fact, maybe partly on caffeine, but primarily on his own adrenalin. He threaded his way between the various desks and knocked on the DI's door. He went in.

Bryce looked up. His face was as cheerless as a wet November day. The office rumour was that his wife had run off with another woman.

'What is it, Constable?'

'It's the man in the river, sir.'

Bryce leaned back in his chair and surveyed Knight. 'You mean the man who was pulled out of the river. The man whom we've identified as being Philip Stubbs.'

'That's the one, sir.' He wasn't going to let Bryce's pedantry spoil his moment. 'We've located him on CCTV from the Bricklayers Arms. The same night we think he went into the river. He's sitting eating his curry with another man. Very matey they look.'

'How many pints did he drink?'

Knight hesitated. He hadn't expected to be asked this level of detail. 'Three. No, four I think.'

'Who bought the drinks? Him or his friend?'

Knight hesitated again.

'Don't you know, Constable? This is basic stuff. You've got him skewered on CCTV, so you make sure you observe every detail. Was his friend buying all the drinks? Or was he? Or were they sharing it? In which case, who bought the first round? That could be significant. How did they pay? Cash or card?'

'Cash.' He could answer that easily enough. Knight felt himself going red, but he tried to pretend he wasn't.

'Have you identified the companion?' Bryce had laced his hands behind his head now and was leaning even further back in his chair.

'Yes, sir.'

'And are you going to tell me his name, Constable?'

'Yes, sir. His name is Paul Reeve. Like Stubbs, he's an ex-con.'

Bryce nodded, but his eyes remained fixed on Knight.

'In fact, sir, until a few weeks ago they were sharing a room at HMP Stonewood. Stubbs was released first, then Reeve a couple of weeks later.'

It was Knight's *coup de grâce* – or so he hoped. This was surely the piece of news which might cause DI Bryce to congratulate him and then (maybe) even underline it with a smile.

Bryce eased himself forward into the upright position. He placed his hands together on his desk. 'So what do you propose doing next, Constable?'

'Try and locate him and bring him in for questioning.'

'Hmmm.' Bryce sucked in his lips. 'Let's suppose he does the "no comment" routine, what then?'

Knight's mouth opened and then closed.

Bryce pressed on. 'Do you have any hard evidence that they had a row? Did they leave the pub together? Do you have any witnesses who saw them after they left the pub? Can you prove that it was Reeve who hit Stubbs? Do you have evidence that Stubbs fell into the river as a consequence of that blow?' Bryce was relentless.

Knight felt as though he had just been cornered in a dark alleyway by a guy armed with a baseball bat. He tried to defend himself.

'Not as yet, sir. But the evidence as a whole is compelling.'

'Is it?' The two words spoke volumes. 'Is this all you've got for me,' he yelled? 'Surely you've got something more than this for me? Why are you wasting my time?' Knight squirmed. He had entered Bryce's office with such confidence. 'Anything else, Constable?' Bryce said sharply.

Knight played his last card. 'Reeve has a history of violence, sir. He was jailed for beating the hell out of his wife and child.'

Bryce picked up a glass of water from his desk and took a sip.

'Look, sir,' Knight said. He wasn't going to submit without a fight. 'They were buddies in prison. They met up after they came out and drank together. That same night Stubbs ends up dead in the river. I may not have enough for the CPS currently, but I refuse to put all that down to coincidence.'

Bryce replaced his glass on the desk with infinite care. He grunted. 'Well, Constable, I think you need to do a bit more digging.'

'Yes, sir.'

Knight felt a surge of relief. Maybe he hadn't done such a bad job after all.

'But don't waste too much time on it. Not unless you can pin the death on Reeve. Not if you want to keep yourself in my good books. Understood?'

Knight nodded and retreated. And as he closed the door behind him, he couldn't stop himself wondering if the rumours about Bryce's wife were true after all.

Sitting at the kitchen table with toast and marmalade and a mug of tea sitting untouched in front of him, Mullen felt like the guy in the circus who spins plates on several different sticks and tries desperately to stop them crashing to the ground. But the circus guy at least knew what he was doing and had practised it in secret for months or even years.

Mullen had slept badly too, and what sleep he had managed had been fractured by lurid and disturbing dreams: decapitated swans (real, not material) with red blood running down their necks and over their white plumage; a dark-suited body swinging from rope in a stair-well, or so it seemed until Mullen became aware that the corpse wasn't wearing a suit, because the 'suit' was alive, a tremulous buzzing horde of flies; and then it was Rex, emerging from under a pile of logs, tail wagging hysterically and an over-sized finger in his mouth. More sur-prisingly, Trish had appeared once too, standing upright, arms down by her sides, motionless. She had opened her mouth to say something, but then suddenly it wasn't her any more, it was the face of Saad, and he was wearing a huge Oxford United football shirt which hung down almost to his knees.

Now that the day had arrived and he was sitting downstairs with the early morning sunshine streaming through the patio windows, the vividness of these images was beginning to fade. He picked up a piece of toast and bit a corner off it. He chewed it and then sipped at his tea.

He needed to concentrate. What to prioritize? Which of the spin-ning plates to attend to first? He had some ideas about Saad, but he had promised Stella that he would speak to the police. That would be easier and quicker. It was a few minutes past eight o'clock. Trent had left him a card with his number on it, but Holden hadn't. He would have pre-ferred to speak to her. Despite her sharp edges, he felt they had some sort of connection and she most certainly had much more clout than Trent. But Trent, he realized, would have to do. He keyed the number into his mobile and was pleasantly surprised to find it was answered almost immediately.

'It's Doug Mullen here.'

'Oh yes.'

'I'm ringing on behalf of Stella Robinson.'

'Who is Stella Robinson?'

'She reported last night that her daughter Trisha had gone missing.'

'How old is the daughter?'

The daughter? Mullen felt his irritation growing with every word that Trent uttered. 'She's just turned fourteen,' he said.

'I see.' The words could have meant anything or nothing. As could the pause which followed while Trent considered his next move. Mullen wondered if Trent was regretting having given him his contact details.

Mullen pressed on. 'I can imagine what you're thinking. Lots of people go missing. Girls of that age go on a night out with a boyfriend whom the parents know nothing about. They sleep together. The girl realizes she'll be in for one hell of a grilling when she goes home, so she doesn't bother. A day or two later, contrite and sullen, she turns up at home to face the music.'

'And what is your point, Mr Mullen?'

'My point is that Trisha is a close friend of Saad Ismat. And that therefore her disappearance ought to be of particular interest to DI Holden and yourself.'

Mullen waited. Trent was silent for three or four seconds. Then, 'OK, I'll pass on the information.'

'Would you like Stella Robinson's mobile number and address?'

'I'm sure it will be on the system.'

'Of course,' Mullen said. But Trent had already terminated the call.

Mullen rang Stella Robinson. She answered instantly and for ten minutes Mullen found himself trying unsuccessfully to reassure her. At least her husband had finally responded to her frantic phone calls and had promised to drive back from Liverpool. She kept repeating how grateful she was to Mullen for speaking to his police contacts, but by the end of the call, an intense gloom had descended upon him, caused above all by a belief that he had given her reason to hope when he felt no such hope himself. What could he do that the police couldn't? Or rather, wouldn't. Because unless Holden decided it was relevant to her own investigations, it was going to be a case of wouldn't. Without her say-so, Trisha's disappearance was going to be pretty low on the police's priority list.

He would speak to Ellie. She was Trisha's best friend, so that was the obvious thing to do. Maybe quiz her about Saad too. In any case, he ought to check out how Natalie was.

He took Rex's lead down off its hook.

'Come on, boy.' Mullen had had enough. Endless introspection would get him nowhere. 'Let's go and pay Natalie and Ellie a visit.'

'Thank God it's you!' It was Mercy who opened the door. 'Come in now, Mr Spade.' She gripped his arm with her hand, as if fearful that he might run off. 'Ellie's friend Trish has disappeared!'

'I know,' Mullen said. 'I've spoken to the police.'

'Oh bless you for that. But what are they doing?'

'They are very used to such situations,' Mullen said, trying to give her the same false hope he had offered to Stella Robinson.

'She's been missing since yesterday morning. She's a very pretty teenager. If I was her mother, I'd be out of my mind with worry.'

'How's Natalie?'

'She's in bed still. She was in such a state last night that Ellie rang me at home after I'd gone to bed. I suggested she give her a sleeping pill.'

'Is Ellie around? Because it's really her I need to speak to.'

'Asleep too, I dare say. But I'll get her up.'

But Mercy didn't need to. There was the padding of feet descending the stairs and Ellie appeared in spotted pyjamas.

She slumped into a chair at the table. Her eyes were red. She had been crying. And Mullen knew in that moment that he had made the right decision. Ellie was his – and Trisha's – best chance.

He waited for Mercy to disappear upstairs with a cup of tea for Natalie, and then he sat down next to her and took his opportunity. It wasn't that he didn't trust Mercy. Quite the opposite. But she was

111

a hindrance. Ellie might well know things about Trisha which she wouldn't want to get back to her mother, or indeed to Stella. So if he was to get the whole truth out of Ellie, his best chance was when Mercy and Natalie were out of the way.

'When did you last see Trisha?'

'The night before last,' she said. 'I went round to her house.'

'What did you talk about?'

'This and that. In between watching *Game of Thrones*.'

'Was she seeing anyone?'

'No.'

'You're sure? And just to be clear, whatever you tell me stays with me. I'm not the police. I don't need to take formal statements. I won't repeat anything you tell me to anyone. Not to your mum or the police or anyone.'

Ellie frowned and dragged her fingers through her hair.

'I think she would have told me if she was seeing someone. And besides, she's still pretty cut up about Saad.'

'Tell me about her parents.'

'Stella is cool. A bit overprotective, but not as much as some mothers.'

'What about Greg?'

'You've met him, haven't you? Trish told me all about it, in graphic detail. He's a control freak, lays down the law. Trish is scared of him and so is Stella.'

'Why do you think they are scared?'

Ellie didn't reply. She appeared to be studying the back of her hands. They were pale, except for her fingernails, which were painted a deep purple.

'Does he hit them?'

Ellie got up suddenly and went over to the fridge freezer. She poured herself a glass of juice and drank half of it. Then she sat down again.

'Not Trish. But I reckon he has hit Stella in the past. Maybe still does. I asked Trish outright once, but she clammed up. Sometimes Stella wears big floaty scarfs round her neck and when she does I wonder what's underneath.'

'So you saw Trish on Monday night. Did you hear from her yesterday at all?'

Ellie picked her mobile phone up from the table. She unlocked it.

'Here,' she said. 'You can see.'

Mullen studied the texts.

At 10.32 on the Monday night: *Home safe. Thx.*

9.48 Tuesday morning: *Off into town.*

11.45: *It's all kicking off on the bus!* There was an attached photograph. A big guy in a scruffy tracksuit, unbrushed hair, stubble on his cheeks. Mouth open, right hand raised, as if he was in the middle of a harangue.

'Any idea who the man is?'

Ellie shook her head.

'Do you mind if I forward it to my phone?'

'No.'

'Good.'

When he had done so, Mullen handed the phone back. 'Would you mind ringing her mobile now?'

'She won't be answering,' she said, but she rang anyway, turning on the loudspeaker. A robotic human voice answered, asking the caller to leave a message.

'Leave one!' Mullen mouthed, and Ellie did, giving a very good impression of not being worried at all. 'I'm really stuck on my Mandarin, Trish. Give me a ring.'

They both fell silent. Mullen got himself a glass of water.

'We were due to meet for lunch yesterday, after her shopping trip in town. But she never turned up.'

'Would you say that was usual? I mean, was she reliable, the sort of person who always turned up when you arranged to meet?'

Ellie shook her head.

'Do you think she's dead, Spade?' Her voice wobbled, on the verge of tears.

Mullen took a sip, buying a moment or two of time. He believed in being honest, but sometimes honesty could be too brutal.

'I try not to think like that. She could have met someone, someone her parents wouldn't approve of. Or gone to a rave. Or maybe Saad has been in touch with her.'

'Saad?' There was a frisson in her voice, as if that possibility had not occurred to her. 'Do you really think so?'

'It's possible.'

'She would have told me,' Ellie insisted. 'I know she would.'

'You can't know for sure,' Mullen said. 'If there's one thing life has taught me, it is that people can behave in quite unexpected ways.' Which was sort of true.

'But you think she's dead? Do you think Saad is dead too?' Ellie was demanding an answer. And maybe reassurance too. 'Just tell me. No lies. No trying to spare me.'

'No,' he said. 'I don't think either of them are dead.'

Ellie looked at him. Her eyes seemed to bore right through him. 'You're a bad liar, Spade,' she said.

The postcard came through the letterbox at half past nine that morning. If Mercy hadn't come down and insisted on making Mullen a cup of tea and a couple of slices of toast with marmalade – 'honestly, I don't know how Ellie could have been so rude not to offer you something' – he would have already gone home and thus missed it.

Natalie had come downstairs while he was eating. A thin blue and white summer dress accentuated her frailty. She seemed to float across the kitchen, before settling ever so softly into the pink Lloyd Loom chair by the patio door.

She eyed Mullen uncertainly. 'Spade, isn't it?'

'That's right.'

There was the clack of the letter box plate.

'I'll get it,' and Mercy was gone, as ever a whirl of helpfulness and action. 'A load of junk mail,' she announced on her return. 'Oh, except for this card for you, sweetie.'

Natalie took the postcard and stared at the picture on the front for a long time. She turned it over and stared at the writing too. Mullen, who had now finished his second breakfast, wondered if he should offer to help. Was she having trouble reading it? Mercy had switched on the dishwasher and was wiping the surfaces. She seemed unconcerned about Natalie.

Mullen got a quick flash of the front of the card as Natalie turned it over again. Her face was screwed up in concentration.

'What's the picture on the card?' he said, trying to start a conversation.

Natalie looked across at him as if she didn't understand the question.

'A giant spider,' Mercy said. She was wiping the front of the fridge.

'I hate spiders,' Natalie said to no-one in particular.

Mullen downed the dregs of his tea and stood up. There was the thump of more feet coming down the stairs. Ellie appeared, now dressed in her usual black garb. She didn't do ironing as far as Mullen could see. (Who was he to talk?) But her spiky hair had clearly received a lot of attention. She went over to her mother and took the card out of her hand, as if Natalie was the child and she was the parent vetting it for indecency.

She read it, then turned it over. 'Fuck!' she said.

'That's quite enough of that language.' Mercy didn't even pause in her wiping of the fridge door.

'Look!' Ellie thrust the postcard towards Mullen. 'You're the detective, Spade.'

Mullen looked and read it. *The truth will out!!!* Three exclamation marks. Otherwise nothing except Natalie's name and address. A

Swindon postmark. Which meant it could be from almost anyone. All the mail originating in Oxford went via the Swindon sorting office, as presumably did mail from a wide area south, west and east of Swindon.

He turned the card over and finally got a proper look at the picture on the front. It was a giant spider. Mullen, like Natalie, wasn't that keen on spiders. Not that this was the sort of spider that he might have encountered in his bedroom, abseiling down the wall. Rather it looked like it could have walked straight out of a science fiction film. He turned back to the other side and noticed this time the printed caption. It was from the Tate Modern Museum in London, so it was clearly meant to be art. On the other hand, he had no idea who the artist Louise Bourgeois was.

'I've seen that.' Ellie's voice was wobbly. She gripped Mullen's arm. 'A few weeks ago. When we went to London for the day. Me, Trisha, Alice and …' She paused. 'And Saad.'

A couple of minutes later, Ellie had pulled herself together and suddenly announced she was going out or she'd be late. As she ran upstairs, Mullen headed for the front door.

'I just need to let Rex cock his leg,' he lied.

He opened the door and almost collided with someone wanting to come in. Rick North.

'Steady up, ship mate. Nearly had a nasty collision there.' Given that he was carrying an assortment of equipment, including a hedge trimmer, he wasn't far wrong.

'Sorry, I thought Rex was going to urinate on the carpet,' Mullen said, blaming it all on the dog.

'How's things inside?'

'So, so.'

'Ah, keeping stum are you, mate? Fair dos. I try to keep out of the way of Ellie. She can be a right little madam. When she made me a cuppa the other day, she put a pile of sugar in it and I hate sugar. Speak of the devil.'

The door opened and Ellie appeared. She paused, perplexed by the two men blocking her path.

''Scuse me.' North edged past her with a scowl and into the house. 'Got bushes to trim.'

Mullen moved too, but only so that he was positioned firmly in front of the little cast-iron gate.

'Shut the door,' he said quietly, and rather to his surprise Ellie did.

'What are you not telling me?' he said.

'What do you mean?' She was looking at his chest, refusing to look him in the eye.

'What did you do in London?'

'We went shopping in Oxford Street. We went to the Tate Modern. We came home.'

'And you went and looked at that spider exhibit?'

'Yes.'

'So putting my detective hat on, I'd say that either one of your friends sent the postcard to your mum, or it was someone you met in London.' He paused. 'Or, of course, there is another alternative.'

Mullen was watching her face closely. The face of a pouting, disinterested teenager. She said nothing, so he pressed on.

'Was it you who sent it to your mother, Ellie?'

The pout disappeared much faster than it had arrived. Ellie swore. 'Me? Is that what you think? That I'd try and scare the shit out of my own mother?'

'You wouldn't be the first teenager to do so.'

'I'm late.'

'Late for what? You meeting someone?'

'Blimey, Spade. What's it to you? You're not keeping tabs on my social life, are you? Are you going to follow me around all day? Because if so, you'll get pretty bored.'

'Just answer my question.'

'I'm going to my church youth group. We arranged to meet up.'

'Which church?'

'What does it matter?' She rolled her eyes like a hyperactive drama queen. 'St Nathanael's, if you must know.'

Mullen started to move away from the gate to allow Ellie to pass, but then stopped. He knew he needed to back-track fast or he was going to lose her goodwill and co-operation.

'Look, Ellie, I apologize. I didn't really think it could have been you,' he lied. A smallish lie, but a lie nevertheless. 'I've seen you with your mother. You're a good daughter to her. But I do need your help. Not just with tracking down whoever it was who sent this postcard. But with Saad. I've promised to try and find him. Heck, I've been paid to find him. So I will do whatever I can to find him. But I'm struggling. So if anything happened in London, or if you know anything …'

'He met someone.' The words burst uncontrolled out of her mouth.

'Who?'

'In Borough Market. I was getting some food. So were Trish and Alice, but Saad sort of disappeared and only turned up half an hour later when we'd texted him a couple of times. He said he'd bumped into someone.'

'Someone he knew, you mean?'

'I don't know. I guess so. He didn't say.'

'But who would he know in London?'

She shrugged.

'How did he react? Did he seem pleased to have met this person?'

'Definitely. But he refused to talk about it.'

Mullen sensed that Ellie wasn't being entirely truthful. Not the truth, the whole truth and nothing but the truth. So he waited, still halfway across the gateway.

'Anything else? You do realize that the police have given up on him? It's me or it's no-one.'

'My feeling at the time was that it might have been a girl.'

'A girl?'

'Maybe someone from school. Mr Aitcheson has been encouraging all his students to go and visit the Tate Modern. Saad's a popular guy.'

'Did you discuss this with Trisha? Because she never mentioned it to me when I spoke to her.'

'I suppose because if it was a girl from school, it wasn't relevant to your investigations. But she definitely thought it was. And Trish was jealous as hell.'

'What about Alice? Did she like Saad too?'

Ellie laughed. 'I'm not sure she's into boys.'

'Oh?'

'Or girls. She's into books. She's a boffin. And bloody good at Mandarin. A very useful friend to have.'

'Maybe I should have a chat with her.'

Another laugh. 'You'll have to fly to Shanghai if you want to do that. She's visiting her grandparents there. Summer holidays and all that.'

Mullen walked home in silence. Rex urinated twice, but he spared Mullen the hassle of having to get a little blue bag out of his pocket.

Back in the house, Mullen pulled open the patio door, but Rex went straight to his bed. He looked expectantly at Mullen ('haven't I been a good boy?') and Mullen dug a biscuit out of the tin and tossed it to him. He seemed to be constantly breaking the rules nowadays, but what the heck.

'Don't tell the professor when she gets home,' he said and proceeded to make himself a mug of strong tea. There were all sorts of herbal concoctions in the cupboards, but Mullen had no desire to try any of them.

'So what do I do, lad?' Mullen said as he sat down.

He was glad to have a listener, even one as unresponsive as Rex, who was ferreting around in his basket, checking for any crumbs that had escaped.

'For crying out loud, do something, Doug.' Mullen mimicked the words, as if they were Rex's.

The dog was looking up at him with a doleful face, as if he had almost given up on the hope of another biscuit. But Mullen could imagine Professor Moody scowling in disapproval from her high-rise Yale apartment and he hardened his heart.

'So first there's the problem of who is sending Natalie decapitated swans and giant spiders,' he explained, 'and then there's the question of who killed Ruth Lonsdale and who it was who led me – or rather you, Rex – to her body.'

The dog looked at him. Eyes unblinking, head still. He hadn't quite given up hope because there was a bubble of slobber hanging down from his jowls.

'And then of course there's Saad and Trisha who've both gone missing. Not to mention the threats that Natalie has been receiving. And while we're about it, who the heck is Ruth Lonsdale?' Mullen was looking down at the dog. 'So, Rex, any bright ideas?'

But if Rex had any ideas – bright or otherwise – he wasn't letting on. Instead he gave up looking at Mullen and began to settle himself down in his basket, circling clockwise for a full circuit and a half before deciding he had reached the perfect position. He lay down, gave a short reproachful whine and closed his eyes.

Mullen went and got his iPad out of the kitchen drawer in which it was stored under the tea towels. He wasn't sure whether this was a very clever or a very stupid place to hide it from any passing burglars. But since he rarely used tea towels himself – he had once read that tea towels accumulate vast numbers of germs which you might then pass on to any plate you dry with it – he reckoned that all things considered it was a pretty smart place to choose.

He opened up the iPad, keyed *Ruth Lonsdale* into the Internet browser and waited to see what happened. Top of the list underneath the sponsored links was a link to the *Oxford Mail*. Mullen clicked on it. There was a brief account of the discovery of her body in Bagley Wood, but no mention of his own part in it (thankfully). Ruth Lonsdale, he read, lived at a house called the Arbour in Nettlebed. Ruth Lonsdale was also, he discovered, actually the Reverend Ruth Lonsdale. She was only fifty-nine years old.

Mullen did a bit more searching, but there was nothing else that caught his attention. There was an article which showed her to have been a leading light a few years previously in a protest against the closure of a family centre. There was a photograph of her standing in the middle of a group of the protestors in front of the Council Offices. He studied this for some time before draining his mug. Finally he searched for her in the online BT phonebook and found the full address with postcode. It was time to do something before any other distressed damsel turned up on his doorstep. Or, even worse, the police put in another appearance. He gathered together dog food, water and a banana and took the lead down from its hook.

'Come on, Rex,' he said. 'Time to get detecting.'

Rex unwillingly raised himself from his bed. Even the sight of the dog lead didn't excite him.

'Sorry, mate,' Mullen said. 'Can't lie about all day.'

That was when his mobile beeped. It was a text from Durant asking how he was getting on. Durant who had actually paid him. To whom he was in debt.

'Change of plan,' he said to Rex. 'How would you like to go to London for the day?'

The barman with the greasy grey hair looked up. He had been polishing the bar surface with a singular lack of conviction.

'Oh, not you again!'

'Nice to see you too, Harry.' DC Knight grinned.

'You don't want more CCTV, do you?'

Knight pushed a photograph across the counter. 'Recognize this guy?'

Harry shrugged. 'I get a lot of people passing through.'

'He's a big guy. Overweight. Wears a suit. Was chatting to your friend Phil one evening.'

'Not my friend. Just a customer.'

'I'm not your friend either, Harry. I'm just the police, and if you don't make yourself a little more helpful, I'll make sure you get a lot of visits from the police. At awkward times. Asking questions of your customers. It might not be so good for business.'

Harry drew back his lips. His teeth were discoloured and crooked.

'His name is Ray.'

'Ray who?'

'I don't know the surnames of everyone who drinks here.'

'I'm not interested in everyone. Just this guy.'

Harry looked at him, weighing him up. Knight stood stock still staring back. He was happy to play the game of who blinks first all day.

Harry blinked. 'Costa. Like the coffee. To judge from his clothes, he was doing very well for himself.'

Knight got out his phone and did a search on the name. There were several hits, and third on the list was definitely nothing to do with coffee. There was even a photo. He thrust his mobile in front of Harry's face.

'Is this the guy?'

'Could be.'

'Let's hope it is, for your sake, Harry. Otherwise I'll be back with some colleagues and they'll be wearing uniforms.'

Knight turned away and headed outside. He couldn't resist that last little jibe at Harry, but he doubted very much that he'd need to bother him again. He was pretty damned sure that he'd nailed it.

Mullen's car trip into London was straightforward. The rush hour was well and truly over and the men who make a living out of digging holes in the roads were apparently all on holiday. It was feeling like it could be his lucky day. The only problem was how to find Saad in a city of over eight million people, even supposing that (a) he was still alive and (b) London was where he had gone.

If he was dead, Mullen told himself as he wound his way south past Victoria, then all bets were off. But if he was alive, then London had to be the most likely place. And the best starting point for a search had to be Borough Market, where Saad had met some mystery man or woman. Mullen wasn't convinced by Ellie's supposition that he had bumped into a girl from school. No girls (except of course Trish) had gone missing from school. However, if he had met someone he knew, the other obvious option was a fellow Syrian, maybe a fellow refugee who he knew from home or had met during his escape to the UK or maybe just a Syrian with whom he had got talking. Had he been offered a job? That was the best scenario Mullen could imagine. Another one – more likely, Mullen feared – was that he had been lured into what was effectively slavery. He had read stories of refugees being ruthlessly exploited, promised the earth but given hell.

The five hundred pounds in his bank account said that he owed it to Elizabeth Durant to try and find Saad. But it wasn't just the money which motivated Mullen. By the time he had parked up in a yard-cum-car park south of the Thames for a tenner for the day, he knew he would never forgive himself if he didn't try his damnedest to find the lad and get him back to Elizabeth Durant and a place he could call home.

Borough Market was the obvious place to start. That was where he was going to concentrate his efforts, hoping for a miracle. Not that he believed in miracles, but he didn't have many other options.

He and Rex made their way to London Bridge. It was several weeks since the terrorist attack which had left eight innocent people dead and many others injured. Mullen had read and watched plenty of news reports and witness accounts of the events, but even so it hadn't prepared him for being there. On the left, near the bus station, the huge conglomeration of floral tributes which had accumulated after the tragedy had been removed. The other memorial, the one made up of photos and post-it notes and messages of defiance – Mullen had studied them on his iPad at the time until tears trickled down his face – were also gone. But even so Mullen stood there transfixed, barely breathing, imagining what it must have been like to be caught up in it. He tried to imagine too what drove people to do such terrible things, but he failed. What were they trying to prove – to themselves or to their idea of God?

Mullen shook himself free of such thoughts and turned left, heading for Borough Market. He knew what he was going to do, but suddenly it all seemed hopeless. The odds of finding Saad seemed ridiculously long. But he pressed on, urging Rex to keep up, emptying his mind of everything except the task in hand. The hounds of despair were at his heels, but he refused to acknowledge them.

Borough Market was hectically busy. There seemed to be a continuous stream of customers wanting to buy food. Getting the attention of anyone who worked there behind the stalls was almost impossible. So Mullen changed tack. He looked around and tried to identify the men (mostly) who were bringing extra supplies to the various stalls. The guys clearing up rubbish. The guys for whom Borough Market was not a great place for a leisurely meal or browse, but a place where they ground out a living. He had a simple routine, interrupt them when they had just finished doing something or appeared to be taking a breather and then show them the two photos of Saad. One was a head and shoulders shot, formal, taken at school, and one was a photo of him taken in his Oxford United football shirt at a match. Maybe the shirt would jolt someone's memory.

Or maybe not. Mullen spent two hours in the area and by the end of that time he was desperate. Not a single person to whom he had spoken had recognized Saad, or if they had they weren't letting on. He had studied their faces as they had looked at the photos, hoping that he might spot if their reaction gave a clue that they did recognize him but didn't want to say so, but all he saw was honest ignorance or total disinterest.

Having spent so long near so many beguiling smells, Mullen finally admitted to himself that he was ravenously hungry. So with the queues finally subsiding, he gave in and joined one of the shortest queues where the man was serving what looked and smelled like a very good spiced lamb with couscous. As he paid, he showed both photos of Saad to the man behind the stall, but the response was a familiar one – a quick shake of the head. Mullen withdrew to a low wall where he sat down and began to eat, wondering as he did so what to do next. He tossed the last couple of bits of meat onto the ground for Rex and wondered guiltily if the spices might not provoke an attack of diarrhoea. Not that Rex seemed bothered. He wolfed both pieces down and then looked up, eyes pleading, please, Mr Mullen, can I have some more?

Mullen ignored him and shut his eyes and tried to spirit himself away to somewhere quiet and cool and anxiety free. But it didn't work. Rex started to whine. He could turn on the 'poor me' at the drop of a hat. Mullen forced himself to his feet, conscious of the feelings of guilt which seemed to be part of his DNA. He pulled out the two photographs and started walking, turning left down a narrow street. It was empty except for a lone man who was making his way unsteadily towards them. A local, Mullen reckoned. Not a tourist anyway. So worth a try.

'Excuse me.'

The man looked at Mullen as if he was speaking a foreign language.

Mullen pressed on. 'I was wondering if you have seen this guy? He's about sixteen.'

The man looked at the photos for some time. Mullen felt a glimmer of hope. Usually it was an immediate 'no' or 'don't know'.

'Might have,' the man said cryptically. 'What's it to you if I have?' Mullen wondered if the guy was angling for some money.

'If you can help …' Mullen left his words hanging. He felt uncomfortable. He wasn't sure he was handling this situation very well. As he knew from the past, offering money sometimes backfired.

The man looked beyond Mullen and then behind himself, checking to see if anyone was around, as if nervous that he might be overheard or observed. Mullen held his breath. Hope springs eternal. He wasn't sure where he had learnt that expression, but right now he clung onto it. Maybe he would give the guy some money if he was genuine. If he really had seen Saad.

'They all look the same, don't they?'

It took milliseconds for Mullen to interpret what this meant. The guy wasn't going to help.

Then something hit Mullen smack in the middle of his face. Later he realized it was the man's fist. But at that moment it felt like an explosion that came out of nowhere. Pain lanced through his head and the next thing he knew he was lying on his back, looking up at the blue sky above. The sun was dazzling. He shut his eyes and wondered what the hell he had done to deserve that.

'What's her name?'

Mullen opened his eyes. It felt as though a long time had passed. There was a child peering over him. A girl. She bent lower, blocking out the sun. She had dark brown, serious eyes.

'Is this your dog? What's she called?'

Mullen tried to sit up. He groaned. 'Rex.'

'She's nice.'

Another voice, which belonged to a woman, said something in reply. Mullen looked up. He couldn't understand what the woman was saying.

'Are you all right?' The same voice, but speaking English now. To him.

Pain bounced around the inside of his head as if it was a pinball machine. Mullen forced himself onto his knees and then onto his feet.

'Perhaps I should call an ambulance,' the woman said.

Mullen looked at her, gingerly touching his face as he did so, wondering how bad the damage was. The woman was strikingly beautiful, flawless skin, elegant green hijab, and slightly taller than he was. A low bulge indicated a second child on the way. As for himself, there was blood on his hand and blood spattered down his T-shirt.

'I don't think anything is broken,' he said. He knew from experience what a broken nose felt like and this was different. Besides, he was pretty sure that even a broken nose didn't in these times of austerity justify calling out an ambulance.

'I think the doggie is hungry,' the girl said. She was stroking Rex with slow, soft hands. 'I think she likes me.' The girl looked up at Mullen as she spoke and then she turned to her mother and said something else.

Her mother replied and laughed.

Then she spoke in English. 'Sorry, it's rude to exclude you. I was telling my daughter that the dog is a boy. She wants to know if you would bring the dog to our house to play.'

'Oh.' Mullen was finding it hard to think. In fact the pain hammering inside his head was making it impossible.

'We live round the corner,' she continued. She spoke as if she had made a decision. 'I think we need to clean you up and find you a shirt and then we can decide if you need proper medical attention.'

She took him by the arm as if he was an old man who had lost his walking stick. 'Let's go.'

Round the corner meant round the corner and up six flights of stairs.

'Sorry, the lift is broken,' she explained, as if she was personally responsible for it. Mullen didn't say anything. He was concentrating on getting up the stairs without doing anything stupid like falling back down them.

The flat was refreshingly cool. She had left the windows open and after they had entered she left the front door open too. She sat him down at the kitchen table. The child disappeared, taking Rex with her.

Mullen hoped against hope that she wouldn't pull the dog's ears or anything. As far as he knew, Rex was good with children, but he hadn't any experience to back that assessment up.

'Do you have a name?'

'Doug,' he said.

'I'm Amina.'

She brought a bowl of water over from the sink and placed it in front of him.

'I'll clean you up. If you don't mind.'

Mullen didn't mind. He shut his eyes in the hope that this would lessen the pain.

'We need to take your shirt off.'

The shirt came off.

'Hold this tight over the bridge of your nose.'

He held it.

'These are some pain killers. Strong ones.'

He didn't ask or even wonder why she had strong pain killers. He just swallowed them with the mug of water which she handed to him.

'My husband will be home soon. If you want, he can drive you to Accident and Emergency.'

Husband? Mullen felt a tremor of alarm. Suppose the husband was possessive. Suppose he took a dislike to Mullen. One punch in the face was quite enough for one day.

'He drives a taxi. He knows all the best routes.'

She brought Mullen an olive green t-shirt and helped him ease it over his face.

'You look a lot better.'

She stood there looking down at him, arms folded above her bump, as if she was weighing up her work. She seemed confident, a person who knew what she was doing. A nurse?

'Thank you,' he said. 'I don't know what I'd have done if you hadn't come along.'

She gave a laugh. 'Somebody else would have come along and they would have helped you. People do that round here. I expect people do that round where you live.'

Perhaps she was a teacher. He remembered his teacher Miss Higgins telling him off like that, gently but firmly.

'Now, I expect you would like a cup of tea. Like any good Englishman in a crisis.' She was teasing him. But he didn't mind.

She made them both a mug of tea and put a small plate of biscuits on the table. She went through to the other room and spoke to her daughter before returning.

'They are watching children's TV together,' she announced to Mullen with a smile. She sat down. 'Now tell me, Doug, how did you manage to get into a fight?'

He winced. His money was still on her being a teacher. But maybe that was a reflection of his own past.

'I'm trying to find someone,' he said. 'His name is Saad Ismat. He ran away from Oxford and I think he may have come to this area and...' Mullen dug into his back pocket and retrieved the now rather creased photographs of Saad. Except that there was only one.

'I showed a photo to this man. Not this one. Another one. I thought that he recognized Saad. I thought for a moment that he was going to help me. But he punched me instead.'

'Did he steal your money?'

Mullen didn't think so, but he felt in his pocket to make sure. 'No.'

'Well, that's something.'

'I think he took the photograph though. Why would he have done that?'

'I think he tore it up,' she said. 'Then threw all the pieces into the air. That's what he was doing when I came round the corner. He was tearing something up.'

Mullen opened his mouth to swear, but he bit back on the words just in time. Instead he took a sip of his tea. The pain in his head had receded somewhat, as if it had moved into the next room.

'Why are you looking for him?'

Mullen gathered his thoughts.

'He's a refugee,' he began. 'From Syria. He was living with a woman in East Oxford. Going to school. He even had a girlfriend. He seemed to be happy. Then he disappeared.'

'He ran away?'

'We don't know. I hope so. Because if he didn't...' Mullen couldn't finish his sentence. He didn't want to voice the alternative scenario.

'Why are you looking here?'

'We think he met someone here. When he was visiting London with some friends. They came to the Tate Modern. They bought some food from the market.'

'Just a minute,' she said, and disappeared through the kitchen door. She still had the one remaining photograph in her hand. Mullen didn't mind. He suddenly felt utterly exhausted. He placed his arms carefully on the table, lay his head down on them and within moments descended deep into oblivion.

As Paul Reeve got off the bus and headed for the woods, he wondered again how long it would take to win his daughter back. How long would he have to camp out here? Would he ever succeed? He liked camping, he liked the outdoors. He even liked it that two guys had set up their tents thirty metres away. They drank. Pretty much from morning to night it seemed. He didn't like that. He felt sorry for them. But they were also a stark warning to him of what he once was and what he could become again. Since he got out of HMP Stonewood, he had drunk alcohol only once. That was with Phil, one single pint, because Phil had insisted. Never again.

'Hi, Paul.'

Ken, the one with an east London accent, waved a welcoming hand.

'Got any spare food?'

Already they had learnt that Reeve was a man who knew how to get food. Sometimes, when he was feeling low he would treat himself to something in a café or the McDonald's where Ellie went. But mostly, in order to save money, he scavenged, often in the bins at the back of supermarkets. Occasionally he went to the Gatehouse in Oxford. But he had no wish to become a regular, the sort of person who is always remembered and recognized when he turns up for his handout. He needed to keep a low profile, so mostly he scavenged and looked after himself.

He went over to Ken and gave him a couple of wrapped sandwiches from his rucksack.

'Drink?' Ken waved a can of cheap beer.

'No, thanks.'

Reeve retreated to his own area and sat down on a log. Another day off the booze. Another day nearer salvation.

He ferreted in his rucksack and found the book he had picked up for 50p that day. He had never heard of the author. But the write-up on the back promised a 'taut and thrill-packed read'. It would while away the evening until he was ready to sleep.

When Mullen woke, there was a man in the kitchen. Amina had disappeared, but he thought he could hear her talking in the next room, to her daughter or maybe to Rex.

'How are you feeling?' the man said. He had a long, but neatly trimmed beard, round face and watchful eyes. He was tall, certainly taller than Mullen, but his stomach was fat rather than muscle.

'Better,' Mullen said. The headache inside his head had now retreated to the attic. 'Are you Amina's husband?'

He didn't answer the question directly. There was merely a slight movement of the head which might have meant anything.

'She's told me about you. You come with me. You can leave the dog with Amina.'

Mullen followed him down the six flights of stairs. He hung on to the rail as if he was an old man prone to tripping over.

'Where are we going?' he said when they reached the bottom.

'You'll see.' Which wasn't strictly true because when they reached the eight-seater car, the man insisted that he wrap a scarf around his head over his eyes and lie down in the back of the vehicle. 'Don't move and don't make any noise.' Then he draped a rug over him and slammed the back door shut.

The journey took some twenty minutes. Mullen had thought he'd listen out for noises and hope they gave him some clue as to where he was going, but no sooner had the car started to edge forward than the driver turned on the radio at full blast. Mullen winced in pain and gave up on the idea of tracking their route. He'd just have to see what happened.

It wasn't the most uncomfortable journey he had ever experienced, but he was glad when it came to an end.

'Keep the scarf on.' The man helped him out of the car and led him a few metres through a low doorway ('mind your feet and your head'). Mullen could smell oil and diesel. A hand on his elbow manoeuvred him to a seat. He sat down. 'Wait.'

Mullen waited. He could see no point in disobeying. Was this a car repair workshop or lock-up under a railway? How far had they come? Three or four miles maybe? North, south, east or west? He didn't have a clue. South of the river was his best guess, but it was only a guess, a fifty-fifty chance of being correct. He listened. He could hear the noise of traffic, but nothing which sounded like a train.

Maybe five minutes passed, then there was noise. A door squeaking open, the pad of people's feet, low voices. People were speaking but not a language which Mullen could understand. Then hands removed the scarf from round his face. He looked around. The room was windowless and the only light came from some overhead strip bulbs which flickered uncertainly, as if they hadn't decided whether they wanted to be on or off. Mullen looked down, while his eyes became accustomed to not being in complete darkness. There were three figures. One was the man who Mullen had assumed was Amina's husband. In the middle was an even bigger man, a man who looked in much better physical condition than the husband. He stepped forward to get a better look at Mullen.

But Mullen wasn't looking back at him. His eyes were on the third man, a much slighter figure, and even in the flickering light Mullen recognized him.

'Saad?' he said. 'Saad Ismat?'

'Yes.' It was a whisper, but Mullen saw his lips move and understood. 'Are you all right?'

'Of course he is,' the big man said. 'He would like you to tell Mrs Durant that he is all right and that she should not worry, and she should not try and find him. He is happy here, with us.'

Us? Mullen wanted to ask who the 'us' was, but he checked himself. Instead he said, 'Perhaps Saad can tell me that himself.'

The man shrugged and turned to Saad. 'You don't have to talk to this man. Only if you want to.'

'It is OK.' Saad moved forward a couple of steps. Mullen could see him better now. No obvious sign of abuse. He looked pretty well fed. But his eyes were wary and his fingers refused to stay still. 'Tell Elizabeth that I am OK. I am safe here.'

'Weren't you safe with her in Oxford?'

He looked down at his feet. 'She was kind.'

'But someone else wasn't?'

'Just tell her I am OK.'

'Why did you run away?'

'Enough questions,' the big man said. He placed a hand on Saad's shoulder. What did that signify? Support? Comfort? Or control and a warning? 'Just go home and leave Saad in peace.'

'Was it Trish's father?' There was nothing to lose by making a guess.

Saad looked up sharply, alarm in his eyes. He said nothing, but Mullen had seen the answer.

'Elizabeth really wants you home. She is very sad. She…'

'But how can you guarantee his safety?' The man was taking over again. 'Can you tell him now face to face that you can guarantee he will be safe if he returns to Oxford? I think not. So I ask you, very politely, to go and collect your dog and then to go back to Oxford and not return.'

What if he refused? Mullen doubted the man would remain very polite.

'OK,' Mullen said. He stood up. 'I'll do exactly as you say. But before I go, I want to ask Saad one more question.'

Mullen waited. He needed Saad to be looking at him, but the young man preferred to look at the ground.

'One question,' the man agreed. 'Then you must go.'

'Saad!' Mullen raised his voice and reluctantly the young man lifted his head until their eyes engaged. 'Is Trisha in London too?'

'Trisha?' The alarm in Saad's voice told Mullen that he had certainly got the youth's attention now. Saad stepped towards him. 'What do you mean?'

'Trisha has disappeared.' Mullen delivered the news in bite-sized chunks, as if that might make it easier for the young man to digest. 'Yesterday. She is not answering her mobile. It is turned off. She is not replying to her friend Ellie. We have reported her to the police. We thought she might have come and followed you to London.'

Saad's face crumpled. 'No! No, she hasn't.'

'Saad, I will ask you one more time. Please come back to Oxford with me. Elizabeth misses you terribly. And I need you to help me find Trisha.'

Bryce looked up from his laptop. It was late and he really should have gone home because there was nothing critical keeping him in the office. But there wasn't much to go home to. A large empty apartment.

No welcoming – or even unwelcoming – voice to greet him. Merely a fridge that he had failed to stock up.

'Excuse me, sir.'

It was Knight, and he was looking annoyingly pleased with himself. 'I thought I should update you on the death of Phil Stubbs.'

Bryce waved him to the empty seat the other side of the desk. The company of anyone would be better than the company of no-one.

'OK, where have you got to?'

'I was going through the pub's CCTV again. Or rather the CCTV for the days before Stubbs's death, in case there was anything else that was relevant.'

'Spare me the detail, Constable. Just the highlights will do.'

'Stubbs was a regular there for two or three weeks. Often drinking on his own or propping up the bar. But one evening, ten days before his death, he was sitting at a table with this guy in a suit.'

'And?' Bryce's impatience and exhaustion was close to overwhelming him.

'And the man's name was Ray Costa. And he's a solicitor. And...' Knight held up the index finger of his right hand to underline his big point.

'And what?'

'And he's dead too.'

'In the Humber, you mean?'

'No. He was found hanging in his house. Last week.'

'Was he now?' If Bryce had got ears which pricked up, they would have been halfway to touching the ceiling.

'I checked with the pathologist and he reckons it was definitely suicide.' Knight was talking fast, determined not to stop until he had finished. 'But that's not all, sir. I spoke to Costa's PA, Linda Wiseman. She was really on edge. But she told me that a private investigator from Oxford had been to see her. In fact it was he who went round with her to Costa's house and discovered the body. Anyway, this chap convinced her that a guy who had turned up unannounced at their office ten days previously was none other than Paul Reeve.'

Bryce held up his hand. His brain was barely keeping up. But Knight plunged on. 'If you remember, sir, Reeve had been in prison for GBH against his wife – and his child too. My guess is that Reeve wanted to track them down. They had changed their names and the private eye seemed to think that Costa had helped them to do it.'

'Just a minute. So this theory is actually the private investigator's theory, not yours?'

Knight's face reddened. 'I guess we've both come to the same conclusion, sir.'

'Who the hell is he, anyway?'

'His name is Doug Mullen. Ex-army. Lives in Oxford. Bit of a local celebrity actually, after he saved a woman and her daughter in a multiple pile-up on the M40.'

Bryce held up his hand, the whole of it, not just the index finger, signalling Knight into silence. In a previous era, he would have made a good traffic cop. He leaned back in his chair and stared at the ceiling.

'Any witnesses to a fight or argument between Stubbs and Reeve?'

'No, sir.' It was still the weak point in the case. Knight was well aware of it.

Bryce continued to stare at the ceiling for several seconds before resuming an upright position. Then he stood up, went over to the coat stand and slipped his jacket over his creased white shirt. He had suddenly had enough. He needed fresh air and a dose of crap TV.

'I'm going home,' he said. 'Email me all the paperwork so I can look through it later. We'll meet here tomorrow morning at 8.00 sharp to discuss what to do next.'

Saad slept for much of the journey back to Oxford. After a flurry of questions and anxious speculation – 'maybe she did this, maybe she did that' – he suddenly fell silent and then asleep. Perhaps it was the

WHITE LIES, DEADLY LIES

presence of Rex which soothed him. The dog had settled himself on the youth's lap and resolutely stayed there despite Mullen's initial disapproval.

'I like him,' Saad had said.

Mullen was conscious that, in the event of an accident, Rex would probably be safer if he remained on the floor at Saad's feet, but he wasn't prepared to argue about it.

Mullen had driven back up the M40 in a cocoon of satisfaction – and why not? He had solved the mystery of the missing refugee. But as he negotiated the eastern Oxford by-pass, the reality of the problems which awaited him hit home.

Saad had been found, but Trisha was still missing. Originally Mullen had hoped that she had run off to join him. That had been the best scenario he had been able to imagine. Whereas all the alternatives which jostled inside his head screamed a very different tale: she had been abducted.

Mullen pulled off the road to get fuel from the all-night garage. He filled up and when he got back in the car, he was pleased to see Saad had woken up. It gave him the opportunity he had been waiting for.

'Why did you go to London?' he asked as he eased his battered car back onto the dual carriageway.

'I met someone there. From the boat. I recognized him the day I went to London with the girls. He was the only person I knew, the only contact I had.'

'But why did you run away from Elizabeth?'

He sighed. 'Trisha's father, Mr Robinson, didn't like me. He thought I would get his daughter pregnant. I like Trisha. She helped me with my English too. But it was not love. It was friendship, I think, a really good friendship. But Mr Robinson didn't see it like that. He threatened me. Very nasty threats. So I decided it would be better if I went away. Better for me. Maybe better for her too.'

They completed the journey in silence. Mullen had rung Elizabeth

Durant from London and of course she had insisted on speaking to Saad – a mixture of squeals of delight and tears of joy. But when she opened her door to them, the emotional firestorm was even greater as she flung her arms around Saad and refused to let go. Mullen made himself scarce as soon as he felt confident that she wasn't going to have another fit. It was well after midnight by the time he got home. His head was pounding again. He dug out some pain killers from one of the professor's drawers and swallowed them. He did a final check of his mobile and discovered there the photograph which he had forwarded from Ellie's phone, the one which Trisha had taken on the bus. The one he had done nothing with.

'Shit!' he said to himself. He forwarded it to Trent with the curt message *you need to find this man*. Not, as he later realized, the most informative message.

Then he dragged himself upstairs. The bedroom was hot and humid, and Rex had beaten him to it, jumping up onto the bed and settling himself down on the duvet. Discipline was collapsing left, right and centre, but Mullen was past caring. After opening the windows wide, he stripped himself down to his boxers, sank down next to the dog and fell asleep.

CHAPTER 8

Thursday

THE DRUMMING WOKE HIM. Or maybe the drumming woke Rex and Rex woke him. At any rate, one moment Mullen was marching in the middle of a pipe band whose instruments sounded like bass drums and the next he was fully awake and staggering downstairs, pulling on a T-shirt as he went. It was the front door and he could hear a female voice shouting his name.

He fumbled over the chain and bolt defences which the professor favoured and pulled the door open.

'What about Trisha?' It was Stella Robinson and she was in full cry. 'It's all very well you finding Saad, but what about my daughter?!'

Mullen wasn't sure what to say, so he said nothing.

'You weren't still in bed, were you?' She made it sound like a crime. Mullen had no idea what the time was or whether he had overslept outrageously or not. But she was staring at his boxers as if they were in the worst possible taste.

'You'd better come in,' he said.

'I need a drink,' she snarled.

'Tea? Coffee? Juice?'

'For God's sake, man, a proper drink! Do you have any gin?'

Mullen found a bottle and poured out a double. 'I'll find some tonic,' he said.

'No need,' she said, snatching the glass off him. She drained it without stopping and slammed it down on the table. 'Another one.'

Mullen took it off her, turning his back on her and this time filled it with water.

'Drink this.' He spoke firmly, determined to gain control of the situation. She took a swig without realizing, then spat it out and hurled the glass to the floor in the same moment. It exploded on the tiles into what seemed like a thousand fragments. Mullen looked down in disbelief. He hadn't even got slippers on his feet. Stella Robinson began to wail.

Half an hour later, calm of a sort had returned to the kitchen. The smashed glass had been swept up and deposited in the bin, the gin bottle had been hidden away, two hot cups of tea had been made, Rex had been fed and Mullen had pulled a pair of jeans over his boxers.

While Mullen was sorting things out, Stella had disappeared into the downstairs toilet for what had seemed like an age, but now she was sitting silent and repentant at the table.

It was an awkward silence. There was plenty to say, but Mullen wasn't sure how to start. He thought after the glass incident that he'd let her take the lead and then see where that took them.

'So,' she said finally, crushing yet another damp paper tissue inside the fist of her hand, 'do you think she's dead?' She didn't pause for an answer. 'I'd hoped against hope that she'd run off to join Saad. I really had. At least she would have been safe with him. The worst that could have happened would have been that she'd have ended up pregnant. But now...'

'I think she's alive,' Mullen said. He hoped he sounded convincing.

'You're just saying that.'

'We have to believe that she's alive. We have to operate as if she is. I'm going to keep looking until I find her.'

'But you don't *believe* she's alive, do you.' It was a statement, not a question. 'In your heart of hearts you think she's dead.'

Mullen didn't like being pinned to the wall by Stella. Hoped against hope that Trisha was still alive would have been a more honest description of what he felt. But he wasn't going to say so to her.

'I am not going to give up on Trisha,' he said. 'Maybe there will turn out to be a very simple reason why she's disappeared. Like with Saad.'

Stella Robinson lifted her face and looked directly into Mullen's, and Mullen realized even before she spoke that he had blundered badly.

'What do you mean? What *was* the reason why Saad ran away? Elizabeth wouldn't tell me when I asked her over the phone.'

Mullen tried to work out how he should break the news, but he knew there was no good way of doing it. The truth will set you free. Where the hell did that expression come from? He doubted it would do any such thing for Stella Robinson. He gulped.

'I'm afraid to have to tell you that Saad ran away because your husband made some very unpleasant threats towards him. He didn't like the idea of him being so friendly with your daughter.'

Stella was silent at first. Then her face contorted. Anguish was replaced by raw anger.

'The bastard,' she screamed. 'The bastard!'

Mullen was on his feet, ready for anything and half expecting the mug of tea to go flying across the room. But it wasn't Mullen that she wanted to damage.

'I'll get him.' She stormed to the front door and down the path. Mullen ran after her and tried to place a hand on her arm, but she swung hers away from her body, throwing him off. 'Leave me alone, Mullen.'

'For God's sake,' he said, 'he's not worth it.' Mullen had wild visions of Stella Robinson, stoked up on the gin he had given her (at breakfast time, on an empty stomach – he could imagine how the press would report that!) taking a meat cleaver to her husband. 'Don't do anything you'll later regret. Don't—'

'Regret? Regret?' She began to laugh, a high-wheeling hysterical laugh which stopped Mullen in his tracks. 'What do you think I'm going to do, Mullen? Kill him? I'd love to. I'd love it. But where would that leave Trisha when she comes home, with me in prison? So I'm going to go home and give him a piece of my mind and as soon as he's got out of the house, I'm going to get every external lock on the house changed. And for good measure, I'm going to go and buy myself a Rottweiler so that if he ever tries to come back, he'll get what's coming to him.'

Mullen wondered if he should ring Greg Robinson and warn him. But that, he decided, was not for him to do. Besides, as long as Stella didn't actually stab him, Greg Robinson deserved everything that was coming to him.

It was more important to hassle the police and see what progress, if any, they had made. So Mullen rang Trent's mobile.

'What is it, Mullen?' Trent's irritation was obvious.

'You've seen the photo I sent to your mobile?'

'You mean in the middle of the night?'

'That's the one. Well, it was taken by Trisha Robinson shortly before she disappeared. When she was on a bus.'

'Which bus?'

'If she was heading home, it would be a bus heading down the Botley Road.'

'Wait a minute.' Things went silent for about half a minute and then Trent was back on the line. 'What makes you think this guy is relevant to her disappearance?'

'Trisha sent it to her friend Ellie. She also sent a text message saying *Things are kicking off.* The guy is distinctive and if he was causing trouble on the bus, the driver should remember it. And buses have CCTV. '

'I am aware of that.' Trent had replaced irritation with sarcasm.

'And are you aware of the fact that I found Saad Ismat last night?'

There was the briefest pause as Trent took this in. 'No. I wasn't.'

'In London. He is safe and OK. I told Elizabeth Durant to ring it in.'

'I'll check it's on our system. If it isn't, I've have someone ring through to Durant.'

Mullen wasn't interested in the Thames Valley Police's systems. 'What concerns me is that since Trisha didn't run off to meet up with Saad, then her disappearance becomes all the more worrying.'

'She could easily have run off with some other spotty youth.'

'It's possible. But this photograph is evidence, isn't it? She was on a bus. Something happened. This was the last text she sent to Ellie, her best friend, round about 11.45 a.m. All you've got to do is get hold of the CCTV of the right bus and see if it helps in any way.'

'I don't know why you aren't a chief inspector. You've obviously got it all taped.' Trent was back in sarcasm mode. 'But let me just point out one or two tiny things. Number one, we don't know it was a bus heading for Botley. If she has been meeting someone in Oxford and was doing a bunk with him, she could have been on a bus heading north, south, east or west. Just tracking down the relevant one will take time and resources and money. We aren't a bottomless pit, Mullen. Point number two, if she *has* gone off with a boyfriend, then all this would be a complete waste of time anyway. Point number three, if a guy wanted to abduct her, then the last thing he is going to do is make a terrific fuss like this guy did. Hell, everyone is going to remember him, don't you think?'

It was a very good third point. Mullen imagined that this was what it was like playing Roger Federer. You play a wonderful cross court shot and he blasts it past you like you don't even exist. Even so, he took a wild swing.

'And if she's been abducted?'

'It's not my job to prioritize. I will make sure DI Holden is aware of all of this, and then if she thinks this is something worth pursuing, she'll have to get approval from her superiors.'

'Damn her superiors.' Mullen was on the verge of losing it. 'If and when Trisha Robinson turns up dead, the first thing which will happen is that I will turn the photograph over to the media. When they turn their guns on the Thames Valley Police, who do you think will be in the line of fire? DI Holden's superiors? Or herself and you? Answer me that, Constable.'

'Thank you, Mr Mullen,' Trent said and hung up.

Mullen could feel his heart pounding twenty to a dozen. He sucked in a deep breath of air and then released it slowly. Once, twice, three times. What now? He had done what he could to spur the police into action, but what could he himself do?

The only idea he could come up with was to ask Saad. Now that he was home and now that he was safe, maybe there were things – difficult things – which he would be prepared to talk about. Had they ever talked about running away together? Did they have a secret place they used to meet? Might Trisha have gone there?

Mullen picked up his mobile and rang Elizabeth Durant. It rang several times, but she didn't answer. He left a voice message.

What else? Or rather who else? Trisha might be missing, but Ruth Lonsdale was dead. He knew so little about her. He couldn't bear to sit about and wait for Durant or Stella Robinson or the police or any other Tom, Dick or Harry to ring him up. He had to get out of the house and do something. He went and got Rex's lead and whistled. Rex trotted through. Having slept all night in Mullen's bed, he was apparently raring to go – by his standards at any rate.

It wasn't hard for Mullen to track down the house where Ruth Lonsdale had been living. His GPS took him straight to the road, and after that it was just a matter of walking down it, heading out of the village, until he came across three bouquets of roses laid respectfully down on the grass in front of a chocolate-box thatched cottage. A plain wooden sign with the words *The Arbour* painted on it underlined that Mullen was in the right place.

There were two cars parked on the driveway and he could see movement in the front room. Mullen had no idea who they might be. Family, he guessed, though there had been no mention of grieving children in the newspaper reports. For some reason, he had assumed that she was a loner with, at best, an ancient parent still alive. But why? Why should she not have got brothers and sisters and nieces and nephews?

Mullen knew that death brought out the best and the worst of people. The cynical voice inside his head was telling him that if Ruth Lonsdale had left behind a house and money, then the people who had gathered here were likely to be people who might have hopes of benefiting from her will.

'What are you doing here?'

The sharp question came from behind Mullen and he turned. An elderly man with close-cropped hair was right behind him.

'Come to gawp, have you?' Everything about him screamed ex-army. Or to be precise, officer class ex-army. 'You're not from round here, that's for sure.'

'I'm a friend.' Another lie. They were adding up and this one was of a darkish grey colour.

The man looked at him hard. Then grunted. 'A rubbernecker. That's what you are. Come to glory in people's misery. Well, I'm telling you now to bugger off. Or I'll get my son to come and move you on. Let people grieve in peace. Just stay away.'

The man marched off, swinging his arms as if he had never left the parade ground. He turned sharp left and up the path to a white bungalow. Mullen was shaken. He made as if to walk further up the road while he considered his next step, but Rex had put on his brakes as he deposited his breakfast neatly on the grass. Mullen knelt down, and it was while he was cleaning up after the dog that he heard another

– much more friendly – voice.

'He's a nice little doggie.'

Mullen straightened up and knotted his little blue bag.

'His name's Rex,' he said.

The woman in front of him – short, grey haired, sharp eyes, white blouse and grey cardigan - could have been a dead ringer for a modern-day Miss Marple, except that he couldn't envisage any Miss Marple wearing trousers.

'He's a bit of a mixture, isn't he?'

'Father's a Poodle and mother a Westie. Or maybe it's the other way around.'

'Don't you know?' The woman's surprise was obvious.

'I'm looking after him for a friend.'

She nodded silently, apparently satisfied with his answer. Then, 'Are you a journalist or something?'

'No, I'm not.' That was the truth, if not the whole truth. Mullen braced himself for another telling off.

'Well, you seem like a nice man. But if you're lying…' She cast her eyes upwards, as if checking that God or some other all-seeing judge was up there, monitoring the conversation. 'I don't want to find myself quoted in the newspapers. The press make up such terrible lies. They twist people's words.'

'I can promise you that I am not a journalist,' he insisted, but he could tell by the way she continued to look at him, her head cocked slightly at an angle, that she wasn't convinced. Mullen felt compelled to explain further. 'Actually the reason I am here is that it was me who found Ruth's body.' That was his trump card, his only one. He hoped she hadn't got a better one.

'Really?' she said.

Mullen nodded. He had run out of words.

'I expect your dog could do with some water,' she said to Mullen's surprise. 'It's a hot day. And maybe you'd like a cup of tea yourself?'

*

Rex had had his drink, plus a couple of digestive biscuits – another black mark for Mullen if Professor Moody was somehow keeping count from the other side of the Atlantic. Mullen and Kay Pollock – the woman had finally revealed her name as she opened her front door – were sitting with cups of tea on the patio at the back of her bungalow.

Their conversation had mostly been about Rex, who had briefly explored the garden – north-facing, so ideal for sitting out on a day which threatened to be the hottest of the summer so far – before slumping at Kay Pollock's feet. He was probably hoping to charm her into handing out a third biscuit, but she was no longer giving him any attention at all.

Instead her eyes were looking, in an unfocused way, somewhere above Mullen's right shoulder.

'Well,' she said, 'Perhaps it was all for the best.'

'What on earth do you mean? All for the best?' Mullen, who had been wilting somewhat, straightened himself, suddenly alert. 'I don't understand.'

'The dementia.'

'Dementia?'

'Didn't you know? Poor Ruth developed dementia.'

'But she can't have been that old.'

'She wasn't.' Despite the heat and the cardigan which she was wearing, Kay shivered. 'Early onset dementia. You can get it younger than Ruth was.'

'I didn't know.'

'I only realized she had got it when she wandered into my house one day. I'd left the front door unlocked because I was unloading some shopping and then I needed to go to the toilet and when I came out, she was standing in the hall. "What are you doing in my house?" she said. "And who put all this horrid wallpaper up?"' Kay paused for

147

several seconds as she remembered. 'Such a shame. After all she'd been through.'

She picked up her paper napkin and dabbed at her eyes.

'It must have been hard for you, to witness that.'

'I suppose that was why she retired from being a minister of the church.'

Yes, Mullen thought, that would explain things.

'So was she the vicar here in Nettlebed?'

'Oh no. She was in Oxford. It's bad form to retire to the same parish in which you've been serving. It might make life difficult for the new incumbent. No, I think it was in the Botley area, the western side of Oxford.'

Mullen sat very still. Botley? Something sparked across his brain. Ellie leaving to go to meet her church group friends. 'Not St Nathanael's by any chance?' he said.

'That's right. How clever of you!' Kay beamed at him. 'Definitely St Nathanael's. He was one of the lesser known disciples. But he was one of the chosen twelve.'

It was too much of a coincidence. Whatever else it was, it was too much of a coincidence, surely?

'Still, at least she's at peace now. We can be grateful for that.'

Mullen nodded, as if in agreement. But he wasn't at all sure that he was. Was Ruth Lonsdale really at peace? That was the question that Mullen asked himself as he walked slowly back towards his car. Did death bring peace? In Ruth Lonsdale's case, he did hope so. But as far as he was concerned, a violent death and an unquiet grave under a pile of timber was hard to equate with peace.

Trisha can hear someone talking. She cannot make out what the person is saying. She cannot hear another voice. Perhaps it is a phone conversation. She recognizes individual sounds. They seem familiar, but she does not understand them. She has been asleep for, it seems, a very long time. She recalls dreaming, but the dreams have dissipated like early morning mist. She wonders if it is the morning? She does not know. It is dark. It has always been dark, ever since… She tries to force her mind to make sense of what is happening to her, but she is so filled with tiredness that nothing happens.

There is more sound. She recognizes this. A door has been opened. A shaft of light cracks open the darkness. She shuts her eyes and then keeps them shut. She feels safer that way. If she shuts her eyes and she shuts out the world, then she will remain safe and sound. What sort of threat can she be to whoever it is who has entered the room if she appears to be asleep?

The person is standing very close. Trisha can sense her. Assuming it is a her. For some reason she is convinced it is a her, and for that reason she feels safer.

'Open your eyes.'

Trisha is wrong. The voice is male. She pretends she is asleep, but the voice speaks again and reluctantly she opens them. She cannot see a face. This is because the only light in the darkness of the room is coming from a torch which is being shone directly into her eyes. She shuts them, but the same voice insists that she open them, first one and then the other. The man is examining her eyes. Like the optician. She wonders why he would be doing that, but her brain refuses to give her an answer.

The man is still there.

'Keep still,' he says. Is he talking to her? He must be because who else could he be talking to?

His hand pushes her sleeve up and then there is a quick sharp pain in her upper arm. She feels his fingers pulling her sleeve down again. They linger on her arm. They brush the material as if smoothing out any creases. It is an intimate movement. Intrusive even. She has a distant memory of Saad gently stroking her and tears begin to well up in her eyes. But then a wave of tiredness overwhelms her again, dragging her down towards oblivion. She fights it and tries to open her eyes. She is aware that the man is padding across the room, away from her. The door opens. Another shaft of light. She closes her eyes. It is too bright. The door clicks shut. Sleep descends again and she welcomes it like a long lost friend.

Mercy was on edge. The effervescent cheerfulness which seemed to be part of her DNA had apparently gone AWOL. She was as polite as usual and solicitous, quick to bring Natalie and Mullen a cup of tea, but there was none of her usual, slightly over-the-top bonhomie. Mullen studied Natalie, wondering if she had noticed, but she gave no sign of having done so.

In fact, Natalie was more interested in Rex than anything else. She was smiling at him and he, playing to his audience, was sitting angelically at her feet, staring up at her with pleading eyes.

'Mr Spade.' As usual she spoke slowly, as if picking her way through a minefield of unexploded words. 'Am I allowed to give your...'

There was a delay as she searched for the next word. Mullen waited too. How long to give her before he helped her? He still hadn't worked that problem out. But he was distracted. Mercy had moved away to the patio door and was signing at him. A finger to her mouth and then with that same finger she beckoned him. She went out into the garden.

'I'm going to get some herbs,' she announced loudly.

'... give your creature a biscuit ...' Natalie said, a smile of triumph on her face. 'Is that OK?'

'Just one,' Mullen replied. He stood up. 'My tea is hot. I think I'll go and inspect your garden.'

Outside, Mercy was indeed picking herbs, but as he approached her she moved further down the long strip of grass until she reached a bunch of hollyhocks taller than herself.

Mercy glanced back towards the house. Mullen followed her gaze. Natalie was feeding Rex small pieces of biscuit.

'I don't want to cause alarm,' she said, 'but I've seen a man hanging around outside the house.' Some of the hollyhock stems were leaning over. They needed staking up. But it meant that Mercy could lift one of them up from its 45-degree angle and sniff at its topmost flower. It was deep purple.

'When was this?'

She licked her lips. 'I first noticed him maybe three days ago. Or maybe four. When I put the recycling out in the bin, I noticed this man standing by the bus stop. Five minutes later, when I put out the rubbish, he was still there, as were three or four other people. They were students, but he was older. I went upstairs and made Natalie's bed. I opened the window to air the room, and I saw he was still there. The others had gone, so there must have been a bus, but he was still there. I stayed at the window watching him. I think he must have noticed me, because suddenly he turned on his heel and walked off down the road.'

'And you've seen him since then?'

'Yesterday, when I was getting off the bus in the morning, I saw him walking up the hill. He went past our house.'

'Did he stop? Look at the house?'

'I thought he slowed down, but he didn't stop. He just carried on walking up the hill.'

'Did you see where he went?'

'No. Do you think I should have followed him?'

'No, of course not.'

'It's just that I was running a bit late. I like to get to Natalie's early and take her a cup of tea in bed.' She paused. She was breathing heavily. 'To be honest, I was a bit scared too. Suppose he had realized I was following him. Suppose he had threatened me.'

'What does he look like?'

She frowned. 'Taller than you. Bigger generally. I think he must go to the gym. His hair is short. He wears jeans and black t-shirts and his nose looks like someone has punched him and broken it.'

Was this Paul Reeve? It sounded as though it might be, though the description could match hundreds of people in Oxford. And Mullen had no idea what Reeve looked like. The only photograph he had tracked down was from a press report at the time of his conviction. He hadn't had a broken nose then, but that could easily have happened in prison.

'Do you think we should report it to the police?'

Mullen shrugged. 'Let me think about it.' Which was another way of saying he didn't know what to do.

'Anyway, I need to be getting on,' she said, and she headed back to the house.

Mullen was about to follow her when he noticed a figure on his knees some distance away down the garden. It was a very long thin garden and it dropped away slightly with the slope of the hill, so Mullen could only see the head and shoulders of the man. But as he drew closer to him he realized it was Rick North, the gardener. He was attending to his vegetables.

North turned round, suddenly aware of his presence. 'Hi there, Doug.'

'I want to ask you something, Rick. In confidence.'

North stood up and pulled off his gloves. 'Ask away.'

'Have you noticed anyone hanging about in the road?'

He ran his hand through his hair. 'Like a suspicious looking man in a trilby?' He laughed.

Mullen scowled back.

He held up his hands. 'Sorry, mate. I was joking. It's just that I spend most of my time here in the garden. There's not much to be done in the little patch by the front door.'

Mullen shrugged. 'I know. It was just a long shot. Mercy is a bit anxious. She told me she had seen a man hanging around watching the house and she was a bit concerned about it.'

'You mean like he was casing the joint? A burglar?'

WHITE LIES, DEADLY LIES

Mullen nodded. A burglar suddenly seemed like a good line to pursue. He didn't want to tell North more than he had to.

'Well, at night there are only two women here. A girl and a very vulnerable woman. If someone knew that.'

'What did this guy look like?'

'Muscular, short hair, broken nose.'

'I'll keep an eye open. In fact, I'll eat my lunch in my van in the road. See if anyone matching the description walks past. I could take a photo if anyone does.'

'Best not to mention this conversation to Mercy. I don't want her getting alarmed.'

'I'll say nothing. Cub's honour.' He lifted his hand in the two-fingered salute Mullen knew from his time as a cub scout. 'Dib, dib, dob!' He laughed, delighted with himself. Mullen was beginning to realize that Rick North could be pretty irritating, but he tried not to let his feelings show. He needed any help he could get.

Mullen pulled out a business card and handed it over. 'Don't do anything stupid,' he said. 'It's not a game.'

'Don't you worry, squire.' This time he tugged at an invisible forelock.

Mullen squirmed. Few people got under his wick, but Rick North was in danger of joining that select band.

'Thanks,' he said, squeezing out the word with the utmost reluctance. He turned away towards the house.

'No problem,' North called after him, oblivious to the thoughts inside Mullen's head.

It was only seconds later, as he stepped onto the patio that Mullen heard raised voices from inside, one alarmed (Mercy) and one forceful (a male).

'I've been looking for you.' Greg Robinson stepped through the patio doors and advanced towards Mullen. His face was red, though whether that was the effects of the sun or Robinson's obvious anger, it was hard to tell. He was wearing a tight, short-sleeved shirt which emphasized his broad physique.

Mullen braced himself. This was not going to be a polite conversation.

'I'm sorry, Spade.' It was Mercy, hovering inside the house. 'He insisted he had to speak to you.'

'Don't worry,' Mullen replied, trying to sound as calm. 'You carry on inside.'

'You've been spreading lies.'

'Why don't we sit down?'

Robinson was barely a step and a half away. Close enough to lunge or punch. Mullen sensed a surge of adrenaline through his veins. Was it going to be flight or fight?

'I'm not sitting down with the likes of you, as if we were old chums. You and that Saad boy have been spreading lies about me. Saying that he ran off because I threatened him. If you tell the police that, they'll be round my house asking all sorts of damn fool questions when they should be looking for my daughter.'

'I haven't told the police.'

'Well, I bet Elizabeth Durant will.'

'I think you frightened Saad.'

'Frightened him? I just told him a few home truths. Like while he's over here leeching off us, he should watch himself. And especially that he'd need to watch himself if he ever tried it on with my daughter, because then he'd have me to answer to.'

'I suspect he found that quite frightening.' Mullen tried to sound calm and in control, but he was right on the edge.

'You think?' Robinson laughed. 'In my book, this would be me frightening someone.' And with surprising speed he stepped forward and grabbed hold of Mullen's polo shirt with both hands, yanking so hard and pulling Mullen so close to his face that Mullen could smell the reek of unbrushed teeth. More alarmingly, there wasn't even a hint of alcohol on his breath. It was pure, undiluted aggression.

'Let me go, Greg.'

'Or what?' There was a sneer on his face as wide as Sydney Bridge. 'You don't frighten me, Muggins.'

Muggins. The word was a red rag to Mullen. Memories of school-yard fights and the bully boy gang. He tried to duck and pull away from Robinson's grip, but Robinson anticipated this and gave him a sudden push backwards so that he went flying backwards. Mullen tried to twist and cushion his fall, but that didn't save him. His head cracked against something hard and painful, the wooden surround of one of the flower beds.

He was momentarily stunned, but before he could try and get to his feet, Robinson was standing over him. 'You can either get up and fight like a man, or I'll kick the shit out of you. Your choice, Muggins.'

'Back off, matey.' It was North. 'You need to calm down and you need to leave.' He was holding a hoe in his two hands, and he looked like he was prepared to use it. He stepped forward a pace. 'I won't have you frightening the ladies. Or attacking my friend Doug.'

Greg had backed down, but when Mullen got back home and shut the front door behind him, he realized he was still shaken. The intensity of Greg Robinson's anger had taken him completely off guard. He let Rex out into the garden and tried to come to terms with what had happened. But his heart was still pounding and when he held his left hand out, it was visibly shaking.

He needed to calm down. He needed to switch off. He needed therapy. He looked around the garden. In recent weeks rain had been a scarce commodity in Oxford. There were signs of drought everywhere. Things needed watering and he needed to water them. Maybe he would feel better then. He unrolled the hose, connected it to the outside tap and turned the water on. He could reach the majority of the garden with the hose and as he moved steadily around it, he tried to forget about Greg Robinson and think instead about his trip to Nettlebed.

Two things stood out for him. One was the fact that Ruth Lonsdale had suffered from early onset dementia. The other was that she had been vicar of St Nathanael's Church, Oxford. There was only one church of that name as far as he had been able to establish and it was in Botley. It was the church at which Ellie attended a youth group. So presumably Natalie used to attend it too before the accident. And so presumably she knew the Reverend Lonsdale. The connections were impossible to ignore. And the church was just a short walk away. Mullen lay the hose down. He walked back to the tap and turned it off.

The garden would have to wait. He needed to find out more about Lonsdale. She was dead. It was he who had found her. How could he prioritize watering the garden over finding out the truth behind her death? He called Rex and got the dog lead off its peg. He might as well kill two birds with one stone.

Mullen wasn't an expert in ecclesiastical architecture. He could have counted on two hands the number of churches he had been into in his life. As far as he was concerned, St Nathanael's, tucked away at the end of a cul-de-sac, looked 'quite old'. That was how he described it to an indifferent Rex as he approached it. The stonework was dark and, he felt, somewhat forbidding. Four lime trees lined the front, standing just behind a low stone wall, in the middle of which was a wooden gate with a miniature roof. It was through this that he and Rex passed, before making their way to the entrance on the south side of the church. Mullen wondered if it would be open at this time of day. Was it safe to leave churches unlocked nowadays? After all, churches were not exempt from burglary. Not that it mattered particularly to Mullen whether it was or wasn't open. He had already made up his mind to try the church first and then, if it was locked, to go in search of the vicarage. It was the vicar he wanted to speak to.

Mullen twisted the handle and pushed. The door was heavy, but it swung open smoothly. He advanced a few steps inside and looked around. There were, as far as he could see, no vicars or vergers or indeed any visitors hanging around in the shadows or in the brightly coloured pools of light which streamed down from the stained-glass windows. He felt disappointed, but he walked up the nave towards the altar nevertheless, enjoying the silence which the building offered. He would go in search of the vicar in a little while, but for a minute or two he would hide from the world and the problems which awaited him beyond these hallowed walls. Hallowed walls? Where did those words come from? Mullen hadn't been inside a church for a year or more. He couldn't pretend to be a Christian, but for some reason he felt comforted to be inside St Nathanael's Church on this sticky summer's day with no-one to bother him.

As he looked up at the window in the eastern end of the church – Jesus Christ on a cross, with two other haloed figures on either side – he suddenly realized that he wasn't alone after all. He turned around. A figure stood at the far end of the nave, half hidden in the shadows.

'Can I help you?' she said.

Accompanied by a reluctant Rex – he had found a very interesting smell to investigate – Mullen made his way towards her. She was young and thin. Not what he expected. She was dressed in blue – a blouse and a pair of three-quarter length trousers, and she was holding a basket full of flowers in her right hand. As he drew closer, she stepped fully into the light and Mullen realized that he had got her wrong. The long hair which was piled casually on top of her head was almost white, as were the strands which hung down over her cheeks. She was certainly thin, but unnaturally so as far as Mullen was concerned. Her skin was stretched tight over her cheek bones and words like 'botox' and 'anorexia' jumped into his head.

'My name is Doug Mullen,' he said.

'Is that an assistance dog?' she said, looking down at his feet.

'No.' Mullen glanced down too, fearful that Rex might choose this moment to blot his copybook. But Rex was doing his best to look cute. 'Are dogs not welcome?' he said. He thought about the ten commandments. They had been written up on the panelling behind the altar of the last church he had been in. 'Thou shalt love thine neighbour as thyself.' Or something like that. Also, something about not coveting your neighbour's ox or ass – he remembered that from childhood. But he hadn't heard of a commandment banning dogs from church.

'People don't normally bring dogs in here,' she said. 'However, as long as he behaves himself, I'll overlook it just this once.'

'I come prepared,' he said, removing a blue bag from his back pocket and holding it up.

She didn't return his smile. She didn't seem a very smiley person at all.

'Are you by any chance the new vicar here?'

'No,' she said. Her faced softened fractionally. 'At least you didn't ask if I was the vicar's wife.'

Mullen waited, wondering if she was going to tell him who she was rather than who she wasn't. Or was she actually the vicar's wife, but wasn't prepared to admit it? He would like to have known. But she stood there silent and inscrutable.

'You asked if you could help me.' Mullen decided he had better plunge straight in. He saw no point in beating about the bush. 'Well, I was wondering if you knew the Reverend Lonsdale?'

The woman was clearly startled. 'Oh, well yes, of course I did. She was our vicar. Poor Ruth.'

'It was me who found her body,' Mullen blurted out. As a technique it had worked with Kay Pollock in Nettlebed. Why not use it here? 'While I was walking the dog.'

'Oh!' The woman's voice was little more than a squeak. The basket slipped to the floor. She grabbed the end of a pew to support herself. 'Oh my goodness,' she said.

*

They sat on a pew together. Pam Hickey – she had finally introduced herself to Mullen – placed her basket of flowers (slightly the worse for wear after being dropped) in between them as if it was a chaperone who would guarantee Mullen's good behaviour and her own honour.

'I want to be straight with you,' Mullen said. 'I am a private investigator. I expect the police are conducting their own investigation into the Reverend Lonsdale's death, but given that I found her body, I feel compelled – called even – to do whatever I can to find out what happened to her. Would you mind telling me a bit about her? I understand she suffered from early onset dementia.'

'That's correct.'

Mullen waited, hoping that the silence would encourage Pam to talk. Short of asking her if she knew of anyone who might have killed her demented former vicar, he wasn't sure what other line of questioning he might attempt.

Pam stood up. There were tears on her cheeks. 'If you'll excuse me for a moment,' she said.

She got up, walked to the back of the church where she turned left into the shadows. The toilet, Mullen assumed.

He got up as well. There were two large notice boards at the back of the church. If Pam was unwilling to talk, then he needed to track down someone else who would. The new vicar was the obvious person. There were lots of posters about forthcoming events in the church and around the city. Mission partners. PCC meeting minutes. Christians against Poverty. The Viva network. It was another world. Mullen moved onto the second board. A large A3 sheet gave him the answer to his vicar question, though not the one he wanted. It was a list of persons involved in the hierarchy of St Nathanael's with photographs next to them: church warden and deputy church warden, youth and children's workers, treasurer, cleaner, and administrative assistant to the vicar. But against the heading *Vicar of St Nathanael's*, there was no photograph and just two words: *Post Unfilled*.

'As you can see, we are in an interregnum.' Pam had reappeared at his shoulder.

Mullen frowned. What was an interregnum?

'We are having trouble appointing Ruth's successor. After two rounds of interviews, we thought we had found one, but he got a better offer and turned us down. Mind you, I don't suppose the diocese is too worried. It saves on the salary costs, doesn't it?'

'I suppose so.'

'Definitely so. Is there anything else? Because I really need to get these flowers sorted. We have a fundraising concert here tomorrow night.'

'You're sure there's nothing you can tell me about the Reverend Lonsdale?'

It was a bad question. Or maybe it was the way he had said it. He could feel the air between them chill dramatically.

'You want me to dish the dirt on her?' Her voice was a mixture of incredulity and disgust.

'No, of course not,' Mullen said hastily, conscious he was on the verge of losing her co-operation altogether. 'I just wanted to get a feel of what sort of person she was, what she spent her time doing, did she have a husband or—'

'No husband,' she said very sharply. It was as if steel shutters had dropped suddenly. 'Married to the church, like many a good minister. Very popular. Weddings and funerals of course. Brilliant with the old and the young. Very hands on. Worked herself into the ground. In fact, come with me.'

She turned around and headed back towards whence she had come, except that this time she turned right rather than left. They entered an office.

'This will give you a good idea of her life here at St Nathanael's.'

There was pride in her voice. 'We put this together at her leaving do. A celebration of her ministry.'

The photographs were of variable quality. But in all of them, the figure of Ruth Lonsdale took centre stage, always with a smile across her face. Mullen wondered what it took to be always on display and always cheerful. Hadn't she ever wanted to scream or cry or just have a sulk?

'It was appalling how quickly the dementia gripped her,' Pam continued. 'The day she left was a terrible one. We held a party. People took photographs of course. People loved her, but it was as if the person known as Ruth Lonsdale no longer existed. Her face was vacant. She was confused by what was going on all around her. I deleted all the photographs I took from my phone. I couldn't bear it.'

Mullen was only half listening to what she had said, because something had caught his eye. It was a photograph at the bottom right-hand corner of the board. Ruth was there in the middle of a huddle of children. But Mullen's attention was focused on the four adults standing to one side. He pointed at one of them.

'That's Natalie Swan, isn't it?'

'You know her? Yes, that's Natalie. She's had it tough too, as you must know. And that there is her daughter Ellie.'

Mullen looked at a girl whom Pam had pointed at. He hadn't recognized her at first glance, but that was probably because her hair was long and flowing and brown. The look on her face however – sullen and disconsolate – was familiar to him. It was most definitely Ellie. There was a minibus in the background. It must have been some sort of trip.

'Tell me about Ellie.'

'Look, I am really not prepared to talk about individual children to a man I have never seen before and will probably never see again. So if you don't mind, I'd like to finish what I'm doing and lock up the church.'

She was rattled. Mullen could see that. Was it because he was a man, or because he was asking a lot of questions or because she had suddenly realized how vulnerable she was on her own with a stranger inside the church?

'OK,' he said. He pulled out his mobile and without asking, took a photo of the photo.

'Oh, I'm not sure you should have done that.'

'It's for Natalie,' he said quickly. It was a pale grey lie. 'I'm seeing her tomorrow. I thought it might cheer her up.'

'Well, it's been nice meeting you, Mr Mullen,' she said, but without conviction.

'Likewise.' Mullen got out his wallet and extracted a business card. 'If you think of anything else, just ring.'

She took it reluctantly with the tips of her thumb and first finger, as if by accepting it she was putting herself in danger of catching the bubonic plague.

Mullen changed direction. 'Are you a professional florist?' he said.

Pam seemed to grow an inch or two in height. Her facial expression certainly changed.

'Not exactly professional,' she said, 'but I do often arrange flowers for church events and friends' parties. l pride myself on my floral skills.'

'Do you have a card by any chance? My sister is getting married next month. They don't have a lot of money.'

Pam was clearly uncertain whether to trust him.

'Please,' he said and held out a hand. 'The flowers will be my gift to them. They will be so pleased.' Another lie, but Mullen liked to think it was much closer to white than black.

'As it happens, I do,' Pam said.

'Thank you,' Mullen said. He glanced down. Rex was looking up at him with reproachful eyes, as if he understood everything and was disappointed with his master's moral code. Mullen ignored him, but as he walked out of the church into the sunshine, the words of an old rhyme rang loud and accusingly in his ears. 'Liar, liar, pants on fire.'

CHAPTER 9

Friday

'How do I look?' she said.

He appraised her in silence. She had an extraordinary capacity to change and blend her appearance and manner. He wondered how it was that she had never quite made it as an actor. She was certainly a determined woman, but he suspected that somewhere along the way she might well have annoyed too many people who could have helped her up the greasy pole of ambition. But whatever the case, right now she looked the part.

'You are both unrecognizable and unremarkable,' he said.

'Good. In the circumstances, I shall consider "unremarkable" as being a compliment.'

The silence which followed was cool and awkward. He wondered if she was thinking what he was thinking – that they had reached the point of no return. Though in truth they had already passed that point the moment Lonsdale had died.

'You'll be all right?' he said at last.

'Why shouldn't I be?'

'You're sure you're happy to do this?'

'Happy?' The word seemed to disturb her. 'It's what we agreed and

163

planned. It's our insurance. It'll keep the police off our tails.'

'I hope so.'

'You hope so?' Her anger flared and words flew out of her mouth like tracer bullets. 'You were the one who lost your temper. Have you forgotten that? With a demented clergywoman for crying out loud.'

'She was hiding stuff. She was as guilty as hell. Are you trying to tell me she wasn't?'

She stepped closer to him, and placed her forefinger on his hard bony sternum. She tapped twice.

'What I'm telling you is that what's done is done. The die is cast. You know that, and I know that. However you like to look at it, this is what has to happen next. And remember, I'm going to be the one doing it. All you've got to do is drive to the house and then wait for me. How difficult can it be?'

'Suppose Mercy isn't there? What then?'

'Then I'll make a phone call. I've fooled Doug Mullen. And I can do it with Mercy McAlister.'

Mullen's mobile rang just after he had pushed a mouthful of granola into his mouth. Natalie Swan's name flashed up on the screen. It was unusual for her to ring.

'Hello, Natalie.'

'It's not Natalie,' a wild voice said. 'It's me. Mercy. I don't know what to do. Should I ring the police? Perhaps I should have rung the police. But then I thought, Spade will know what to do. I'll ring Spade.'

'What's happened?' Mullen said very firmly, conscious that Mercy was on the edge of hysteria.

'They aren't here. Natalie and Ellie. Neither of them are here. They've gone.'

'Have you tried ringing their mobiles?'

'Of course I have. Do you think I'm a complete fool? Ellie isn't answering. It goes straight into the answering service. And I found

Natalie's on her bedside table.'

'Just wait,' Mullen said. 'I'll be round in ten minutes.'

Mullen was round there sooner than that. He realized he had no time to waste walking at Rex's pace, so he bundled him into the car and drove.

Mercy in person wasn't any calmer than she had been over the phone. If anything she was worse.

'Where would they have gone? Natalie never gets up early. There's no school. So where could they possibly have gone? It makes no sense.'

Maybe Ellie had taken her mother into town on the bus for breakfast, Mullen told himself. Why not? But he wasn't convinced. He scouted around the house. Ellie's bed was unkempt, as if it had been taken over by a family of restless chimpanzees. He wondered if she ever made her bed. Looking around her room, with clothes, make-up, jewellery and God knows what else strewn everywhere and anywhere, he decided probably not. By contrast, Natalie's room was immaculate. All clothes tidied away in cupboards and drawers, a few ornaments displayed carefully on surfaces and her bed as neat as apple pie. Mullen looked in the bathroom. There were two electric toothbrushes and two different toothpastes, one for sensitive teeth. Certainly no sign they had decided to go away for a couple of days. He made his way downstairs.

'Do you make Natalie's bed for her?'

'Yes, of course I do. I'm her carer, aren't I?' She spoke as if he had cast aspersions on her professionalism.

'And have you made it this morning?'

'No.'

'It looks very tidy, as if it hasn't been slept in.'

'Oh!' As far as Mullen was concerned, he had made a very simple deduction, but Mercy looked at him in bemusement. 'Oh!' she repeated as the implications of his words began to sink in. 'Maybe she made it herself.' But Mercy didn't sound convinced.

'I think we had better ring the police,' he said. 'Don't you?'

DI Holden and DC Trent arrived within fifteen minutes of Mullen making the phone call. They were accompanied by another man who introduced himself as DC Knight. Northern accent of some sort, a touch of Yorkshire and something else. Holden sat down without delay and fired off a barrage of questions at both Mercy and himself. Mullen was impressed. Finally, it seemed, they were taking it all very seriously. He would have liked to have asked them how they were getting on with their investigations into Ruth Lonsdale's death and Trisha's disappearance, but there was no opportunity.

'We'll see if we can trace their mobile phones. If they're turned on, we'll locate them. Even if they are not, we should be able to find out where Natalie and Ellie were when the phones were turned off.'

'Natalie left her phone behind,' Mullen said.

'Oh.' Holden looked at him as if she held him personally responsible. 'We have reason to believe that Paul Reeve, Natalie's ex-husband, may have wanted to abduct them. We don't have a mobile number for him, so we can't track that, but we have got a recent photograph from when he left prison, so that should help. If he is in the Oxford area, we'll find him.'

Holden sounded confident as she rattled through her plan, but Mullen wasn't so sure. After ten years in prison, Reeve would know all the tricks. He would also have had plenty of time to plan things down to the last detail. If Reeve had abducted them, he would surely not have been so stupid as to allow Ellie to keep her mobile. He would have taken it off her and disabled it straight away.

'It must have been him I saw the other day.' Mercy burst into alarmed life. 'I told you, Mr Mullen, didn't I? You told me to keep my eyes open and I did.'

Trent produced a photograph and thrust it forward. 'Do you think it could have been this man?'

Mercy frowned. She closed her eyes briefly and mouthed some-thing silently. A prayer perhaps. 'I'm having a bit of trouble with my eyes these days. I think it could have been him, but I wouldn't swear it was.'

'Whatever the case,' Holden said, 'I think I should stress that we see Paul Reeve as potentially very violent. I strongly urge you to take all possible security measures.'

'Why would he be interested in us?' Mullen wasn't prepared to accept without question the official police line. 'If he's got hold of Natalie and Ellie, then we are an irrelevance.'

'You think so, Mr Mullen?' Holden turned and nodded to Knight.

Knight leaned forward as if fearful that there might be people listen-ing in. He spoke briskly but softly. 'Several days ago, a man's body was fished out of the River Humber. We have reason to believe that this was a case of murder rather than accidental drowning. We also know that this man shared a cell with Paul Reeve at HMP Stonewood. We know that they met and drank together on the night of the man's death.' He paused and looked hard at Mullen. 'We also know, as of course you do, Mr Mullen, that Paul Reeve visited a solicitor called Ray Costa in Hull and that Mr Costa died in his house a few days later. In short, we believe Mr Reeve is not a man to be underestimated. Anyone who gets in his way is at risk.'

It was Holden's turn again. 'So, Mr Mullen, I am hereby warning you to desist from any investigations which you may be undertaking on your own behalf or indeed on behalf of anyone else. This is now a major police investigation and when Paul Reeve has been arrested and brought to trial, you will yourself be an important prosecution witness. Do I make myself clear?'

'Yes,' he said, 'totally clear.'

'I do hope so.' She stood up. The meeting was emphatically over. 'There's no reason for either of you to stay. We will be making a search of the house and taking away any relevant electronic devices, and a uniformed officer will remain on duty in case either Natalie or Ellie return. For the time being, this house will be treated as a crime scene.'

'I think I left my phone upstairs,' Mullen said. 'If you don't mind.'

Holden looked at him as if he had just asked if she minded him taking off all his clothes and running naked round the house. But she gave him a curt nod nevertheless.

Mullen made his way upstairs. He had lied, but he knew this was his last chance to look round. He could hear Mercy talking loudly to Holden downstairs. Her anxiety levels were stratospheric. Maybe that would give him a few extra moments, though quite what he was expecting to find he really had no idea.

There wasn't time for a thorough search. Only a quick scan of one of the rooms. Whose? Natalie's or Ellie's? He opted for Ellie's. Her room was a complete mess, in no sort of order, and as such it was surely more likely to offer up something that would help him answer the question which was uppermost in his mind. Was it merely a coincidence that Natalie and Ellie had attended a church headed by Ruth Lonsdale? Somehow he doubted it. It was possible, but Mullen wasn't a great believer in coincidences.

He padded as quietly as he could into Ellie's room. What are you looking for, Mullen, he asked himself. Where is the most promising place to look? Where might Ellie had hidden something in the midst of such domestic chaos? Where, oh where?

He started with the chest of drawers next to the bed. If you've something you want to hide, he reasoned, you'd hide it somewhere close to hand. Especially if it was something you might want to look at occasionally in private.

He pulled open the top drawer. Pants in several different colours. Sanitary towels, some of which had escaped from their packaging. A photograph. Ellie, Trisha, Saad and a Chinese looking girl. Was that the Tate Modern? Where the spider had been?

Drawer number two was less interesting. Creams, make-up,

hair-dye and various gothic jewellery. Mullen slid it silently gently shut and tried the bottom drawer. He pulled it open. Folders of school notes as far as he could tell. He hadn't put her down as a diligent student, but rebellious exteriors are often nothing but masks. Why shouldn't Ellie be a young woman with the drive and ambition to get on in life? He picked them out, folder by folder and there, at the very bottom, inside a see-through envelope, was a photograph of a man.

He picked it up, and almost immediately he heard footsteps on the stairs. There was no time to think. He slipped the photograph inside his shirt, thrust the files back into the drawer, pushed it shut with his foot and hurried across the bedroom floor. He met Trent at the top of the stairs.

'Come on, Mullen. Hop it now. And take that dog with you. He's getting in the way.'

'Sorry, Constable. He's a friendly little chap.'

Trent made a noise which indicated that he didn't agree. Mullen headed down the stairs. He reckoned Rex had earned an extra treat when they got home.

When Mullen got home, he gave Rex the dog chew he had silently promised and pulled open the patio windows. He made himself a strong mug of tea and went and sat in the garden. The sun was already well established in a flawless blue sky, so he positioned himself in the gentle shade of the false acacia and prepared to examine the photograph from Ellie's room. He pulled it out of the envelope.

The man was standing half turned away from the photographer. His eyes, however, were looking straight at the camera, as if afraid that the photographer might at any second do a runner. His face was emotionless. Hair that almost touched his ears, a beard of several days' growth and broad, muscled shoulders. Mullen looked at the back. There were two letters at the bottom, a capital 'D' and small 'x'. He went inside and found his tablet. It didn't take long for him to find what he had been looking for. It was an article from ten years previously which he had read twice already. But it wasn't the article he was interested in seeing, just the photograph which accompanied it. He stared at it for some time, imagining the man on the website ten years older, and in the end he knew there was no doubt: the photograph in Ellie's drawer was of her father, Paul Reeve. 'D' was for 'Dad' and 'x' – well, it was obvious what 'x' meant. That Paul Reeve loved his daughter. Or thought he did. Mullen wondered how Ellie felt about him. But as soon as he wondered, he knew. If she hated him, then why would she have kept this photograph tucked away in her drawer? Out of sight of everyone, especially her mother.

The questions began to flood into Mullen's head. How did she get hold of this photograph? Did he post it? Or had they met up? And if so, where and when? But that seemed to make no sense. Remember the swans, their heads cut off. That was a clear enough threat. What about the spider postcard? If anything, Ellie had been more alarmed by that. And now she and her mother had both disappeared. Had they done a runner to escape him? Mullen doubted that Ellie and her mother could have possibly managed that on their own. Had they been kidnapped? More likely. Or were they dead? Mullen tried – and failed – not to think like that. And what about Trisha? Was she dead too? What could she have possibly done to incur Reeve's wrath, beyond being one of Ellie's best friends?

Mullen stood up, unable to bear sitting still anymore, and that was when he noticed the other photograph. It must have been tucked inside the envelope behind the other one. It was only passport sized. He picked it up and turned it over. The face that stared at him was extremely familiar and it caused his brain to spin even faster. He began to pace around, pulling up weeds here, pruning roses there, in the hope that the activity of gardening would calm him down and in so doing would enable him to think clearly. It didn't work.

What was it they said about the emperor Nero? That he fiddled while the city of Rome burned all around him. Well, he wasn't going to be a Nero. Not while there was a chance, however remote. And whatever Detective Inspector Holden said.

Mullen's mobile phone rang and he jumped in alarm. He couldn't imagine a phone call which didn't bring bad news. He pulled the mobile out of his back pocket and looked to see who was calling. It was Elizabeth Durant. In the circumstances, that was the best he could have hoped for.

'Hello?'

'This is Elizabeth Durant. I got your message.'

'Thank you so much for ringing back. Is Saad there?'

'Might I ask what you want to ask him? It's just that I don't want him feeling pressured. I don't want him running off again. I just want things to get back to normal.'

Normal! What was normal about the current situation? Mullen didn't say that, but he easily could have. Instead he said, 'I want to talk to him about Trisha.'

'We've already seen and spoken to the police. So many questions, including about Trisha. They obviously think she's in London. Hiding out. Maybe even pregnant.'

'I don't.'

'Can't it wait for a couple of days?'

Mullen sighed. He hoped she could hear it. 'It is not just about Trisha. Ellie Swan has gone missing too, and so has her mother Natalie.'

'Oh! They didn't tell me that.' There was a long pause before she continued. 'Seeing as it is you, Mr Mullen, and you have done so much for both of us, then of course you can speak to Saad. But if you don't mind I'd rather you came and spoke to him here.' Polite, but definite.

Saad was sitting in an armchair in Elizabeth Durant's front room. He seemed tense. Knees drawn together, hands clasped in his lap, his eyes down. He had barely acknowledged Mullen. Durant was organizing a drink for the three of them. Saad had apparently taken up the English habit of drinking builders' tea.

Mullen tried a few conversational gambits, but none of them provoked anything beyond a 'yes' or 'no' or a slight twitch of the head. Mullen tried to imagine what the young man had undergone in his short life. The bombing of his home, the violent death of family and friends, being smuggled by unscrupulous people traffickers – he had read about that sort of thing in the papers and watched documentaries on the TV – but the truth was he knew very little about the youth sitting in front of him.

Durant brought each of them a cup of tea.

'Thank you,' Mullen said. And then, before she could sit down, 'Do you mind if Saad and I speak one to one?'

She looked at Mullen. For a moment he thought she was going to refuse, but instead she nodded. 'I'll be at my computer if you need me.' And she disappeared upstairs.

Mullen took this as a cue to begin.

'Has Elizabeth told you about Ellie?'

'Yes,' he said. But his eyes remained lowered.

'And her mother?'

Another 'Yes'.

'And Trisha is still missing.'

He lifted his head. For the first time he looked at Mullen. 'I don't know where they are,' he said. 'If I did, I would tell you.'

'Last night you told me that you and Trisha were just friends.'

'Yes.'

'So Trisha was not pregnant?'

Alarm flashed across his face. 'No. That is not possible. I do not sleep with her.'

'Perhaps she had other boyfriends?'

This seemed to catch him by surprise, as if this possibility had never occurred to him. He examined his hands again. 'I think not.'

Mullen picked up his tea cup and took a sip.

'Tell me about Ellie,' he said.

'What about her?' Saad picked up his cup too, but hastily so that some of the tea slopped over the edge into the saucer.

Mullen waited for him to raise the cup to his lips. 'Did you have sex with Ellie?' he said.

Saad's whole body twitched violently. This time, tea spilt down his chin and T-shirt.

'I'm not going to tell anyone,' Mullen continued as calmly as he could. 'I am certainly not going to tell Elizabeth or the police. In fact, I don't care if you had sex with Ellie or not or whether she is pregnant or had to use the morning after pill. I care only about finding her and Natalie and Trisha.'

Saad remained silent. He was trembling.

Mullen took out two photographs and laid them on the table in front of him. 'I found these in Ellie's room, hidden under her school books. A photograph of a man who I think is her father and a photo-graph of you.'

Saad picked up the two photographs and held them close to his face. Mullen waited. The last thing he wanted was for Saad to clam up or even worse, freak out and run off to his bedroom.

'Only once.' Saad was breathing heavily, as if he had just run up a steep hill. 'It was not meant to happen. We were just holding each other. And then it was like a madness. I did not have a condom. I did not plan any of this. Because she is very young. It was very stupid.' Saad began to cry, though softly, as if afraid that the noise might alert Durant and bring her running down the stairs. But the grief was pal-pable. 'Afterwards I was so scared. If Ellie got pregnant, if Elizabeth find out I sleep with her, it would be the end for me. So I decided to run away.'

'You told me yesterday Mr Robinson threatened you and that is why you ran away.'

'Yes. He said he would beat me up if I touch his daughter. I like Trisha. She is beautiful. But with Ellie it is different. She understands suffering. So I go away to protect both of them.'

Mullen pointed to the larger photograph. 'Have you ever seen this man?'

Saad frowned at it. 'No,' he said. 'I think not.' He continued to study the man's image. 'But I think you are right, Mr Mullen.'

Mullen was puzzled. 'In what way am I right?'

'This is Ellie's father. Look. They have the same eyes.'

Mullen looked at the photo again. It had never occurred to him, but he could believe that Saad was right.

'Did Ellie ever talk about her father?'

'No. Not in detail. She said her father had been locked in prison for a long time, but she didn't want to talk about him.'

Mullen nodded. He tried to formulate another question, but Saad hadn't finished.

'Ellie texted me. She told me she had met her father.'

It was Mullen's turn to stare. 'When was this?'

'Last week. While I am away, we exchanged texts once a week. Always at the same time on the same day. For three or four minutes. Then we both delete all the texts so that no-one will know.'

'Did she say anything else about her father?'

'I think she was very pleased to meet him. But scared for her mother too.'

'So she didn't tell her mother?'

'I think definitely not.'

It made no sense.

Mullen had left Durant's house in such confusion that as soon as he got home he let Rex into the garden and then followed him out with a pair of secateurs in his hands. His earlier foray into the garden had reminded him how much he had been neglecting it. He started with a

174

couple of pink roses. Pruning was a thing he did as if it was his second nature and by the time he had moved further down the garden to where the hollyhocks were ranged along the wooden fence like drunken soldiers on guard duty, his brain had calmed down and had started to process what he had learned over the last few hectic hours.

For a start, there was the revelation that Ellie had met her father, and had done so without the knowledge of her mother. Was she not afraid of him after what he had done? Did she not remember the drunken rages, the cigarette pressed against her thigh? Mullen himself did not remember much about being three. But if he had been exposed to such things, what then? Would he have remembered? Or would he have suppressed such horrors so deep that they disappeared from his memory? He had heard about that sort of thing. But if you repressed your memories to that degree, what if you then encountered your abusive father ten years later in the flesh? How would that play out? What distorted recollections and hatreds might then come bubbling to the surface? Or indeed what desire for revenge?

Mullen felt in the back pocket of his jeans and took out the two photos, the one of Saad and the one of the man he assumed was Paul Reeve. How did Reeve see things? Did he love his daughter and hate his daughter's mother? That would make sense. That would explain why he and Ellie had met in secret. So why would he have absconded with them both? If it had been just Ellie, that would make some sort of sense, but Natalie too? Familicide! The word popped into his head from somewhere. That was one answer. There had been enough cases in the news. A man kills his wife and children because he can't bear the reality of his current situation, or maybe so that they can be together in heaven or hell or in whatever life there was after death. Mullen knew it happened, but he couldn't get his head round it. And Mullen, optimist that he was when it came to human nature, could not quite believe it. If Ellie had met her father and shown a willingness to relate to him, then why would he wish her any harm?

Mullen's mobile began to ring. He hastened over to the garden table on which he had left it.

It was, to his surprise, DC Trent. He hesitated before answering. It could only be bad news.

'Is that you, Mullen?'

'Yes.'

'Detective Constable Trent here.' He sounded very pleased with himself. 'I thought you might like to know that we have apprehended Paul Reeve.'

'What about Natalie and Ellie Swan?'

'We expect Mr Reeve to tell us where they are. It will be in his best interests to do so.'

Mullen swore. 'So you haven't found them?'

'Not yet. He was living in a tent out near Eynsham.'

'But are there any signs that they were there with him?'

Trent didn't answer the question. 'We will find them,' he insisted. 'One way or another we will find them.'

'You mean dead or alive.' Mullen didn't mean to actually say this out loud, but the words popped out of his mouth. Trent hung up. Maybe he hadn't even heard them. Maybe he was already moving on to the next thing. Maybe he had only rung up Mullen because DI Holden had told him to. Mullen didn't like him at all. And it wasn't only because he sounded like a posh git.

Rex gave a bark. It was more a yap than a bark in reality and Mullen, back to his own reality, watched him as he came running up to him. Rex had something in his mouth. Probably a chew which he had redis-covered and dug up somewhere in the garden. But for the briefest of moments Mullen was back in Bagley Wood and Rex was running up to him with Ruth Lonsdale's finger in his mouth. And for several less brief moments Mullen could taste regurgitated food in his throat. He choked back the impulse to spit it all out.

He steadied himself. Poor Ruth Lonsdale. Who the hell would have done that to her? Forced her to slide under a pile of logs and then blown her brains out.

He tried to stop thinking about her death. What about her life? She knew both Natalie and Ellie. Was that significant? There was that photograph in the church. He should have asked Pam Hickey more about it. Why hadn't he? Mullen got out his wallet. The first card he saw, tucked next to his paper money, was the one which she had given him for her flower arranging. He punched her number into his phone. Never say never.

She answered almost immediately, a rather wary 'Hello', the sort you give to an unrecognized number.

'It's Doug Mullen. We met in the church yesterday. Do you remember?'

'I do.'

'And do you remember that I was looking at a photograph of the Reverend Lonsdale with members of the youth club and with various parents?'

'I do.' Her voice was still wary, as if she would rather she didn't remember anything of the sort.

'Am I right in thinking that Trisha Robinson was also in that photograph?' He was pretty sure she was. He had checked his own photo of the photo again and the girl behind and half obscured by Ellie certainly looked like a younger Trisha.

There was a distinct pause before Pam answered. 'I imagine she would have been. She and Ellie did everything together. They were great buddies and stalwarts of the youth club.'

'What was the occasion of that particular photo?'

'Gosh, I'm not sure.'

Not sure. Or not wanting to be sure? Mullen pressed on. 'It's just that I remember what you said about how you helped to assemble the display, so I was thinking that if anyone knew, it would be you. If it is of any help, I did notice that there is the bonnet of what appears to be a minibus in the background.'

'Well, it must have been a trip, then. Obviously! I really don't think I can tell you any more than that.'

Mullen didn't need psychic powers to sense that she was on the point of hanging up, but he wasn't going to make it easy for her to do so.

'I expect you've read in the *Oxford Mail* about Trisha's disappearance,' he said.

'Yes.'

'Well, I am very sorry to have to tell you that Natalie and Ellie have also disappeared. The police are extremely concerned, and so am I. If we are to find them,' he continued, making it sound as though he and the Thames Valley Police Force were linked by an umbilical cord, 'we need all the help we can get. So let me ask you again: please tell me everything you know about that photograph.'

This time there was an undecipherable noise from Pam, a groan or sob or something else. 'If my memory serves me well, Ruth took a group of them, all girls, to Cornwall two years ago.'

'And Natalie, Ellie and Trisha were all on it.'

'Yes, I believe so. Natalie was one of the adult helpers.'

'Did something happen during the trip?'

'Why on earth do you think anything happened?'

It was Mullen's turn to stop in his verbal tracks. He had an answer to Pam's question, though it had only materialized in his consciousness as they were talking. It might be a stab in the dark, but the more he thought about it the more he liked it. There was nothing to be lost by saying what he wanted to say. The worst that could happen was that she would terminate the call.

'Well,' he said, 'it's quite simple. The fact is that the Reverend Lonsdale appears to have resigned within weeks of that trip. So I am wondering if the two things are connected.'

Mullen pressed his mobile closer to his right ear, anxious not to miss her reply. But all he heard was a harsh guttural sound just before the line went dead. Mullen waited a few seconds and then tried ringing back, but this time there was no answer.

Mullen stood unmoving in the professor's kitchen. The grand-mother clock in the hall was striking, but he didn't register the noise, let alone the number of hours struck. He was thinking about Pam's refusal to answer his question and the way in which she had instead terminated the call. Those two things together spoke volumes. Pam could have told him the timings didn't match his theory. She could have laughed him out of court. Instead she had hung up in alarm. And that, Mullen hoped, was because he was getting close to the truth.

Mullen went and located his iPad. He wasn't a natural techie, but the fact was that the internet had opened a whole world of information to people like him – and indeed to people not like him.

He keyed in his four-number password and opened up his inter-net browser. He began to search – first St Nathanael's and then Ruth Lonsdale, throwing in Cornwall as an afterthought. He was looking for something that had happened round about two years previously, something sufficiently shocking or sad that it got into the news. And before long he had found it.

Mullen didn't stop there. He continued searching and came up with more information that brought him to a grinding halt.

There was a single uniformed police officer outside Natalie's house. She looked as though she couldn't wait for her shift to end.

'You can't come in here, sir,' she said firmly.

'I know,' he replied. 'I'm Doug Mullen.' He had a business card ready in his hand. He held it up. 'May I see your ID?' He grinned. 'Fair's fair.'

PC Lynn Benning hesitated as if this was something she hadn't been trained to deal with. Reluctantly she held her warrant card out for him to inspect.

'Thanks. I was here earlier, with Mercy McAlister when she reported

Mrs Swan and her daughter missing and I wanted to see—'

'You may not enter the house. It is still currently viewed as a potential crime scene.'

Mullen bent down to the ground and picked up Rex. 'Sorry,' he said, 'Let me explain. I need to return Ms McAlister's dog to her.'

'She went home hours ago.'

'I expect she has. I know the officers had to question her. Quite right too. That is their job. But she was in quite a state because she felt responsible for Natalie and Ellie. So I said I'd look after her dog for as long as it takes. But now I'm in one heck of a hole because my mother has been taken ill in Portugal in the Algarve, and I need to fly there, but obviously I can't take the dog. So I just need to ring her so I can return the dog. But the really stupid thing is that I don't know where she lives and I don't have her phone number. I gave her my card, but she hasn't rung me and I need to catch a plane to Portugal a.s.a.p.'

He hugged Rex more tightly. 'So I am hoping against hope that you've got some contact details.'

PC Benning looked at him as if she couldn't decide whether Mullen was deranged or a conman. Mullen lifted the dog. 'He's a sensitive little chap, but if you can't help I'll have to put him in a kennels and hope for the best.'

Mullen wasn't sure he had any more cards to play, beyond deploying his little-boy-lost face, so he tried that too. And maybe it tipped the balance because the constable dug into her pockets and produced a small notebook and a mobile.

'Thank you so much,' Mullen said. 'I'll just copy the number down and leave you in peace.'

'No, you won't.' She wasn't so stupid as to give away personal details. 'I'll ring.'

Mullen waited. She rang twice, and the second time she swore. 'Damn. No answer. Her phone must be switched off. Why do people switch off their phones?'

'She could have given you a dud number.'

'Why would she have done that?' PC Benning was suddenly alarmed, as if she might be missing a trick.

'No worries,' Mullen said cheerfully. 'Did she give you an address?'

'Yes, of course.'

'Well, if you give it to me, I can drive round there and see if she's in.'

'So you can give her the dog?'

'Yes.'

She laughed, a harsh disappointed laugh. 'I bet she doesn't have a dog. In fact, I bet the dog is yours. And I bet the whole story about your elderly mother being ill in the Algarve is a load of hogwash.'

Mullen paused, uncertain whether to continue with his deception or come clean.

'I'm sorry. You're right,' he said. 'Absolutely right.' Maybe he could redeem the situation. 'But what is true is that I strongly believe Ms McAlister is involved in the abduction of Natalie and Ellie Swan. Think about it. You've just discovered she gave you police a dud phone number. If I drive round to her address and I discover that it doesn't exist or that it does exist, but she doesn't live there, then that pretty much confirms that she is a liar and she is involved. In which case I will tell you, and you will inform Detective Inspector Holden and hopefully we will catch her and you will get a commendation for your intelligent initiative.'

The constable's face was transparent. She wanted to believe him, but she was having great difficulty in doing so. 'Why on earth should I trust you? Just because you've got the smooth patter and all the answers?'

'I just need the address,' Mullen said. 'Then I'll go round there and I'll see if Ms McAlister lives there or not. Then I'll ring you. It's as simple as that.'

Mullen's assumption was that – just like the mobile number which Mercy had given the police – the address which Mercy had given would turn out to be a dud. But his GPS took him straight to the postcode and

181

he was relieved to see at the end of the cul-de-sac a four-storey block of flats.

He got out of the car and went to the entrance. Three times he rang the bell for flat 12 – with a thirty second gap in between – and three times he waited in vain for an answer. He lifted his finger to ring flat 11 when he heard a voice right behind him.

'That's my flat.'

Mullen turned to see a short, bald man with a tightly clipped beard, dressed in a grey tracksuit. His face was red with perspiration.

'I'm an old friend of Mercy's in flat 12,' he said. 'My name is Doug,' and he held out his hand. The man didn't shake it. 'She's not answering her bell,' Mullen said.

'She must be out. Probably at work.'

'She's not at work,' Mullen said.

'That's unusual. She cares for this lady who had a crash.'

'I think the lady has gone on holiday,' Mullen lied. 'Would you recognize Mercy's car?'

The man looked around the parking area very slowly, as if he was a camera panning gradually across a scene in a film.

'It's not here,' he said eventually.

The man seemed a bit on the simple side, Mullen thought. Learning difficulties, he corrected himself. There was something about the way he spoke and presented himself.

'Thank you for your help,' Mullen said.

'She gives me chocolate sometimes. She's very kind.'

'Do you know her mobile number?' Mullen said. 'She told me it, but she's not answering.'

The man got his mobile out and after several seconds read the number out. The same number as she had given to Benning. Mullen cursed silently. So much for that theory! She must just have turned the phone off. Was that so she couldn't be tracked?

Mullen tried another tack. 'Has she been living here for long?'

'Not as long as me. I have been here three years. She only arrived earlier this summer, just before the tennis.'

Mullen thought about that. It fitted with his theory. Mercy had come to Oxford to care for Natalie because she had another agenda. She wanted to get close to her, not to look after her.

'Well, thank you very much,' he said.

The man nodded and opened his door. He shut it firmly behind him. Mullen heard the tell-tale sound of a security chain being slipped into place.

'So are you going to charge my client or not?' Althea Potter had been strikingly silent while Paul Reeve was interviewed by Holden and Trent. She wrote detailed notes inside a lined A4 book. She listened intently, her eyes forever on Holden (for it was Holden who did nearly all the talking). And she whispered advice to her client as the situation required.

Then, like a cat that has been watching a naive fledgling sparrow, she pounced. 'The evidence which you have presented has all been circumstantial. The fact that my client had a drink with the deceased proves nothing. There is no witness to the moment at which the deceased fell into the river. Indeed there is no evidence that a crime was committed at all. All we know for sure is that the deceased was drunk at the time of his death and that he drowned in the river. My client served time for a domestic dispute gone wrong while under the influence of drink. He has lived with that for the last ten years. He has stopped drinking. My overwhelming impression is that you think my client is an easy person to pin the deceased's death on, just because he has a criminal record. So I must insist that you either release him or charge him and face being ridiculed in court.'

Holden sat very still. The other occupants of the small interview room seemed to stop breathing. It was pin drop time, but no-one was going to do that.

Holden gathered up her folder and hugged it to her body.

'Mr Reeve is free to go. In the meantime we shall continue to gather evidence.' She got up and opened the door, but before she got any further Reeve was on his feet and right behind her.

'What about my daughter?'

Holden turned. She was not a woman easily intimidated. 'Let me assure you, Mr Reeve, that we shall continue to search for both your daughter and your ex-wife with every resource at our disposal.'

'It's my daughter I'm interested in. While you've been wasting time trying to pin a non-existent crime on me, she's been missing. For all I know, she's dead. So let me warn you, Detective Inspector—'

'Paul!' Althea Potter put a restraining hand on his arm, but he shook her off.

'Let me tell you that if anything has happened to Ellie, it's you I'll hold responsible, so help me God.'

The man in flat 11 thought about what had happened all through the time he cooked his dinner, all through the time he ate it and all through the time he drank his cup of tea and watched the TV. But when the programme he was watching was over and he turned off the TV, he realized that he had made a mistake.

The man Doug had been so nice. He had been very polite and had tried to shake his hand. Thinking about it now, he realized he had been too trusting. His mum had always told him he was too trusting, and even though she had died twelve years and three months ago, she had been proved right yet again. The fact was that Doug could have been anyone. For all he knew, Doug might not be Doug. He might be Alan or Graham or John.

When Doug had asked him about Mercy, he had been caught right off his guard. But he felt pleased that he hadn't given her away. 'You must be careful with strangers who come to your door,' Mercy had warned him. Mercy was like his mother now. Always giving him good advice. And chocolate! He smiled.

She would be pleased that he hadn't said anything about her car. Of course it was sitting out there where it always was. She always parked it in the same place if it was free. But he wasn't going to tell a stranger that. Especially when that stranger had been about to ring his doorbell. That was very odd.

He opened his door, shut it behind him and then rang Mercy's bell. There was no reply. He opened her letter box flap and called her name. Still no reply. He got out her key. She had given it to him so that he could water her plants. He would go in and water them now and see if she was all right. Maybe she was ill in bed. He could make her a cup of tea or cocoa. She liked cocoa. He slipped the key in the lock and let himself in.

The curtains were drawn. Perhaps to shade her from the sun and keep the room cool.

'Mercy?' he called. No reply. He switched on the light. 'Oh my God!' he said.

Mercy was lying on the floor. She was still. He felt frightened.

'Mercy!' he said again.

But she remained very silent and very still. He peered closer. She didn't seem to be breathing. He knelt down next to her and touched her shoulder to give her a little shake. Still nothing. He looked at her face. She didn't look peaceful at all. Her hair was all messed up. Her eyes were wide open. And there was a mark on the side of her neck. It was a bit swollen and there was what looked like dried blood in a runnel as far as her blouse. He touched the blouse very carefully. There was a dark brown stain on the white material. It was, he thought, definitely blood.

'If you are ever in trouble,' his mother had told him, 'ring 999.'

This was definitely trouble. He got out his mobile phone and rang 999.

*

It took Mullen just over five hours to get to his destination. He stopped once on the way, allowing Rex to meet all his natural needs at a service station on the M5 halfway between Bristol and Exeter. He relieved himself too, though not on the grass alongside the dog. He bought himself an Americano with an extra shot to keep himself alert and also (because he was hungry and it seemed appropriate) a Cornish pasty. He wasn't so gullible as to suppose it would taste as good as one purchased in a quaint Cornish delicatessen, but it would do for the time being.

He also (finally!) made the phone call which he had promised to PC Benning.

She sounded surprised. 'I thought that was the last I'd ever see or hear of you. Typical man. Get what you want and then bugger off.'

'I am a man of my word,' he said. Which was sometimes true and sometimes not. 'I meant to ring earlier, but I got distracted.' The lies were piling up. 'I've been to Mercy's flat. She does live there, but she's not there now. I wasn't able to get into it, of course, but I did speak to a neighbour. He said her car wasn't there, so I reckon she must have done a runner. And incidentally, the mobile number which she gave you is correct. It's not a dud. So she must have turned it off to stop us tracing her movements.'

'So where are you? What the heck are you doing? You should have rung me ages ago.'

'I'm going to Cornwall.'

'Cornwall?' She sounded alarmed.

'That's right. When you ring DI Holden, you can tell her that Doug Mullen says that Paul Reeve is not a killer. You can also tell her that Mercy very likely is. And that the story began in Cornwall and will very likely end in Cornwall.'

And with that, Mullen terminated the call and powered his mobile down. He needed to get moving or he'd be too late.

*

PC Benning knocked on Holden's door and pushed her way straight in. DS Trent was there, but she ignored his disapproving glare. 'I've had a phone call from Mullen.'

Holden looked at her. 'When?'

'Just now, Guv. I've just finished my shift guarding the Swan house.'

'Why on earth was Mullen ringing you?'

'He came round to the house earlier.'

'Please don't tell me you let him in.'

'No, ma'am. But he asked me for Mercy McAlister's phone number. He was insistent. I didn't give it to him, but I did ring the number on my phone. Twice in fact. But she never answered. She must have turned off her phone.'

'That's not a crime, Constable.'

'The next thing was Mullen asked me for McAlister's address.' Benning paused. 'So I gave it to him.'

'What the hell for?' This was Trent. But Holden held up her hand and motioned her to continue.

'Mullen wanted to go round there and see if Ms McAlister was in.' Benning left out the story about the dog and Mullen's mother being ill. She didn't want to invite more ridicule. 'I asked him to report back to me straight away, but actually it was nearly three hours later that he rang me to say that Mercy wasn't in the flat.'

Trent interrupted again. 'Maybe she's gone shopping.'

'Quiet, DC Trent,' Holden growled. Her eyes remained on Benning.

'Mullen said he was on the way to Cornwall.'

'Cornwall? Why?'

'He said that he was convinced Reeve had not kidnapped his daughter or the others. He said he believed that it was probably Mercy McAlister who had done it. And that he believed the story began in Cornwall and will end in Cornwall.'

Seconds passed and then the bulky figure of Detective Sergeant Fargo bundled into the room, brusquely pushing Trent to one side.

'There's been a 999 call, Guv. From the flat occupied by Mercy McAlister. Medics are there. I've sent two detectives round too. Mercy McAlister is dead. Very probably not natural causes. It looks very much like someone stuck a needle into her neck. We're waiting for confirmation of that.'

'So Mullen got it wrong.' Trent was sounding rather smug about this. 'If Mercy's dead, she's hardly the abductor.'

'If Mercy is dead, Constable,' Holden hissed, 'then it's hardly a joking matter. And if Mercy is dead, then there's a reason for it and it must be because she knew or suspected something.'

Mullen pulled up in the hospital car park shortly after 7.30 p.m. He gave Rex a chance to pee, locked him back inside the car and then headed for the hospital's main entrance. He had given it a lot of thought on the journey down and he had come up with a plan A. It seemed like a pretty good plan, but he had various lesser plans B and C tucked away at the back of his head in case he should need them.

He waited patiently for the receptionist to finish hammering the keys of her computer and gave her his broadest smile.

'You on the night shift?'

She gave a curt nod, unimpressed by his obvious flirting. 'Can I help you, sir?'

'I've come to visit someone, but I'd quite like to go and gather my thoughts and prayers first and …'

'Go to the double doors along that corridor.' She pointed. 'First right through the doors, then second left.'

'Thank you so much.'

The receptionist looked down.

Mullen made his way to the quiet room. Of course, once he got through the double doors, he realized there were signs and so failing to find it even in a sizeable hospital would have been difficult. He pushed his way cautiously in, concerned that he might disturb someone's prayers or an intimate tête-à-tête between a desperate relative and a priest or Rabbi or Imam. The room was empty.

Mullen sat down on a chair on the right-hand side and tried to think. Perhaps he should be praying in a place like that? Except that he didn't know how. He wondered how long he would have to wait before a minister came and when he did come in, what were the chances of he – or she – being able to help? He thought about the woman Jade Sawyer, who he thought was at the centre of all of this, even though she was now dead. He thought too about her daughter and he tried to imagine what it had been like for the people who loved them. He thought about Ruth Lonsdale and Natalie and Ellie and Trisha and he wondered if he had got it all totally and utterly wrong.

Mullen never noticed the man come into the room or sit down, but he became aware that he wasn't on his own any more. Perhaps he had dropped off without realizing it. He wasn't sure. But in any case when he raised his eyes, the man was sitting opposite him. He was dressed in jeans and a blue shirt, and he could have been anyone had it not been for the discreet dog-collar at his neck.

'Hello.' He spoke very softly. His hair was thin and grey and he had an oval serious face.

'Hello.'

He opened up his hands in a gesture of welcome. 'I hope I didn't interrupt your prayers. If you would like to talk or would like me to pray with you, then I'd be happy to do so. Or I'd be happy to leave you in peace.'

'I wasn't praying.' Mullen looked around the room. He wasn't sure why. 'We can talk here?'

The priest smiled. 'Where better? If someone else comes in, we can always go somewhere else more private if you wish.'

Mullen gathered his thoughts. The priest sat absolutely still and waited, his eyes on his knees. Was he praying? Mullen hoped he was. Maybe it would help.

Mullen began. 'Do you remember Jade Sawyer? She died in this hospital three or four months ago. She had cancer.'

The priest looked up. Mullen had got his attention. 'I think I do,' he said.

'Her little girl died a couple of years before. She fell over a cliff. Did she tell you about that?'

'She did.'

'Can you tell me what she told you?'

'No. I'm afraid not.'

'Why is that?'

'Firstly, I have no idea who you are or why you are asking. And secondly, she spoke to me in confidence, so I have to respect that.'

'You mean the seal of the confessional?'

He looked surprised. 'You're a Catholic?'

'My mother was. I'm not.'

'Nor am I.' He smiled. He seemed pleased with himself. 'And for the record, Jade didn't make a confession.'

Mullen felt a flash of temper arc through him. He hadn't come all this way to engage in a battle of words and intellect. He wanted help. He waited for his irritation to subside before continuing.

'OK, you want to know who I am? My name is Doug Mullen. I'm a private investigator. And I am asking you to tell me what Jade Sawyer told you because I am trying to save the lives of three people.'

'Well, Doug, my name is Matthew Ledger.' He was completely unruffled. 'I am an Anglican minister and I think I need you to tell me more, a lot more. Only then can I decide to what extent I am able to help you.'

So Mullen told him more. About how he had saved Natalie and Ellie on the M40. How Natalie had had a stroke and he felt compelled to 'keep an eye on them'. He told him about the murder of Ruth Lonsdale and the disappearance of Trisha Robinson and then of both Natalie and Ellie. He didn't mention the complications of Saad Ismat or Greg

Robinson or Paul Reeve because they (he insisted to himself) were not relevant. Eventually he ground to a halt.

Ledger buried his head in his hands for several seconds. Then he sat up and started talking.

'Jade was very ill. Her cancer was in a very advanced state. There was no hope for her. She should have been in a hospice, but there weren't any places and she had no-one to care for her at home. She told me about Lucy's death. How guilty she felt even though Lucy hadn't been in her direct care at the time. She had been hired to cater for a church group and Lucy had gone with some of them to the cliffs and she had fallen to her death. They didn't find her body for two weeks.'

'Did Jade have any visitors while she was in hospital?'

'Lucy's father. It was quite a surprise, as I understand it. He had run off to New Zealand a couple of years after her birth. Apparently he found it difficult to deal with the fact that she had Down's Syndrome. But at least he came back eventually.'

'Lucy had Down's Syndrome?' That was news to Mullen. He didn't recall reading that in the reports of her death.

'Yes, she did.'

'Did Jade have any female visitors?'

Ledger held up his hands. 'Really, I don't know. I tended to pop in outside of visiting hours, so I wouldn't necessarily have met other visitors. But she did mention a sister. I got the impression that there had been some friction between them in the past, but things had improved. In times of crisis, family tends to rally round, doesn't it?'

He paused. Mullen said nothing, because the Reverend Ledger's words had just rung a very loud alarm bell in his brain. When Ledger talked about families rallying round, he was thinking about people putting aside past grievances and offering support. But Mullen's brain had taken a more cynical turn and central to this was Jade Sawyer's money.

'Anyway,' Ledger carried on in sudden haste, 'with Alex being on the scene again I felt comforted that she wasn't on her own. As you can imagine, I have to spread myself quite thinly. And I don't think she was that keen on men of the cloth like myself. But if you want to know more about who visited her, maybe I could ask around the nurses for you.'

'I haven't time for that.'

'I see.'

'How did Jade seem with regard to her daughter's death? Accepting? Forgiving? Bitter?'

Ledger put his hands together, fingers interlocking. For a moment Mullen wondered if he was going to burst into public prayer. Instead he said, 'I'm afraid to say that Jade departed this life in an unforgiving frame of mind.'

'Oh.' Mullen was confused. He had convinced himself that Mercy was at the centre of this affair, but Ledger was fast undermining that theory.

Ledger stood up and took a card out of his wallet. 'Look, I'm due to do some more visiting. But if you have any further questions, don't hesitate to ring me.'

Mullen took the card.

'Actually, there is one other thing I ought to tell you. Jade changed her will two days before she died.'

Mullen almost swore. 'Are you certain about that?'

'Am I certain?' He laughed. 'I was one of the witnesses. One of the nurses summoned me. It was the last time I saw her.'

'Do you know in what way she changed it?'

'I only witnessed the signature. I didn't read the small print. But I imagine she was changing it in favour of Lucy's father.'

'Even though he walked out on her and their daughter?'

'But he came back. Like the prodigal son. And to be fair he seemed very supportive of her. He visited her every day. Sat with her for hours. Slept in the chair by her bed some nights. None of us are beyond forgiveness. We only have to repent.'

'And she left her money to him.'

'It's only a guess.'

But Mullen wasn't to be distracted from his line of thought.

'Was she wealthy?'

'She didn't appear to be so. But she had a house overlooking the sea. She wanted to go back and die there, she once told me. She wanted to be near Lucy. But it never happened. In the end her death came very quickly. It was a blessing, I think.'

'And this guy walked off with her money.' Mullen was finding it hard to hide the distaste he was feeling. 'What was his name?'

'Alex something. I really can't remember his surname.'

'Who drew up the will?'

'I'm not sure. I merely witnessed it.'

'This isn't a game. This is life or death.' Mullen didn't care if he was being rude to a man of God. He needed answers. A "can't remember" just didn't cut it as far as he was concerned.

'There can't be many solicitors in this town,' he said, pressing hard.

Ledger pursed his lips together as if he had just bitten into lemon.

'Tolman,' he said. 'I think it was John Tolman. He has an office at the top of the High Street.'

'Any idea where he lives?'

'No. I really don't. I would try his office in the morning.'

'Describe Alex to me.' Mullen pressed on to a new subject, conscious that everything about Ledger was screaming 'I've had enough of talking to you'.

'Gosh. I'm not very visual, but I'll try. Late thirties I'd say. Long light brown hair. He tied it back in a pony tail sometimes. He had a funny looking face, not quite symmetrical and hid it with as beard. About six feet tall. Spoke with a slight twang. Maybe that was the result of living in New Zealand. Lean looking. He told me he liked to jog. And surf of course. The call of the sea was how he described it.'

Mullen tried to visualize the man minus the hair and the beard. He found himself returning to the same person. The name was different, but apart from that.

'I really must go.' The priest had had enough. He extended his hand. 'Perhaps you should share your concerns with the police.'

'I have.'

'Good. And the best of luck.'

DS Fargo had decided it was going to be a long night. He had just bitten into his sandwich from the Co-op when DC Crane rang from Mercy McAlister's flat.

'This is good,' Crane said with relish. In Fargo's book, Crane was a bit of a prat, but he was pretty competent when push came to shove. 'Definitely murder. Highly unlikely she could have stabbed herself in the neck by our reckoning. More interesting though, she had a hand-kerchief clutched in her hand. And guess what?' Crane paused.

Fargo bit off another piece of sandwich. He wasn't a man to play guessing games. So he waited for Crane to tell him.

'There's a nametape on it! Would you believe it? Name of Douglas Mullen. Now how lucky is that!'

'Too lucky, maybe.' This was Fargo voicing his thoughts to Holden five minutes later. He liked Mullen. He had seen him up at close quarters a year previously and he couldn't easily see him as a killer. 'Simple enough to plant the evidence. To draw our attention to Mullen.'

'It's stone cold evidence,' Trent snapped. 'What more do you want? The murder weapon with a pretty label attached to it. "This is the possession of Doug Mullen. I did it." McAlister is dead because she got in the way and he has abducted them. They'll be dead soon or maybe they already are, dumped in a ditch somewhere.'

Holden and Benning were the audience as the two men sparred. Experience and gut feeling versus ambition and the confidence of youth. Not to mention a clash of class and temperament.

'Why would Mullen save mother and daughter in a car crash and then decide to kill them?' It was Fargo's turn. 'He's one of the good guys.'

'Good guys can do bad things,' Trent replied, wheeling out the debating skills he had honed at university. 'All they need is a motive—'

Benning interrupted, 'Well, we know he is heading to Cornwall.'

'Do we?' It was Trent again, dismissive as ever. 'You mean he told you he was. He wants you to think he is going to Cornwall. He's probably driving in the opposite direction.'

'He was very convincing,' Benning said.

'He's ex-army,' Trent sniped. 'The blood probably runs ice cold in his veins.'

'Enough.' Holden slapped her hand hard on her desk. 'Quite apart from two unexplained deaths, we've got three people missing.' She spoke deliberately. The anger was there, visible in her eyes and her flushed cheeks, but she was under control. 'Two of them are children. If we fail to find them or if we find them dead, I'm the one who will have to face the press and explain to the world why we failed to save them. We have just had to release the man who was previously our prime suspect. So sitting here arguing is not an option. Fargo, Benning and I will drive to Cornwall in pursuit of Mullen. You, Trent, will oversee the monitoring of Mullen's mobile and an ANPR search for his car. You will keep me informed of every development as soon as it happens. If Mullen turns out to be heading towards John O'Groats or anywhere else, we will turn round and follow him there. Any questions?'

It was almost ten o'clock and Mullen was sitting in his car outside a large square house on the outskirts of town. He had found only one Tolman in the area when he did a search on his mobile of the BT phonebook, and this was the address. He leaned over to Rex, who seemed to have taken out a long-term lease on the passenger seat. Mullen removed his collar. Then he picked him up and got out of the car.

'Time to demonstrate your acting skills, mate, then I'll find you a treat.'

Rex whimpered, though whether this was excitement or anxiety, Mullen didn't know. Maybe he was starting to miss the professor. Maybe he was very attached to his collar. Maybe he was finding Mullen's lifestyle just a bit too unpredictable.

Mullen walked up to the door, which was set back under a porch supported by two classical columns. Mullen wasn't impressed. The house screamed money, but nothing much else.

He hammered the fancy lion's head knocker and waited. There was movement inside. A light went on in the hall.

'Who is it?' a voice said. 'It's very late.'

Mullen had already positioned himself in front of the spy-hole. He lifted Rex up so that their two faces were close to each other.

'I nearly ran over this dog. He ran into the road. No collar or tag. So I was wondering if you were the owner or if you knew the owner.'

After a delay during which Mullen tried to come up with a plan B, the door opened. Two men stood there, both over six feet tall, one built like a rugby prop, the other like a ballet dancer.

'Oh, he's cute. But he's not ours and I really don't know who he belongs to.'

'Definitely not from round here,' the other one said. 'Perhaps he's been abandoned by some beast of an owner.'

'I think he may be hungry,' Mullen said, playing to his audience.

'Poor little chap.' The ballet man stretched out a hand and stroked Rex. 'I am sure we could find something. There's some ham in the fridge, or maybe he wouldn't say no to some cat food.'

'Thank you.' Mullen eased himself into the house. Not for the first time, the words 'liar, liar, pants on fire' were ringing accusingly in his head.

Rex ate with a will and Mullen accepted a cup of tea and they were all getting on so famously that Mullen felt a complete shit. So after he

had got about halfway through his tea and eaten two very nice chocolate chip cookies (much superior to the own-brand stuff he was used to
buying), he broke cover and made his confession.

'Is one of you John Tolman, by any chance?'

They both looked at him in alarm.

'I'm afraid I've not been entirely truthful,' he continued. 'The dog is
mine,' he said, still not being entirely truthful, 'and I desperately need
to talk to John Tolman if I'm to stop three people being killed.'

The big guy, the one who looked like he would be a pretty handy ally
in a street brawl, stood up.

'What the hell are you talking about?'

'I'm a private investigator. I've driven all the way down from Oxford.
If you don't believe me, you can ring Detective Constable Trent of the
Thames Valley police. He'll vouch for me. Or the Reverend Ledger
from the hospital.'

The other one, who had a very contented Rex on his lap, raised his
hand. His eyes studied Mullen as if seeing him for the first time.

'I'm John Tolman,' he said softly. 'I think you need to fill me in on
the details.'

Mullen was getting used to telling his story, albeit each time fine-
tuned to meet the expectations of his audience. Tolman listened
intently. He didn't ask any questions, not until Mullen had got to the
end.

'So you think this Alex Pike has kidnapped Natalie and the two
girls?'

'Yes, I do. What I need to do is find him. The Reverend Ledger told
me that he witnessed a will which you drew up for Jade shortly before
her death. He also said that Jade had told him she owned a property
overlooking the sea and I need to know where that is. Because if the
new will made this Alex Pike the sole beneficiary, then I am guessing
that is where I will find him.'

Tolman looked down. Rex was revelling in the attention he was getting. Tolman was caressing his ears with intense concentration and Mullen felt a pang of guilt that he himself so often took the dog for granted.

'For the last two and half years of her life, Jade lived on the north coast.' Tolman spoke precisely, measuring his words as if they were a legal document. 'She moved there after Lucy's death.'

He slipped Rex off his lap and rose to his feet. He located a tablet and went and perched on the arm of the chair in which Mullen was sitting.

'Here, Doug,' he said after a minute or so of searching. 'This is where she lived. Baldrock is the nearest village, a couple of miles away. Rather lonely I'd have thought, but she bought it because it was only a mile or so from where Lucy died. She told me she walked there on the coastal path every day. I worried that one day she'd walk there and decide not to walk back.'

'So did she leave the house to Alex Pike?'

'Not just Alex. She left her estate to be shared between Alex and her own sister Dee. I have to say it was against my advice. After what he did, she would have been better advised to leave her will as it was, divided between Dee and the Down's Syndrome Association. Pike had abandoned Jade with Lucy. He only came back when he heard she had cancer. Initially she couldn't stand seeing him again, but then one day I got a phone call from him saying Jade had been readmitted to hospital and she wanted me to visit her. It was obvious to me what he was after. When I saw her, I urged her to think very carefully, but something had changed. She had become very dependent on Pike. He was even living in her house. Anyway I drew up a new will and the Reverend Ledger witnessed it.'

Mullen nodded. He was concentrating on Tolman's tablet, taking in every detail of the map until he was certain he could find the house. Finally he handed it back.

'Thanks very much. You've been very helpful.'

'Sadly there's no law against being a complete bastard,' Tolman said.

*

Mullen set the GPS for the village of Baldrock. That would get him close enough and after that it was just a matter of driving two miles south-west along the coastal road until he saw the house on the right, just past a series of tight bends. It wouldn't be difficult to find.

He switched on the engine and pulled out into the road. Tolman's house was on the edge of town, and Mullen immediately found himself in the dark. No street lights out here, no visible moon, and a low cloud which obscured things even further and left droplets of water on the windscreen. He drove steadily. Driving fast on roads he didn't know and in such murky conditions was not going to get him there much sooner than driving more cautiously. In any case, getting there a minute sooner or later was unlikely to change anything. Either Natalie and the girls would be there or they wouldn't. Either they would be dead or they wouldn't. The important thing was that he arrived there in one piece.

The headlights of a vehicle came into view in his rear mirror. They drew closer. A local driver who knew the road and didn't want to hang about. Soon the van – for that was what it was – was on his heels, pressing. Mullen felt his irritation levels rising. He hated people who hugged his bumper. He hated people with badly adjusted headlights. He slowed down a little, hoping the guy would overtake. He didn't.

Then another thought jumped unbidden into his head. The guy was following him! And that thought was followed by a memory of a film he had watched as a teenager sprawled across his mum's shabby sofa. He couldn't remember its name, but it was directed by Steven Spielberg. In it, a man in a car is mercilessly chased by a guy in a huge lorry. Throughout the film the lorry seems always on the edge of driving the car off the road and throughout, the lorry's driver remains a threatening unknowable character, face hidden behind sunglasses, never speaking. Mullen felt the sweat on the palms of his hands. The van's driver unquestionably knew the area. He had a big van at his command, his headlights were ridiculously bright and he was almost touching Mullen's rear bumper.

Up ahead, a petrol station came into sight. The BP sign was comfortingly visible. Mullen felt a surge of relief and began to signal left, but as he got closer he realized that there were no lights on in the shop and not a single other vehicle to be seen on the forecourt. For a critical moment or two, he froze, undecided whether to pull in anyway or carry on. It was now raining hard and the van driver, still right on his tail, hooted and flashed his headlights. Mullen decided to get out of the guy's way and pull into the garage. He wrenched the steering wheel left and hit the brake with his right foot. That was a mistake. Whether it was the pool of water which his wheels hit or maybe a slick of oil or both, Mullen's car skidded like a drunk who has just stepped on sheet ice wearing leather-soled shoes. He swore. The dog barked. There was a thump as the underneath of the car bounced heavily and hit something solid. Mullen fought with the wheel, easing his foot off the brake and then pressing it again as the pumps loomed alarmingly close. The rear end of the car twitched hard to the right, but then suddenly the tyres found their grip and Mullen brought the car to a shuddering halt.

Up front on the road, the van was hammering off into the dark rain, his rear lights already disappearing from Mullen's view.

For several seconds Mullen sat, conscious of how close he had been to disaster. He realized with a start that his whole body was trembling. He closed his eyes and took three deep breaths.

'Fuck,' he said to the darkness.

Rex whined.

'Sorry,' he replied. 'Naughty Mullen. Bad Mullen.'

Mullen made it to the village of Baldrock without any further incident. The heavy rain had ceased almost as suddenly as it had begun, and with it visibility had improved. He pulled into the side of the road next to a small green space. It was empty except for a wellington-booted figure walking a Collie type dog across it. Mullen attached the lead to Rex's collar and got out. It was an opportunity to give the dog a final chance to do his business and to allow himself a few moments to think. He turned on his mobile. The battery was even lower than he thought. There was a signal, albeit not very strong. Rex stopped halfway across the grass. Mullen waited, gathering up the small turd in one of his little blue bags. Just as he was knotting it, there was a series of beeps as four texts popped up, all from the same mobile number. First *Where are you, Mullen? PC Benning*, then two more each half an hour apart and asking the same question in heightened tones. *We are worried about you. Contact me urgently.* And finally *DI Holden is concerned for your safety. Contact us please!!!* The other text was to tell him someone had left him a voice message. That was from Benning too and along the same lines, though more emotional. *I thought we were trying to help each other. I did you a favour. Why aren't you answering your phone?*

Mullen considered all this as he followed Rex across the grass. He could feel the water seeping into his sock of his left foot. He knew he ought to reply. So he did. *Baldrock, north Cornwall. Headed for Cliff View Cottage.* His battery was down to less than ten per cent, so he powered the mobile off. If things went wrong, then at least they would know where to look. But he wasn't going to wait for them to come charging to the rescue like the Seventh Cavalry. He couldn't waste any more time.

'Come on, Rex!' He pulled on the lead and headed for the car.

Holden, Fargo and Benning were just about to cross the border from Devon into Cornwall when Mullen's text message arrived on Benning's mobile phone. Benning didn't respond. She was asleep in the back seat. She should have been back home in her flat, spread-eagled on her bed after a long day, but when Holden had suddenly announced that they were going to Cornwall after Mullen, that had changed.

'Any questions?' Holden had said in a manner which dared anyone to question her decision making or indeed anything else. Benning's face, however, must have shown her surprise and possibly a hint of dismay. 'Do you have a problem with that, Benning?'

'No, ma'am.'

'Because if we find the three of them, or rather when we find them, I'll need another woman and given that Mullen has been talking to you, you're the obvious person. Make sure you bring your mobile and a charger for the car.'

'Fargo will drive us,' Holden had continued, apparently oblivious to any atmosphere in the room, and now not looking at either of them. 'We leave in five minutes.'

Within minutes of leaving Oxford, sirens and lights on, Benning was, under Holden's instructions, texting Mullen and then leaving a pleading voice message. 'Say what you like, as long as it gets him to contact us,' Holden had said. After that, Benning had shut her eyes and tried to get some sleep.

'Wake up, Constable!' Back in the present, Holden's barking voice woke her out of a dream which involved Mullen, the dog and a UFO. (She never did work out the significance of the UFO.)

'You've had a text, Constable. Read it for God's sake. Out loud. That's what you're here for.'

Benning read it.

'Where the hell is Baldrock?' Holden's lack of sleep wasn't improving her volatile temper.

'North coast, I think,' Fargo said in his usual unemotional tones.

Holden leaned forward and reset the GPS. A quick recalculation and it displayed its new ETA. Holden snarled again.

'Give me your phone, Benning.' She rang Mullen's number and swore. 'He's turned the bloody phone off.'

'Maybe his battery is low.' Benning was feeling anxious and defensive about Mullen. She did hope she hadn't misjudged him. Holden would never forget.

'For crying out loud, Fargo!' Holden had turned her fire on her sergeant. 'Did you pass your advanced driving test or not? Put your bloody foot down. An hour and a half is way too long.'

And with that, as Fargo pressed his foot even further down on the accelerator, Holden lay back in her seat again and shut her eyes.

'Wake me when we get there,' she said.

Peace descended.

Mullen was nearly one and a half miles along the coastal road when he reached the series of sharp bends which told him he was getting very close. They wound their way up a surprisingly steep hill – he hadn't realized that when studying the map on Tolman's tablet. The heavy rain had stopped, but Mullen found himself climbing into low cloud. He switched on his wipers again to clear the screen, but this didn't do much to improve visibility. By the time he had reached the top, he had dropped two gears. He peered ahead, as he now moved carefully through the murk, scanning the right-hand side for any sign of a drive or house.

Despite that, he was almost past the entrance before he saw it. He had no intention of pulling straight in. He wanted to scout it out as best he could, but apart from light from a downstairs window and the vague shape of the house, there was nothing to see. He drove another half mile before he was able to pull into a gateway on the left and turn his car round.

He began to drive back from whence he had come. You're an idiot, he told himself. You have no weapon. Suppose they are all there. Are you going to mount a one-man rescue? How stupid can a man be? But he wasn't listening. Like the 600 men of the Light Brigade, it never seriously occurred to him to not charge in.

Actually, it wasn't a charge. Once he had reached the entrance, he turned left in between the stone gate posts and slipped into neutral, killing his lights and gently applying the brake. He didn't wait. He had his plan and he got straight out of the car. But plans sometimes go wrong and almost immediately movement-sensitive security lights came on. Mullen didn't panic. He moved away from the car, heading for the shadows of the trees while keeping his eyes on the house. Surely someone would come out. When you live in a place as isolated as this and your security light goes on, you don't ignore it.

Inside the house, the only light which Mullen could see went off. He froze, listening for a sound, any sound which would alert him to where his enemy was.

The sound when it came several seconds later was a door opening. Then a bright beam of light from a torch slowly scanned 180 degrees, from the garden on the far side of the house, across the lawn, then the shrubs and then finally Mullen's car where it settled.

'Sorry!' Mullen shouted. Play it needy and helpless until you know who is here and whether you've got it horribly right or (even more hor-ribly) wrong. He advanced a few cautious steps towards the light. 'I've broken down,' he said. 'I went through a big puddle at speed. Maybe you could lend me that torch so I could check it out.'

There was no reply but the torch began to move uncertainly around, as if the person holding it had been drinking or was extremely old. Mullen waited, holding up his hands like a bad guy surrendering to a United States marshal in the wild west. And then, very suddenly, he found himself enveloped by its beam. He looked down and stood very still, anxious to appear as unthreatening as possible.

'Oh my God, it's you!'

He wasn't sure about the voice. 'Thank the Lord that it is you. I've been beside myself with worry. You've no idea what that man has put me through.' But it sounded like Mercy.

The torch beam began to bounce up and down. She was stumbling hurriedly towards him.

'Oh, Doug,' she said, 'you are an answer to my prayers!'

Mullen wasn't sure how to react. The torch was still dazzling his eyes, but he was relieved to know that Mercy was alive, but what about the others? And what about Rick North, assuming that it was him that she was talking about? Mullen felt the multiple tensions in his body ease as Mercy drew nearer. And then he heard another noise. It might have been a foot snapping a brittle branch on the ground – but it certainly wasn't Mercy. It was behind him and it was close. Mullen tried to turn, but he knew he was too late. He knew that he had been fooled. An excruciating pain flashed through his body. He had read about being tasered, but that didn't prepare him for the pain which arced through him. It was as if thin serrated knives had been thrust deep into his back down the length of his spine and then twisted vigorously. Mullen felt his legs collapse under him and he crashed to the ground. As he lay spread-eagled on the ground, it was as if every muscle and nerve within him had been shredded. His arms and legs jerked uncontrollably, and the pain in his head was like a thousand shards of glass.

The beam of the light was still directed onto him. He tried to open his eyes a fraction, but that only brought on a fresh onslaught of agony. He was aware of a dark shape above him, a man he thought, breathing heavily, legs splayed wide apart. But he couldn't see who.

'Great performance, doll,' a man said. That definitely sounded like Rick North, but Mullen wasn't sure of anything any more.

He shut his eyes in surrender and wondered if he was about to die.

The hill was steep and the bends sharp, but Fargo didn't seem to notice. The roads were wet, but the possibility of skidding had apparently not entered his mind. Benning sat very still and hoped that Holden couldn't sense the anxiety she was feeling. She was way out of her comfort zone.

'Less than half a mile,' Holden said, now fully alert. Her eyes moved up and down from her phone to the road to the phone again.

Fargo grunted as he swung the wheel hard left. He was halfway across the white line, but at this time of night – as Benning tried to tell herself – there would be plenty of warning from oncoming lights if he needed to get back onto the left-hand side of the road.

'Slow down!' Holden's desire to control and always be in control was as strong as ever. 'There, on the right.'

Fargo had to brake faster than he had anticipated and for the first time in over 200 miles there was just a hint of him making a mistake. The car seemed to shimmy for a moment, the back end sliding to the left, and then the tyres gripped again and Fargo brought them lurching to a halt five metres from a battered metallic blue Ford Focus.

'That's Mullen's car.' Benning had his registration seared into her brain, as well as his mobile phone number. Not that there was any point in ringing it. She had tried (again) five minutes earlier without any success.

They got out as one. Holden held up her hand in warning as she led them cautiously towards the car. She had a torch in her hand, as did Fargo. Benning had nothing except for her mobile, still turned on, but at least mobiles had torch applications nowadays. Benning wondered what they were going to find in the car – a dead Mullen, his brains splattered all over the interior of the car? That was her negative fantasy.

They had all three reached the car when Rex barked. Benning jumped in alarm. Fargo swore. Holden peered in.

'That's his dog, isn't it?' It was a question, but it sounded more like a statement of fact.

'His name's Rex,' Benning said helpfully. Ever since she was a little girl she had called dogs by their name. It had become second nature. 'He's rather cute,' she added unnecessarily.

But Holden had already lost interest in the dog. 'Where the hell is Mullen?'

Her eyes were scanning the house, but there was no light coming from it and no sign of life there at all. In fact, all around, it was dark.

Not even the hint of a moon.

Fargo was scanning his torch around the car and on the ground near where they were standing.

'My guess is that he went this way.' His torch was focused on a rough piece of grass that didn't deserve the term lawn. After the heavy rain, the foot-prints were clear enough. Fargo had lowered himself onto his haunches. He gave the impression of a boy scout back in his element. 'Not just him, by the looks of it. At least one other. Two in fact, I would reckon. And look there.' He stood up and moved a couple of paces. 'From the shape of it, this could be where a body lay. Mullen maybe.' He fell silent. No-one spoke. 'Maybe,' Fargo concluded, 'we should wait for back-up. Just in case.'

'I haven't driven all this way to wait for back-up,' Holden said loudly. Of course, strictly speaking it was Fargo who had done the driving, but neither he nor Benning were going to split hairs with her on that point.

Holden was standing upright, head raised. She was listening. It was remarkably quiet. A vehicle in the far distance. Possibly a hint of the breaking sea. But otherwise nothing.

She walked back to the car and opened the passenger door. Rex was cowering on the driver's seat. He looked at her. 'Not you again,' the look said.

'Come on, doggie,' Holden said with her most encouraging (and rarely used) voice. 'Let's go find him.'

The dog continued to look at her.

'Come on, Rex!' This was another voice. It was Benning, hoping against hope that he would remember her. 'Let's find Doug, shall we?' Rex looked at her and then, to her surprise, got up and jumped out of the car.

Mullen was having trouble staying on his feet. As far as his addled brain could make out, it was something like half an hour since he had been tasered, but the effects had not dissipated. The official police line is that tasering is very short-lived, but when you have been tasered for twenty or more seconds, the official police line is a load of horseshit. His back was the worst, but every step was a new agony too. It felt as if his knee – both knees – had been skewered, ready for a barbecue.

They were walking in single file. In the front was a woman. Not Mercy, Mullen thought. He didn't quite see Mercy as a hoodie type and the woman was thinner and taller. Behind her came Natalie, Ellie, Trisha and Mullen, each of them with hands tied behind them. Behind Mullen was Alex Pike, alias Rick the gardener, alias the bastard who had electrified him like he was part of the national grid. They were walking towards the sea as far as Mullen could work out, but he couldn't be sure because his brain didn't seem to be working. It was hard enough to put one foot in front of another, let alone come up with a plan as to how he was going to get out of this mess.

Neither Mercy nor Pike had told them where they were going, but Mullen's not fully functioning brain knew three things. First, the little girl Lucy had died falling from the top of a cliff. Second, as Tolman had told him, Jade's house was only a mile from where Lucy had died. Third, they were being taken step by painful step towards those very cliffs. It didn't matter how Mullen added those three facts together, the answer was always the same.

Mullen peered as best he could into the dark. As far as he could see, Natalie was walking without difficulty, whereas the two girls were staggering and intermittently sobbing. Mullen would have liked to offer them encouragement, to have fatuously told them to be brave and try not to worry, but he couldn't because like them, his mouth was gagged.

When Trisha tripped and fell over, Mullen stopped by her, trying to offer her silent psychic encouragement. But Pike snarled with fury.

'Up, you bitch. Get up. Or you'll be the first.' He grabbed her by her upper arm and yanked her to her feet. 'Don't you dare do that again! Now get on with it.'

She struggled on, trying to catch up with the others. Mullen struggled on too. He was trying desperately to will his brain into working order. What the hell was he going to do? If he didn't come up with something soon, it was going to be too late. He would die and so would they.

At the front, the woman stopped and turned round, shining the torch directly into their faces. 'Recognize this, girls? Do you know where we are now?'

No-one said a thing. Someone moaned through her gag.

'Get a move on, Mullen.' This was Pike's voice. Mullen felt something jab into his back and let out an involuntary yell. 'There'll be more of that if you try playing silly buggers with me.'

Mullen wondered how he could buy them all time. If PC Benning had got his message, if they had been driving like a bat out of hell, then how long would it take for them to arrive? Or what about the local coppers? It surely wouldn't take long for them to turn up – and yet there was no sign of them at all.

Mullen tripped and stumbled. It was a simple ruse.

'Get up!' Mullen tensed himself for another sharp prod on the back, but instead there was an explosion of pain in his ribs as Pike's boot crashed into them. 'If you don't get up, I'll finish you off here and now.'

Mullen clambered to his feet, no easy task with his arms behind his back. But he didn't want to be dead. And he didn't want Natalie or Ellie or Trisha to end up dead either.

They walked in silence for the next five minutes, apart from the occasional whimper of terror. Then the woman at the front turned round again.

'Well,' she said, 'isn't this fun? A bit of a reunion. Except that it isn't a proper reunion because how could you have a proper reunion without the star guest – without Lucy. You remember Lucy, don't you?' She paused. Her breathing was fast and laboured. 'Or maybe you don't remember her as Lucy. Maybe you remember her as the annoying Down's Syndrome kid?'

She looked around at them as if she expected them to make some sort of answer despite being gagged.

'Lucy was my niece. Aunty Dee she called me.'

Someone moaned. Natalie's body was shuddering as if she might be going into shock or about to fit.

But the woman wasn't interested. Her focus shifted to Mullen.

'Worked it out yet, Mullen? Don't you remember me, Mr Private Detective?' She gave a shriek, a mixture of pleasure and hysteria. She pulled her hoodie back and switched voices. '"I want you to find poor little Saad?" Don't you remember?' She shone her torch on herself, holding it under her chin. 'It's amazing what a wig and a serious bit of make-up can do to one's appearance. To one's whole persona.'

It was the change of voice, to a rather squeaky home-counties warble, which did it for Mullen. Of course he remembered her. How could he not? The voice and the way she waved her arms around like she was trying to catch a taxi from the central reservation of the M25. It all came flooding back. And when she had shone her torch on her face and he had seen the mole on her chin, that was the clincher, if he needed it. Elizabeth Durant – the fake Elizabeth Durant, not the real one. But he couldn't tell her so because he was gagged.

He looked back at her and tried to hold her stare. He forced his mouth into a grin, as if he found her quite ridiculous, as if she was the most laughably pathetic person he had ever encountered. He looked at her and hoped for a miracle.

'What are you fucking smiling at?' It was as if someone had flicked a switch. Dee's face transformed into a mask of fury. She strode forward. Mullen continued to hold his sneering grin. She swung her right hand back and slapped him hard round the face. Compared with what had happened to him already that evening, a slap was barely worth a mention. He grinned even more broadly.

'Careful,' Pike growled, though whether he was talking to the woman or to Mullen wasn't clear.

The woman leaned forward and wrenched Mullen's gag down.

'I'll wipe that smile off your face, Mullen, if it's the last thing I do.'

'Well, you're in charge, aren't you, so I guess you can do whatever you want to.'

'Why the hell did you save them on the M40? If you had just let them burn to death, we wouldn't have had to go to all this trouble.'

'And you wouldn't have had your chance of revenge.' He paused. 'I'm right, aren't I? It's not the truth you want, is it? You want revenge. To make yourself feel better? For failing Lucy? For failing your sister? Where the hell were you and Alex when Jade needed you?' These were mostly stabs in the dark. He didn't know for sure. But he wasn't after truth either. He was trying to survive.

'They are responsible.' She waved her hands at Natalie, Ellie and Trisha. 'They were meant to be looking after Lucy. Instead they killed her. And after they had killed her, they covered it up. They and that bitch of a vicar.'

'Lucy fell into the sea. It was an accident.' Mullen knew he had to keep going. Now that he could talk, he had a weapon. Delay things. Try to avert the inevitable. Hope against hope that help would come. 'If you think otherwise, you're deluded. Crazy!' If that didn't wind her up, nothing would.

Mullen's right leg exploded with pain and he fell down again, but only onto his knees. Pike's voice sounded above him. But where Dee was volatile and emotional, he spoke as if he was under control.

'That's pretty much what the Reverend Lonsdale said to us! But she was the one whose brain had half gone. She wasn't so far gone as not to claim the privacy of the confessional. "Whatever people tell me in confidence, I am bound by God to keep it secret and take it to my grave." That's what she said and that's what she did. She took it to her grave. We saw to that.' He laughed. 'But she made a mistake. By saying what she said, she confirmed what we suspected, that there was a secret around the death of Lucy, a secret which they were all covering up.'

'People shouldn't have secrets,' Mullen said, trying to be conciliatory. He forced himself back onto his feet and stood there, swaying slightly, wondering if he would get another kick.

'You've got it wrong, Mullen.' Dee too was calmer now, as if she had remembered what the purpose of everything was. 'I want the truth, but I also want revenge. And that's what we are all here for. That's why we've come back to the place where Lucy died.'

Pike stepped forward, away from Mullen and towards Natalie and the girls. One by one, he removed each of their gags, threatening each of them as he did so against shouting or trying to run.

Mullen knew that time was running out fast. The two of them were working together now, back on plan, conscious no doubt that they only had a limited amount of time to work with. He had had no doubt at all that this plan involved all four of them being pushed over the cliffs and into the sea below.

'Trisha, tell me what happened to Lucy.' Dee was standing in front of her. 'If you want to save yourself, you must tell me the truth.'

'It wasn't me.' She was sobbing as she spoke. 'I was playing rounders. It was Ellie's turn to look after Lucy. Lucy got in the way when we were playing, so Ellie took her off for a walk. I didn't see Lucy fall, but it was just an accident.'

'How can you possibly know that it was an accident, if you didn't see it?'

There was a scream of agonized grief. Natalie. 'It was my fault. Mine and the Reverend Lonsdale. We shouldn't have given that responsibility to someone as young as Ellie. We thought it would be good for her. She needed to learn responsibility.'

'But she didn't learn, did she? All she learned was how easy it was to kill someone.'

'It was an accident!' Natalie was whimpering.

'So tell me about the accident,' Dee said.

'How can I tell you? I wasn't there.'

'OK.' Dee turned to Ellie and shone her torch full in the girl's face. '*You* tell us—'

'Just a minute.' The interruption was from Pike who moved past Mullen and grabbed Natalie by the upper arm. He marched her several metres away, towards the dark and the sound of the waves. 'If you lie, Ellie, or if you refuse to tell us what happened, I'm going to push your mother over the cliff and I'm going to make sure you have a grandstand view. Do you understand?'

Ellie stood rigid and terrified, overwhelmed by the horror that was unfolding all around her.

'Do you understand?' he shouted louder and grabbed Natalie by the hair with his free hand, yanking it hard so that she screamed.

'Yes,' Ellie sobbed. 'Yes!'

'So you tell us, and you speak nice and loud so that we can all hear.'

'I went to the cliffs when the others were playing rounders,' she said, hurrying – and stumbling – over her words. 'I was meant to be in charge of Lucy, but she was so needy. All the time. She used to follow me round like a lost dog and say stupid things and I just wanted some peace. So I didn't take her to the cliffs. I tried to slip away when she wasn't looking. I thought I had succeeded. I had a favourite rock which overlooked the sea. Trish and I used to go there and pretend we had run away from home to a deserted island. Anyway I got there and I'd just lit a cigarette when who should come panting round the corner? Lucy, of course.' Ellie was breathing heavily, as if she had just completed a half-marathon.

'And?'

'And I told her to go away, but she clambered up beside me and sat down. I tried to ignore her. I took another drag on the cigarette, sucking the smoke into my lungs, but then I got into a terrible coughing fit. "Smoking is bad for you," Lucy said. There I was on my private bit of rock, just wanting peace, and the stupid girl wouldn't let me have it. Even there I wasn't free of her. I remember thinking I hated her.

And what did she say, in her silly little girl voice? "Ooh, you shouldn't smoke," she said. "I'll tell your mum." So I said, "All right, Lucy, I'll stub my cigarette out. Just to please you." And that's what I did. I pulled up her dress and stubbed it out on her thigh, where it wouldn't be obvious, where nobody would notice. But she gave this wild squeal and then her whole body seemed to lurch backwards and before I could do anything, she just disappeared over the edge. Oh my God. It all happened so quickly. One moment she was there and then next she was bouncing off the side of the cliff like a rag doll and then into the sea with a splash.'

All this time, while Ellie was talking, Mullen was waiting and hoping for the moment when Pike and Dee were so distracted that he would have an opportunity to do something, but Pike's hands continued to grip Natalie. In addition, Mullen found himself, like everyone else there, mesmerised by what Ellie was saying, by what she was admitting.

As Ellie felt silent, Natalie began to cry, huge sobs which shook her body from top to bottom.

'It was my fault. I shouldn't have given her the responsibility. I shouldn't have covered up the truth. But what was I meant to do? Tell everyone and ruin my daughter's life?' She wailed. 'Kill me,' she keened. 'I'm her mother. Please kill me. She's only a child.'

Mullen looked at Natalie and Pike, standing there so close to the edge. For a moment Natalie's gaze fell on him. Could he? Should he? Suppose he got it wrong? But it felt like Natalie was giving him permission to take the risk of causing her death. He tensed himself, measuring the distance he would have to traverse.

That was when a dog barked. Not any dog either. Rex. Mullen recognized his bark. Not that Rex was big on barking. A low growl when an intruder got on his patch. The occasional yap, usually when he wanted attention – to go outside or for a bit of petting or supper. But this was Rex as Mullen had only occasionally heard him, in Bagley Wood for example or once when they had encountered a pit bull (fortunately on a lead).

'Where the fuck has he come from?' Pike was momentarily distracted and in that moment Mullen charged. And as he charged, he like Rex, uttered a war cry, a deep-throated roar that started somewhere far down inside his chest and seemed to propel his body forward like a human cannon ball.

If Pike's hands hadn't been attached to Natalie, one twisted into her hair, the other trying to hold her upright by the arm, then things might have turned out differently, but it bought Mullen the milliseconds that were the difference between triumph and disaster. Halfway across the space Mullen stumbled and, arms still clamped behind his back and unable to give him balance, he very nearly fell. Pike gave a yell. Only later did Mullen discover it was because Rex had bitten him on the ankle. Some more milliseconds passed and as Pike finally disentangled himself from Natalie and kicked viciously at the dog, Mullen's head – now behaving like a torpedo just released from a Fairey Swordfish – crashed into Pike amidships.

Mullen was expecting resistance, but Pike was off-balance. As Mullen crashed to the ground, he had the briefest of glimpses of Pike, arms outstretched, toppling backwards into the dark void. He heard a desperate cry, suddenly truncated, and then another cry, much closer. It was Natalie, motionless, pointing outstretched arms towards her daughter, who was being dragged across the grass towards the cliff edge by Dee. Mullen tried to stand again, but this time his legs refused to respond and he watched in horror.

Another scream cut through the dark, but this was not Natalie. Mullen watched in astonishment and relief as Detective Inspector Holden almost flew across the ground.

'Stop!' she was bellowing at the top of her voice.

Dee hesitated and before she could react Holden was on her. There was no human cannonball or torpedo treatment from Holden. A stab of two fingers into the face, a wrench of her arm, and Dee was down on the ground. It was all over faster than Mullen could have imagined. Pike dead, Dee pinioned on the ground by a huge detective whom Mullen recognized from a previous time, and Ellie enclosed by the arms of Holden, as if she was fearful that the girl would, after all their efforts, throw herself over the cliff. Mullen allowed himself to shut his eyes for a few moments, in the vain hope that the pain which was again criss-crossing his body might subside.

'You're not going to die on us, are you, Mr Mullen?' He opened his eyes. It was the nice police constable. Benning. He felt like crying.

'Not if you give me the kiss of life.'

He shut his eyes again. The pain was flashing round his body like a bush fire. Actually it wasn't a kiss of any sort which he desired. It was a dose of morphine.

EPILOGUE

Tea

MULLEN HAD GIVEN UP on the pain killers. He had a box of them at home, still three-quarters full. The fact was that he didn't believe in them. It was better to put up with the pain, better to know which bits of you hurt and need looking after, than to wander around feeling numb and listless. Mullen could be damned stubborn when it came to pain.

Rex was being very well behaved. He seemed to like the fact that Mullen was hobbling rather slowly along the pavement rather than striding out like a man on a mission. Actually Mullen *was* on a mission of sorts. He had been asked to tea by Natalie and Ellie. He suspected it was going to be some sort of 'thank you' celebration. Mullen was a modest sort of guy, but not so modest as to object to being a little bit feted, especially when he was feeling a little bit sorry for himself.

'Try to arrive promptly at three,' Ellie had said over the phone. She must have been put up to it, because Ellie didn't seem the type to worry about precise time-keeping.

But old army habits – however unspectacular his army career had been – die hard and Mullen was rather pleased to find himself approaching the gate at 14.59 hours. He paused and studied his phone. Thirty seconds to kill. He knew it was a little bit pathetic, but he waited until the digital display flicked over to 15:00 hours before approaching the door and pressing the bell.

Natalie opened the door. 'Spade, it's you.'

Mullen felt awkward. Was this a kiss on both cheeks occasion? He moved forward to do so, but she wrapped her arms around him and clung to him as if he was her long lost son. Pain flashed around Mullen's ribs, but he wasn't going to cry out or ask her to stop. Instead he placed his arms loosely around her frail body and waited for her to let him go.

She waved him into the sitting room at the front of the house. 'Be with you in a minute.'

Mullen went in. There was a man sitting there. Something about him was familiar, but Mullen didn't place him immediately. A tough looking face, close-cropped brown hair, the stubble of a man who hadn't got around to shaving, navy blue polo shirt, jeans (much smarter than Mullen's scruffy pair). The man in the photo he had taken from Ellie's drawer.

'I'm Paul Reeve,' the man said. 'Ellie's father. I expect you've been told about me.'

A shiver of apprehension ran down Mullen's spine. What the hell was this all about? A happy ever after reunion? In which case, why had he been invited? Were they expecting him to act as some sort of referee? Or bodyguard? God, he wasn't in any position to do anything if Reeve got nasty.

'Doug Mullen.' He held out his hand. Reeve ignored it. 'A friend.'

'You rescued my daughter.'

Mullen nodded. Daughter. No mention of his daughter's mother.

'Twice. On the M40 and in Cornwall. I owe you.'

Mullen wasn't sure he wanted Reeve to be owing him anything.

'You did what I couldn't do,' Reeve continued.

Mullen remained silent. He was beginning to wish he hadn't come, but at the same time, whatever it was all about, he was glad to be there.

'I'm trying to rebuild my relationship with my daughter. I've served my time. I've stopped drinking. I deserve a second chance.'

There were noises coming from the kitchen, cups being clinked, whispered conversations, a cupboard door being shut. Then the door opened and they came in. Natalie was in front. She sat down on the sofa. She linked her hands together on her lap, but said nothing. Ellie followed behind, carrying a tray with the teapot and cups and a plate of scones piled with cream and jam. She placed the tray on the low table in the middle of the room, and then poured out the tea. She passed out plates as if they were incapable of doing it for themselves and offered each of them a scone. But for all the appearance of calm practicality, her hands trembled as she did this. She sat down next to her mother.

The door squeaked open. It was Rex, still licking his lips from some treat he had been offered in the kitchen. He surveyed his options and jumped up on the sofa between Natalie and Ellie. Two pairs of hands greeted him, but it was Natalie's lap that he chose.

Natalie feels the creature's hair between her fingers. It is curly and soft, but she cannot remember the creature's name. She can remember the word creature. She has sung 'All creatures great and small' many times in her life, but she cannot remember the name for this little creature even though she knows it is a short one. She knows 'cat'. She doesn't like cats. But this little chap she likes and does not know what to call him.

'Mum.' Ellie touches her hand and breaks into her reverie.

Natalie looks around. Spade and Paul are sitting opposite her. Spade makes her feel safe. He will look after her. But Paul makes her very nervous. She looks at him and her body twitches. She remembers what he did to her, time after time. She wishes he had died in prison. She wishes he was not here. She wishes she and Ellie could disappear and start new lives again. But running is not the answer. She knows that now. For the last ten years she has lived in fear of him turning up on her doorstep. She has dreamt nightmares in which he has been released early and tracked her down and taken Ellie away from her. Every time she has taken a bus into town, she has looked around, scanning the other passengers just in case. When she goes for a walk, she imagines he is following her, hiding behind a tree or bush.

So now she realizes that the only answer is to confess. To hope that God forgives her and Mullen protects her. She has no idea what Paul will do.

The creature on her lap whines. It is a whine of pain. Natalie loosens her grip on his hairy coat. The creature settles back down.

She looks at Paul. 'I have a confession to make.'

He says nothing. He waits. They are all waiting.

'You remember the night you came home drunk.' She pauses, assembling the chaos of her thoughts into order. 'Actually you were always coming home drunk. I am talking about the *last* night you came home drunk. Do you remember?'

He nods. 'Sort of. It's a bit hazy to be honest.'

'You were very drunk and you had a cigarette in your mouth.' She could remember that night very clearly. She had been stone cold sober. 'When I asked where you had been, you hit me right across the face. Twice. Very hard.'

He looks down at his hands. Then up. 'I'm sorry.'

'You hit me in front of Ellie. You had been making so much noise that you woke her up. She came downstairs and she saw you hit me. And when you saw her, you swore at her and yelled at her to go to bed. And she ran back upstairs like a terrified little mouse.'

He looks at their daughter. Natalie thinks he looks ashamed, but experience has taught her not to trust him. At all.

'I don't really remember,' he says.

As if that is an excuse! Natalie feels anger. She often feels fear and anxiety. But she has almost forgotten what anger feels like. It is like molten lava bubbling up inside her.

'You lay down on the sofa and fell asleep. And while you were asleep I did what I had to do to keep Ellie safe. I rammed my face into our bedroom wall until I couldn't bear to do it any more. Then I went next door to Ellie and I lit one of your cigarettes and I pulled up her nightie and I stubbed it out on her thigh.'

'What?'

Natalie ignores him. All that matters now is to get to the end. She turns her eyes onto Spade. She feels safer telling him. 'My beloved daughter screamed. Hurting her was the worst thing I have ever done. But I held her tight, for a very long time, comforting her until she finally fell asleep again and then I rang the police.'

Her ex-husband rises to his feet. 'I was in prison for ten years.'

Natalie flinches. She sees and hears his anger, but she will not give way to him.

'You deserved it. You were a bastard when you were drunk.'

'Have you told the police this? Made a formal statement to them?'

'Of course she hasn't.' It is Ellie speaking. She has slipped her arm through Natalie's arm and they are leaning on each other. It is them against him and Ellie is speaking up for her mother. 'And she's not going to.'

'Well, I will.'

'Not if you want to see me again.'

Natalie looks at her daughter. She is astonished. In profile, with her heavy black make-up, piercing eyes and the set of her mouth, Ellie looks every bit as tough as her father.

'Besides, it would be your word against Mum's. No-one would believe you. No-one would want to believe you.'

Paul looks at them all, one at a time. Eventually his eyes settle on Spade.

'They would believe Mullen.' He smiles disconcertingly. He leans towards the man she calls Spade. 'You wouldn't lie, would you, Mullen? In court. Under oath. Hand on a Holy Bible.'

Natalie thinks of a washing machine, tumbling the clothes around inside it. It is how she feels now. What will happen to them? The truth, the whole truth and nothing but the truth. The words are engraved on her heart because she herself has lied on oath and the guilt has perched on her shoulder ever since.

'Remember what you said earlier.' Spade speaks slowly, one deliberate word after another. Natalie is confused.

'What was that?' Paul asks.

'You said you owed me, Paul. Because I saved them twice. You remember?'

Paul shrugs. 'It was just a way of saying thanks.'

'Well, if I had to, I would save them again, whatever the cost.'